Tainted DREAMS

TAINTED Book One

KIMBERLY QUAY

Turnit Publishing LLC

I

Turnit Publishing LLC
112 Bartram Oaks Walk #600981
Jacksonville, FL 32260

eBook ISBN: 979-8-9867417-6-5
Paperback ISBN: 979-8-9867417-5-8
ASIN: B0C179N24X

Printed in the United States of America

To those who find beauty in the darkness.

Contents

Playlist

"Addicted" by Saving Abel
"Goodbye" by Cannons
"In Dreams" by Ben Howard
"Fire for You" by Cannons
"Mr. Sandman" by SYML
"Bringing Me Down" by Ki: Theory (feat. Ruelle)
"Black" by Peal Jam
"Nothing Else Matters" by Metallica
"Grey Street" by Dave Matthews Band
"Bad Romance" by Lady Gaga
"Closer" by Nine Inch Nails
"Two Ghosts" by Harry Styles
"One Way Or Another" by Blondie
"Creep" by Radiohead
"Stronger" by Kelly Clarkson
"Wide Awake" by Katy Perry
"Go Your Own Way" by Fleetwood Mac
"The 1" by Taylor Swift
"I Knew You Were Trouble." By Taylor Swift
"Burn" by Ellie Goulding
"Woman" by Mumford & Sons
"The Reason" by Hoobastank
"Monster" by Mumford & Sons

Content Warning

To my readers,

This book contains content that may be difficult for some, such as graphic violence, explicit sex scenes, profanity, a possessive anti-hero, murder, stalking (light & welcomed), mention of past child and domestic abuse, mention of drug use/addiction, and death of a parent (mother).

It's possible I've unintentionally left something out, but I trust you to know your limits before continuing.

Overall, the book is about overcoming the demons of the past and finding the light in the dark.

At its core, it is a love story.

Much love and happy reading, Kimberly Quay

Chapter One

Skye

With the glow of the sunrise at my back, I sat in my small art studio, taking a moment to look at the paintings lining the walls. The sounds of the city faded as my eyes swept over the canvases. Each one was full of raw emotion, the hauntingly beautiful colors and brushstrokes portraying pain and despair. Each one captured the same woman in various stages of torment.

The painting on the back wall always struck me the most. She sat hunched over with her head in her hands. Her hands hid her face from view, but her agony was palpable.

Her defeated posture combined with the dark, moody backdrop of a seedy bar screamed anguish without the viewer having to see the tears falling from her eyes. There were countless others of her. Each piece of work revealed another level of her inner turmoil and her downward spiral into hell.

There was one, hidden behind all the others, of her when she was happy. It was a stark contrast to the rest, showing her in a moment of pure joy and happiness. The setting was the woman's art studio during her daughter's seventh birthday party. She stood in the center of ten little girls, all of them trying to smear paint on her face. She had her head thrown back in laughter, her eyes sparkling with joy.

Of all the paintings in the room, it hurt the most to look at. The emotions it evoked tainted its beauty. It was a reminder of the happiness fate had cruelly ripped away from her. A painful vision of what could have been and was no longer possible.

I'd painted it five years ago and hadn't looked at it again.

To shake off the weight of my thoughts, I let my gaze settle on a painting I'd done nearly two years ago. It was the only one in the room that didn't feature the woman. Instead, it depicted a tall man wearing a crisp, gray suit clearly tailored to fit his broad, muscular frame.

I'd seen him one afternoon on my walk back from the market. I couldn't take my eyes off him as he slid into a sleek black Bentley SUV while his driver held the door open for him. As I passed by, our eyes met for just a moment.

It happened so quickly. I barely remember what the driver looked like, but the man getting into the car had been seared into my memory.

Except his eyes. I had been too far away to see the color of his eyes, and it was the one detail missing, the one thing that prevented me from finishing the painting.

I had hoped to run into him again, to catch a glimpse

of his eyes and finally complete the piece. Despite making the same trip countless times, I never saw him again. It was as if he vanished, leaving me wondering if he was even real.

Looking at the painting, I couldn't help but feel a sense of longing. Just the thought of him had my pulse quickening. He'd caught my attention, not only because he was insanely handsome, but because his dark brown hair had fallen to cover one eye.

It had surprised me because I expected someone dressed so impeccably, someone with a freaking driver no less, to have perfectly styled hair with not one strand out of place.

That one unruly lock of hair made me think that the immaculately dressed businessman had a wild side to him, and I found myself yearning to explore it.

That's when it happened. He'd turned his head ever-so-slightly to blow the wayward lock from his face and our eyes met. In that split second, a butterfly took flight in my stomach and prickles of heat danced over my skin.

We'd seen each other for only a millisecond, but the impact had lasted well into the night as I sat in my tiny workspace and painted him. It had been the first time I'd painted anyone other than the woman in years. His face had been burned into my memory, demanding to be captured on canvas. The need to possess him in some way, in *any* way, had been overwhelming, and the only release I could find was through my brush strokes.

Shaking my head, I reluctantly tore my eyes from the man and turned to the canvas on the easel in front of me. The heartbreak and beauty of it washed over me. Even though the woman's profile only displayed half of her face, it was no less striking than if she'd been facing the viewer head on.

There was a single tear falling from her dark blue eye, which mirrored the swirl of angry clouds in the sky. The storm represented the darkness brewing within her. The dark, roiling ocean in the background was a perfect reflection of the tempest she felt inside and of the hell she lived in every day.

As it always did when I picked up my paintbrush, time melted away. I'd been working for hours without fully noticing the ache in my back from sitting for so long. Standing from the stool, I stepped back to admire my work, feeling a sense of satisfaction and a pang of remorse.

While my art may be dark and moody, painting was a form of meditation for me. Better than journaling or therapy, a blank canvas gave me a way to expel any negativity. My paintings were reminders that life could be intense and disappointing, but they also provided a way for me to find beauty in the darkness.

My phone alarm chimed, telling me it was time for work. Before turning off the light, I blew a kiss to the painting. "See you later, mom," I whispered as I turned away.

A SMILE PULLED AT MY LIPS as I stood at the front of the class, my eyes scanning the room while everyone filed in. As I watched them unroll their mats, I could see the nerves and anticipation on their faces. I smiled wider and took a deep breath, preparing myself for my first class of the day, which was their first yoga class ever.

"Welcome everyone," I said calmly, trying to soothe them. Putting the students at ease was a big part of the work. If I was tense, *they'd* be tense and that wouldn't work on the mat. "My name is Skye, and I'll be your instructor today. We'll start with some basic poses and breathing techniques to help you connect with your body and relax your mind."

As I spoke, I walked around the room. I could see the tension in their bodies ease as I answered their questions. "Alright, let's get started," I said as I took my place at the front of the room.

Once everyone settled onto their mats, I led them through a series of warm-up stretches, encouraging them to listen to their bodies and move with intention. As we moved into more challenging poses, I offered modifications to help them find what felt good for them.

As we neared the end of class, I watched as they each pushed themselves past their comfort zone and gained even more confidence in themselves.

"Take a moment to be proud of yourselves for taking this first step on your yoga journey," I said. "Remember, yoga isn't about being perfect or doing something the exact way your neighbor does it. It's about listening to *your* body and honoring where you're at in the moment. Keep returning to the mat and you'll keep surprising yourself."

After four more classes, two intermediate and two

advanced, it was time to hand the reins over to Layla to close out the day. I always knew the second she entered the building, even if I couldn't see her, I sensed her. It was as if the air became electrified when she entered a room. She exuded confidence, grace, and sex appeal no matter where she was, what she wore, or what she was doing.

At five-seven, she was only two inches taller than me, but her irresistible personality made her seem seven feet tall. Wherever she went, she had a gift for being the life of the party and making friends. Even on the first day of third grade, when *we* first met. We hit it off right away and have been close ever since.

Even when Layla Montgomery traveled the world as the prima ballerina for a top New York ballet company, we stayed close. Our bond grew stronger after a nasty fall resulted in a broken ankle, ending her career too early. She hadn't let it get her down for long.

After Layla healed, she'd given me advice that helped me get my yoga studio up and running. Once it opened, she'd started working as an instructor. As a former ballerina, she had been practicing yoga for much longer than I had and taught me some new techniques.

"Hey Skye, how'd it go today?" Layla asked as she slid her purse into my bottom desk drawer.

I wandered into my office, accepting the cup of tea she handed me. "Same as always. You have three classes and then you're free for the night."

"Nice. Want to grab dinner later?"

"Not tonight. I have some things I need to finish up at home. First class starts at six tomorrow, so I'll be in bed by nine."

"You can't keep yourself locked away forever, babe. There's more to life than work."

"I know, but I can't show up to work half awake. How about we go out Friday night?"

"Deal." She shifted her feet, a move she rarely did, but one I knew all too well. "Are you going to see her tonight?"

My gut clenched the same way it always did when I thought of her, but I forced my lips into a smile. "Not tonight. Like I said, I have some stuff I need to do at home."

She moved around the desk to stand in front of me. "When you go next, you know you don't have to go alone."

I leaned in and gave her a hug. "I know and thank you for always offering. See you tomorrow."

My trip home was quick, seeing that I lived in the loft apartment above the studio. As I stepped into my small apartment, the sounds of the outside world faded away, replaced by the quiet hum of my window-unit air conditioner.

I'd been beyond lucky to find the spot. Being a flourishing neighborhood for trendy and wealthy young people, The Verve was not a cheap place to live, but the rent for the studio included the living space which made it more reasonable—as reasonable as rent in the city could be.

Every time I stepped inside, a sense of peace enveloped me. I loved my apartment, even if I had to use the generous walk-in closet as a makeshift art studio and hang my clothes on dress racks. Living in the city came with sacrifices, and I was willing to make them.

As I did every time I walked by that closet, I peered inside at the painting of *him*. The longing to see him again hadn't lessened over time. Instead, it had grown stronger every day, and I was beginning to think that desire would never be satisfied.

THE NEXT FEW DAYS FLEW BY. Skye Yoga had gained several new clients, so new client meetings and beginner classes had filled my days. By the time Friday had finally arrived, I was more than ready for a night out with Layla.

After a few months of poor attendance on Saturday mornings, I'd changed the first class to later in the day. That way, I had less hungover students and I could sleep in after a night out with my friends.

"Ready to get sloppy and stupid?" Layla asked as she locked the door.

I let out a laugh. "Lay, you know no matter what I'm doing, I never get sloppy."

"There's a first time for everything." She led the way up to my apartment, giving me an unobstructed view of her too-perfect behind. "I invited Chelsea. I hope that's okay."

Chelsea Sinclair's father was a prominent political correspondent for a leading international news channel. After her mother passed away, her father raised her the best he could with his demanding schedule.

She attended the best private schools and graduated early with top honors because of her intelligence. She knew six different languages, as well as the proper etiquette for interacting with domestic and foreign dignitaries. To her father's dismay, she also pursued her passion for culinary arts by attending the world's top culinary schools.

She was not only one of the most popular chefs in the world—there was a years-long wait list to get a table at her restaurant, Harvest & Hearth—but she was also one of the most devoted students at the studio. Not to mention a great friend and an even better person.

"Of course it's okay. I'm surprised she had a night off. Is she coming here or meeting us... where are we going anyway?" I perched myself on my bed as I watched Layla scrutinize the few choices I had for a night out.

"She's meeting us there. It's a surprise." She gave up on my dress rack and unzipped the overnight bag she'd brought with her. "Here. You're wearing this."

My face scrunched up at the tiny piece of black fabric she was holding out to me. "Uh-uh. No."

"Yes." She waved it around. "You need to wear something other than leggings and a Skye Yoga t-shirt. Let that body out, show it off."

"That's easy for you to say. Look at you!" I gestured at her dancer's body. "I don't have the figure for that dress."

She wiggled her butt while shooting me a smirk. "Girl, that is not true. You have a gorgeous body. This dress will emphasize your curves and long legs. You'll look like a runway model, I swear."

"Long legs? I'm five-five, Lay. Unlike you, I'm hardly runway model material."

Knowing she'd win in the end, I took the dress from her and placed it on the mattress beside me, then stood to strip out of my work clothes before making my way to the bathroom to apply my makeup.

Once that was done, I reentered the room to find Layla dressed in a slinky gold halter top and tight black skirt that had a slit running from her ankle to her hip. Her needle thin heels matched her top and added to her height, making her statuesque. Her sleek black hair was in a braided twist I'd never be able to achieve in a million years.

"Damn, Lay, you look *hot*," I said self-consciously as I picked up the dress she'd chosen for me. "Where is it we're going again?"

"It's a surprise," she repeated as she passed by me to the bathroom to finish her makeup. When she came out again, she looked stunning. The bronze eyeshadow she'd chosen made her jade green eyes pop even more than they did on their own. "Let's go. Chelsea is already there."

I slid on the pair of strappy black heels she'd dug out from under my bed and stood to straighten my dress. "I feel naked," I said, turning in front of my full-length mirror.

Layla moved up behind me. "You look amazing." She rested her hands on my hips and gave them a squeeze. "Look at us. Young and hot. We're going to make a statement tonight."

"I'm still not getting sloppy."

Taking my hand in hers, she pulled me toward the door. "We're only twenty-five. I have plenty of time to get you stupid drunk and sloppy at least once in your life."

If anyone could, it'd be Layla. Even during her ballerina days, she was the partier, the resident wild one of our little trio, and she enjoyed every moment of it.

As we walked down the street, people noticed us. Not just Layla. *Us.* While she barely noticed the attention, because she was used to it, I felt uncomfortable and kept tugging at the hem of my dress.

"Your ass is covered. Stop stretching out my dress," Layla said as we descended the steps to the subway.

"You didn't tell me we were taking the train. I would have worn a coat."

"You'd have stuck out like a sore thumb in this heat. You look amazing, your ass is covered, now stop worrying and have fun."

I sighed as I lowered myself into the seat beside her for the ten-minute trip to wherever we were going. The secret destination was a short walk from the train and when I saw where she was leading me, my jaw dropped.

"You're kidding. We're going here? We can't be going here," I said as we approached *X*, the city's hottest nightclub. It was normally impossible to get inside. The line was always wrapped around the block and most everyone went home disappointed after a night of standing on the sidewalk.

"The owner ate at Chelsea's restaurant last week. He's smitten and," Layla said as she pulled me to the front of the line, "we're on the list."

On the list. I'd never been on a list before. Well, at least not one that granted me access to somewhere fun. As we entered the club, a chorus of shouts and groans floated in behind us. I'd have felt guilty about it, but the thrill of actually getting in outweighed my compassion. Chelsea met us just inside the door, and a squeal escaped her lips when she saw us.

"I'm so happy you came out," she said with her lips pressed against my ear so I could hear her. "You look yummy."

"You look pretty tasty yourself," I replied, eyeing her outfit of a black sleeveless crop top and skin-tight black leather pants. "Should we get a drink before we dance?" I asked, hoping they'd say yes.

"No! I want to dance," Layla exclaimed as she led the way into the club.

The club was a mosaic of strikingly beautiful and glamorous people, and the music pulsed through my body, making it hard not to dance-walk through the room toward the dance floor. The air itself felt alive as the beat of the music brought on the swaying of countless hips, and I let myself get lost in it.

As soon as we stepped onto the dance floor, Layla yanked Chelsea and me to the center, clasping our hands tightly in hers. We moved together, letting the rhythm of the music guide us. I could understand why Layla liked it so much. It felt amazing to drop my inhibitions and dance like no one was watching.

But someone *was* watching. I could feel their eyes on me, a tingle between my shoulder blades, working its way down my spine. I turned around but didn't notice anyone right away. A gasp escaped me when my gaze found my observer.

It was *him.* The man from my painting. He'd grown a beard since I last saw him, but I knew it was him.

After all the hoping, all the longing, there he was leaning against the bar with a glass of amber liquid in his hand. I stopped dancing as our eyes met. His eyes held a brooding intensity that I thought only existed on the pages of classic gothic novels. There was a darkness within him that inexplicably drew me in, and before I knew what I was doing, I took a few steps in his direction.

The heat from his gaze caused the butterfly from two years ago to take flight in my stomach, along with hundreds of its friends. The desire to go to him was so strong I started walking toward him again, but before I could get away, Layla grabbed my arm to pull me back.

"Where do you think you're going? The song isn't over yet."

"I need to go to the bar. There's..." When I turned to point at the guy, he was gone.

"What?" she yelled.

"Never mind," I muttered as I began to dance again while I searched the crowd for him, but he had vanished. I did my best to shake off my disappointment and went back to dancing with my friends.

The night flew by, and all too soon the houselights were on, telling us it was time to leave. Layla and Chelsea came to my place for a sleepover. My apartment was bigger, but not nearly as nice as either of theirs. We always ended up crashing at my place because we would end up at the yoga studio the next day anyway.

We grabbed a pizza and ice cream on the way home and stayed up eating and talking until dawn. Even after we'd settled into my thankfully king-sized bed, I couldn't shake the memory of the guy at the club.

The look in his eyes. The way they felt on me. The urge to touch him. Who was he? Would I ever see him again? The thought of never seeing him again did something strange to my stomach. No one else had ever stuck with me like he had. There was something about him that called to me, pulled at me, and I couldn't get him out of my head.

After a while, I drifted into a restless sleep with dreams full of *him*.

Chapter Two

Killian

I took a sip of scotch as I watched the sunset from the windows of my living room. From the height of my penthouse apartment, I could see the entire city with the sun's rays glinting off the buildings while dusk settled into night. The view was stunning, but work consumed my thoughts, and I didn't fully appreciate it.

My mind was on my latest target. My guys had gotten what we needed only the day before and had already struck the killing blow.

Business wasn't business to me. It was an invigorating and calculated game of chess. For me, there was nothing quite like the satisfaction of toppling a rival and reaping the benefits. As the saying went: to the victor go the spoils. And I was always the victor.

My company mainly took over struggling businesses and restructured them for success or liquidated their assets. Those were the easy, boring deals that kept the books clean and the prying eyes off me. My most recent endeavor was one of the fun ones.

The pictures of Silverstone & Co.'s CEO snorting lines of cocaine off the abdomen of an underage prostitute had sealed his fate. He'd ignored my attempt to make a deal, but after seeing a taste of what I had on him, he had no choice but to accept my revised terms. It was just too bad for him that the new terms were even more weighted in my favor.

The new deal gave him nothing but the promise of keeping his indiscretions a secret. Had he accepted the first time, he'd have walked away with enough to keep him comfortable. His arrogance and the threats he'd tossed my way had cost him everything.

I hadn't built my fortune by playing fair, but then again, neither had the assholes I took down.

The taste of victory over swine like Randal Silverstone greatly surpassed the decadence of my prized forty-year-old scotch. I imagined his face when he saw the photos and a smirk pulled at my lips as I took the last sip of my drink. Just when I placed the empty glass on the coffee table, my phone rang.

"Is it done?" I asked without a greeting for the caller.

"Yes, sir, Mr. Asher."

"Good. You know what to do next," I said before hanging up, not bothering to wait for a response.

My guys knew not to look for praise or lengthy conversations. There was no room for sentiment in my tainted world, and anyone who worked for me learned that quickly. If they didn't like how I handled things, they were welcome to leave. No one ever left because I paid well. Exceptionally well.

Before I could put my phone down, it rang again. The call was from a blocked number, but I knew exactly who it was.

"Silverstone, I figured I'd hear from you," I said into the receiver, keeping my tone light.

"Fuck you, Asher. You've sunk too low this time." His tone was anything but light. Instead, he was frantic and belligerent. Just the way I liked my fallen adversaries.

"I didn't pay a sixteen-year-old to fuck you. Your downfall is on you. You should know better, Randy."

"If you breathe a word of—"

"Are you about to threaten me?" I asked quietly, barely above a whisper.

He sputtered to a stop, gasping in a breath. "What? Uh, n-no. I-if those pictures..."

"As long as you don't fuck with me, those pictures will remain where they are. Go slink off into a hole somewhere, Randy, and never show your face in public again."

"How can I know you won't release them?"

"My guys gave you the terms of our deal. The pictures will stay where they are unless you break the agreement." I paused. "I'll add one more term. If you touch anyone underage again, paid or not, those pictures will be the least of your worries. Are we clear?"

"I-I didn't kn—"

"Are. We. Clear?"

He gulped in another breath. "Yes. Yes. I—"

Whatever he was about to say went unheard as I

ended the call and slid the phone back into my pocket. I grabbed my glass and rose to stand, but something caught my eye in the pile of mail on the table. An advertisement for a yoga studio in The Verve. It wasn't the discount for first timers that caught my eye. It was the woman in the center of the ad.

She'd pulled her long, golden-blonde curls into a ponytail while her plump, red lips formed the most dazzling smile I'd ever seen. Her bright blue eyes held a sparkle mine had lost eons ago. The ridiculous urge to touch her slammed into me.

That's when I realized it was *her*. It was the chick from the club the other night. I'd struggled not to go to her while I watched her dance with her friends. When she'd spotted me, nailed me with those eyes, a primal need filled me.

I'd lusted after women, but with her it was different, more visceral. The desire to press my lips to the hollow of her neck, to glide my hands over her hips, and to feel her body beneath me had been so strong, so foreign, I left before I tackled her in the middle of the dance floor. That level of need was unlike anything I'd ever felt, and it had unnerved me.

I shook my head. What was it about this random woman? I'd dated supermodels, actresses, some of the most beautiful women in the world, but this photo of a chick in a Skye Yoga t-shirt had my dick reacting as if I were still a virgin.

"Skye Yoga? What the fuck is that anyway?" I muttered just before my eyes settled on the tiny print below her picture: *Skye Larsen, owner and head instructor.* "Ah…"

The women I usually dated understood there would be nothing more than a nice meal and a fantastic fuck. They were okay with it as long as I posed for a picture or two so they could prove they'd been with Killian Asher, the 'most eligible billionaire on the east coast.' They fed off the media attention for a few months and they were happy. Well, as happy as they could be in their superficial, materialistic world.

Quick, meaningless relationships worked best for me. I didn't have time for romance and emotions. With Skye Larsen, something told me there'd be nothing quick and meaningless about it.

Annoyed, I crumbled the ad into a ball and tossed it in the trash before placing my glass in the sink and heading to bed. It was after midnight, and I had a busy day ahead of me. Takeovers or take*downs*, it didn't matter. They both produced a lot of clean up, and I liked to oversee everything.

Dreams of a perky yoga instructor made my sleep restless, which left me groggy the next morning. How could one picture have had such an effect on me, Killian fucking Asher? I'd fucked the daughters of foreign and domestic dignitaries, princesses, hell, even a queen. Why should some small business owner keep me tossing and turning?

There was no time to dwell on the insanely erotic dreams or the confusion they'd caused. Work beckoned and required my entire focus. After a long, cold shower, I headed out the door in a crisp, dark blue suit ready to get shit done.

My driver, Neil, was already waiting for me with my usual coffee order in hand. With a small nod for him, I took the cup and slid into the backseat. As we drove, I checked my emails for any last-minute snafus. There weren't any. Which is what I expected.

I'd hand-selected each member of my staff because of their extensive knowledge in their chosen field of work. Whether they were an administrative assistant or IT gurus (a.k.a. hackers) or clean-up geniuses (a.k.a. hitmen), they were all the best in their field and knew I expected them to take care of things with zero fuck ups.

While I'd slept—sort of—they had been busy getting everything in place for the liquidation of Silverstone & Co. The press would undoubtedly be all over the news that the company was closing its doors after several decades at the top. My staff would have already reached out to my contacts in the media, both print and television, with a prepared statement from Randal Silverstone. It's always helpful to know the right people.

Next up were meetings with the buyers and the signing of the paperwork to make it all official. The meetings would take all damn day. Breaking up a multi-billion-dollar real estate development company and selling off the assets took time.

It also took a lot of pleasantries and patience, two things I have in short supply on a good day. Without sleep, they were nearly nonexistent.

I took the last sip of my coffee as we pulled up to my office building. I aimed a nod at the security officer before stepping into my private elevator, which I used more for the comfort of my employees than mine. No one wanted to be trapped in a small box with their grumpy boss. On the flip side, I didn't want brown-nosers kissing my ass on the ride up to my office.

When it stopped on the top floor and the doors slid open, my assistant, Amelia, was already waiting for me.

"Mr. Asher," she said, handing me a second cup of coffee. I rarely have more than one, so I assumed Neil warned her during the drive. "Mr. Brady, his son, and their lawyer are in meeting room one. Mr. Landry is in room two with his people. Lastly, Mrs. Smythe is in room three with her, um, advisor." Her brown eyes twinkled, and her lips quirked upward for a millisecond. Mrs. Smythe's 'advisor' would be her latest boytoy, who would be at least twenty years her junior. "Would you like me to sit in on the meetings?"

"No. Call the caterer and have them set up—"

"Already done. A selection of pastries and muffins, as well as coffee and tea, are in each room," Amelia replied. Before I could make my next request, she smiled and added, "I started the recorders, and the signed releases are on your desk."

I nodded my approval to her as I made my way toward my first of many meetings of the day. One of her best qualities was that she didn't want or need my approval. She knew she did an excellent job. She also knew I appreciated it, even if I didn't tell her. I had ways of showing my appreciation without words.

After the meetings were over and the signatures were dry, I tried replying to emails, but the yoga woman kept sneaking into my thoughts.

"Amelia," I called. When she popped her head into

the office, I held out a piece of paper. "Look into this for me. Report back to me with whatever you find. Do not breathe a word of this to anyone."

"Understood," she said, taking the strip of paper without looking at it. "Claudia called three times."

"Fuck." I'd forgotten about my date, and it was the last thing I wanted to do. Normally I didn't mind them, but sitting across from a woman who only wanted me there so she could make headlines was less than appealing.

Amelia could read me like a book. She pulled her lips into a soft smile as she headed out of my office. "I'll call her and cancel."

I was missing out on a night of mind-blowing sex. Claudia was adventurous and up for anything, but my mind was too full of Skye Larsen and what she looked like doing a downward dog. That image made supermodel Claudia Lobos look like a troll.

My preoccupation with Skye Larsen had plagued me throughout the day. Her face, that dress, and the body it covered were at the forefront of my mind. She tempted me like a moth to a flame. Her pull was hard to resist, and it was difficult to focus on anything else.

Amelia knocked once on my door before letting herself in. "Here's what I could find. There's not much on the surface, but I have my guy looking deeper. I should have more in the morning," she said as she slid a piece of paper onto my desk.

Her dark eyes examined me. She saw something in my expression and wanted to say more. I could see her debating whether voicing her opinion was worth it. Amelia was only thirty-three, but she had the intuition of a much older woman. She also had amazing connections and could keep her mouth shut. She was so good at keeping shit quiet, I still had no idea if she was married, dating, or single. Her lack of chitchat was one of my favorite things about her.

"The woman, Skye, had a rough childhood, but seems to have come out of it pretty well." I grunted in response, and she took a deep breath. "Is she a target?"

I glanced up at her. "In a manner of speaking, yeah."

The way her lips twisted proved she'd caught my drift. The way her eyebrows lifted revealed her surprise at my interest in a yoga instructor. The way her eyes lit up told me she approved. "All right, Mr. Asher. If that's all, I'll be leaving for the night."

"That's all. Goodnight," I muttered as I read over the information she'd left for me.

"She lives in the apartment above the studio," she called out as she headed toward the elevators.

I couldn't stop the smile that played on my lips. Amelia Reid was a remarkable woman.

She'd also been right. There wasn't much on Skye Larsen. She'd been raised by a single mother who bounced from man to man and bottle to bottle. There had been no money for rent, which meant there was none for college. That hadn't stopped Skye from working her way through school and graduating with minimal debt and a bachelor's in business.

Her degree clearly came in handy, since her yoga studio had been a success from the start when she'd opened the doors three years earlier.

I'd know more in the morning. The temptation to drive by her place just to catch a glimpse of her was so strong. My hands fisted, and my jaw tightened as I fought against that urge. Stalking wasn't a hobby I'd ever done or even considered, yet I debated picking it up for Skye Larsen.

I slid my phone from my pocket and shot off a text. The reply was almost instantaneous. Claudia Lobos and her lack of inhibitions were what I needed to get my mind off the yoga instructor, after all.

Chapter Three

Skye

T he slow rhythmic beeping of the heart monitor filled the space around me. The air in the room was thick and heavy with the sterile smell only found in a hospital. Every blip from the monitor sent another wave of anxiety through me, but still I smiled at the nurses and doctors. Hiding my feelings was something I'd mastered over the years. What good would it do to let them see through my façade anyway?

Their sympathetic looks didn't hide their judgment as well as they thought. As the nurse needlessly took my mother's blood pressure for the millionth time, I let my face relax, and my eyes wander around the room, taking in the familiar surroundings. I knew every inch of the room, every crack in the ceiling, every scratch on the floor, every cheaply framed piece of so-called art on the walls. It was all too familiar after spending countless hours there, watching her fade away.

I looked back at her frail form, lying motionless in the bed. Meadow Larsen was a shadow of the woman she'd once been before succumbing to addiction ten years earlier.

Her once bright and playful eyes were dull and unseeing. Her ashen lined face had once been so beautiful that a smile from her could win over the heart of any man. Protruding bones had replaced the curves of her body, and her smooth, bronzed skin was yellowed and sickly. Her formerly flat stomach was so swollen it looked as if she were hiding a basketball under the sheets.

The nurse finished taking her patient's vitals and covered my hand with hers. "How you holding up?"

"I'm doing okay. Thanks, Tiffany," I said with one of my well-practiced bright smiles. "How'd Jimmy do on his math test?"

At the mention of her little boy's name, Tiffany smiled, a real, heartfelt one, not the sad, pity-filled smile I was used to seeing. "Thanks to you, he got a B. If you hadn't given me that tip, I don't think he'd have done as well."

I let out a light laugh and shook my head. "That's not true. Jimmy's a smart kid."

"Thanks," she said, her eyes turning sad again. "You know she doesn't know you're here."

As much as I'd already known that, it still hurt to hear. "Yeah. I know."

She leaned in closer to me. "It's none of my business, but why do you do this to yourself?"

You're right, it's not your business, I thought but said, "I'm all she has left."

"You're a good person, Skye. A *really* good person. We get so many patients like her and no one ever visits them. Who knows, maybe on some level she does know you're here."

"Maybe." I shrugged my shoulders and smiled. My face hurt from all the smiling, but I kept that upward turn on my lips until Tiffany left the room and hurried down the hall. Her shift was over and I knew she was eager to get home for dinner with her family.

I returned my gaze to the woman lying in the bed, watching her chest rise and fall slowly. Each breath seemed to take more effort than the last. I'd stopped asking for updates because every time I did, the doctors would respond with, "It's only a matter of time." I'd smile and thank them while inside I screamed, "No shit, Sherlock! Why can't anyone tell me how much time?" I knew they meant well, but it bothered me that they couldn't tell me more.

I reached out and took her hand, feeling the limpness of her arm, the coolness of her skin. The warmth and strength that had once filled her was long gone.

There were no more tears for the woman I'd once admired, for the woman I'd once known as my mother. I'd cried my last tear for her a long time ago. All that remained was a vague sense of duty.

"Miss Larsen," the night nurse said, pulling me from my dark memories, "visiting hours are over."

I smiled my brightest smile and gave her a small nod as I rose to my feet. Still holding her hand, I leaned over my mother and pressed a kiss to her forehead. "I'll be back soon, Mom."

I always walked home after visiting her. The somewhat fresh air of the city helped clear the antiseptic smell of the hospital from my nose and clear my head of the stress of seeing my mother in her condition.

I was three blocks from home when I felt a tingle between my shoulder blades. The sensation traveled down my spine and back again. A frisson of excitement ran over me, causing goosebumps to form along my skin.

It was him. I knew it was him. When I turned around, he wasn't there. Was he hiding? Was it just my imagination? Whatever the answer was, the feeling stayed with me until I was in my apartment. Even then something pulled me to the window to look out onto the street below. I saw nothing unusual. Though there were no signs of *him*, I knew there were plenty of shadowed alcoves in which a person could conceal themselves.

I laid awake long into the night wondering if he was standing out there watching, waiting. What the hell did it say about me that the idea of him doing just that excited me so much, it made my core throb?

I wasn't a religious person, but that night I sent a plea out to the universe to bring the mystery man into my life.

———

"SKYE! OVER HERE," Layla called out.

I jogged across the street to join her at the little café table outside our favorite lunch spot. We ate there most

Saturdays before opening the studio for the day. It was always busy but had quick service and great food. Two tall glasses of iced teas with lemon sat on the table along with a basket of brown bread and honeyed butter. If I were being honest, it was that bread that kept me coming back.

"Hey Lay," I said, leaning in to give her a hug. "Have you been waiting long?"

"About ten minutes. Marco is bringing you your favorite." She wiggled her eyebrows. "He's got the hots for you."

"Funny," I said with a laugh. Even at almost eighty years old, Marco had an undeniable charm that captivated the ladies. Since he made *the* best croissants which made the perfect vehicle for *the* best chicken salad, I was a little smitten with him myself.

Her cheerful face fell, and I knew what was coming. "How'd the visit go yesterday?"

"Same as usual. She's unconscious and dying. The doctors don't know how much longer it'll take."

"Damn. I'm so sorry, babe," she said, reaching across the table to give my hand a squeeze. "I wish there was something I could do to help."

"You're here. That's enough." I smiled up at Marco as he slid my plate in front of me. "Thanks, Marco. Looks delicious as always."

"You're welcome, love," he replied with a grin. "Now if we could only get your friend to eat something more than rabbit food." He grimaced at the green salad with grilled salmon and light vinaigrette that was Layla's regular order.

"Marco, your grilled salmon is the best in town," Layla said with her knee-melting smile.

"Bah, rabbit food," Marco muttered as he walked away while Layla and I tried to hold back our laughter.

"I swear he's the only man alive that isn't charmed by you," I said, picking up half my sandwich.

Layla plucked a piece of bread from the basket and buttered it. "Speaking of men, have you seen Mr. Sexy Stalker again?"

"I never said he was stalking me. I just feel his eyes on me sometimes."

"Hmm, and that's not stalking, how?" She smirked at my groan.

I shrugged my shoulders. "Ugh, I don't know what to call it, Lay. All I know is I get the exact same feeling I did that night at the club. When I'm walking to the market. When I'm going for a run. When I'm eating a chicken salad sandwich with my best friend," I added as I turned in my seat to look for any sign of him.

She gasped, and I heard her fork clatter against the plate. "What? He's here? You feel him?"

I turned back to see her straining her neck to look beyond me. "I feel *it*. The tingle between my shoulder blades. I don't see him though. Maybe it's just wishful thinking. Like I'm imagining it all."

"Wishful thinking? Like you want someone to stalk you?"

I rolled my eyes. "No! No one is stalking me." I took

a bite of my sandwich and chewed carefully before adding, "Though if anyone were, I'd want it to be him."

Layla stared at me like I had two heads then burst out laughing. "Oh, babe, we need to get you laid."

After we finished our lunches, we headed to work together. We were about halfway there when that spot between my shoulder blades began to tingle again. As we got closer to the studio, the more the sensation intensified, telling me he was close.

I unlocked the front door before turning around, and when I saw him, my breath caught in my chest. He was across the street leaning against the light pole, staring at me with an intense look in his eyes.

"Uh, Lay, do you think you can take the first class for me?" I asked. "I just remembered I have an errand to run."

Her eyebrows shot up and a second later her gaze scanned the surrounding area, stopping when they landed on him. "That's him, isn't it?" she asked without looking at me.

"I think so," I replied, keeping my eyes on her.

She finally looked at me. "Just be careful."

"I will. Thanks." I waited for her to go inside and for the door to close again before I turned back to the street.

He was still there, his eyes trained on me. Mixed emotions warred inside me. An inexplicable desire to run to him wrestled with the more logical reaction to run far away from him. So, what did I do? I stood frozen in place staring at him, scared if I looked away, he'd disappear.

I watched in fascination as he started walking toward me. His powerful body moved with the grace of a panther, his muscular frame rippling with each step. My pulse raced as he approached with a dark energy radiating from him.

Without thinking, I took a few steps forward. I couldn't resist the pull he had on me, even though I knew nothing about him. His piercing gaze transfixed me as if he'd put me under some kind of hypnosis spell. There was something about his eyes, it was as if he could see straight through me. Like he knew my deepest, darkest secrets.

As he got closer to me, a shiver of anticipation ran down my spine. I should have been afraid because despite what I'd told Layla, this guy had been stalking me, and he was clearly excellent at hiding himself. Yet I couldn't stop the heat from pooling in my core at the thought of his hands on my body. Something told me his touch would be rough with a passion I'd never experienced. Just thinking about it had my heart racing and my center throbbing.

"Skye," a voice said from behind me, pulling me out of my hypnotized state.

I closed my eyes and swallowed the bile that had risen into my throat at the sound of that voice. I shrugged off the hand that gripped my arm, and when I opened my eyes again, *he* was gone. Frustration roiled inside me as I turned around to face the man who ruined my chance to meet *him.* To meet my beautiful stalker.

"Skye," he said again while grabbing my arm even

harder and using it to keep me from walking away.

"What do you want, Paul?" I asked, knowing exactly what he wanted. He was thinner than he'd been six months earlier. He looked tired and stressed.

"I want to come home. I belong here with you."

He tightened his grip when I tried shaking off his hold. I knew there'd be bruises before the end of the day. "No. I belong here. *Without* you," I said through teeth clenched from anger and pain. "Let go of me. Now."

Paul pulled me into him and lowered his lips to my ear. "I belong with you because you belong *to* me. Don't forget that, Skye."

"I am no one's property, least of all yours. Let go of me or I will scream."

"Do that and you'll be sorry. Remember what I'm capable of. You know what I'll do to you if you misbehave," he whispered against my ear. His breath smelled of cheap whiskey and cigarettes, making me gag.

He was right, I knew all too well what he could do to me. Paul was the reason I kept myself locked away, barely ever leaving the house, even after kicking him out. He was also the reason I'd lost the desire to be with another man.

"I believe she told you to release her," said a voice I had never heard before but recognized instantly. *Him.*

My head snapped to the side. There he stood, my beautiful stalker, even more gorgeous up close. With him standing beside me I could tell he was about six two or six three, making him tower over Paul. He'd rolled up his shirt sleeves, revealing tattoos, starting at his wrists and disappearing under his shirt. My eyes followed the intricate designs over his muscular forearms, and I felt the urge to trace them with my tongue and see how far they went.

Where the hell did that come from? I thought. I'd never wanted to lick a man's arms before, but something told me this man would taste like sin, forbidden and addictive. Then again, maybe I hadn't lost my desire to be with *all* men.

Paul pulled me to the side, keeping a vise grip on my arm. "Who the fuck are you?" he asked.

"That doesn't concern you, but if you don't take your hand off of her, I'll show you what *I'm* capable of." His tone was soft, almost conversational, but there was a subtle edge to it that set off alarm bells in my head.

As far as anyone else could tell, he was just a sexy businessman talking to a young couple. However, from my vantage point, I could sense a dark side beneath his seemingly polished exterior. Something told me he was more lethal than cyanide, and it only intrigued me more.

"Fuck off, buddy," Paul said as he began to walk away, pulling me along with him.

My stalker locked eyes with me, and I shook my head in response to his unspoken question. I didn't want to go with Paul. My stalker got my message and grabbed Paul by the wrist of the hand holding on to me. I heard a *pop* and a split second later, I heard Paul's yelp.

"You broke my fucking wrist!" Paul squealed as he cradled his arm.

He held his wounded limb against his chest, but it took my stalker's hand on the small of my back for me to realize I was free to move. It wasn't Paul touching me anymore.

It was *his* arm around my waist, *his* hand holding my hip possessively. When he pulled me closer, holding me tightly against his side, something happened in my chest. A weird bubbly, fluttering sensation.

He kept his eyes on Paul, patiently waiting for him to stop blubbering about his wrist. "Are you done whining?" Paul just stared at him with tears streaming down his face. "It's not broken. It's dislocated." As he stepped toward Paul, his hand slipped from my side, leaving it feeling cold.

I watched as he took Paul's arm in both his hands and made a jerking motion. Another *pop* sounded and Paul's hand was back where it belonged.

Then *he* settled his arm back around my waist. "I think it's time you left, don't you?"

Paul's gaze darted from him to me and back again. "Who are you?"

"Let's just say, if you ever come near Skye again, I'll be your worst nightmare. Don't even think about her. Understood?"

The blubbering moron turned to me. "Figures you'd end up with a psychopath. I'm done with you."

"You have it backwards, Paul," I said, finally finding my voice. "I was done with you months ago. I kicked you out, remember?"

His face turned red as he started shaking. "Fuck you.

I don't even know why I thought about taking you back. You're pathetic, just like your mom."

My back stiffened as the full force of his words slammed into me. He knew just how sensitive a subject my mother was, and he also knew just how hard I tried not to end up like her. Which was exactly why I'd finally kicked him to the curb.

"Walk away and never come back or lose the use of your legs," my stalker said. "Your choice."

With one last glare for me, Paul turned and walked away. I watched as he disappeared into the crowd. He was gone but the sting of what he said remained.

"Are you okay?" my stalker asked me. I lifted my gaze to his, and for the first time, I could see the color of his eyes. His anger made them the color of storm clouds, a gorgeous shade of gray that had me mesmerized. As his heated gaze roamed over my face, a softness washed over them. "Did he hurt you?"

It was then I realized I was absently rubbing my bruised arm. "Uh, yeah. Wait no. Yes. I mean no." *Oh my God, I'm spewing nonsense at Mr. Sexy Stalker,* I thought, shaking my head and taking a deep breath. "Yes, I'm okay. No, he didn't hurt me."

His eyes narrowed as he gently took my arm to lift my sleeve. His jaw twitched and his nostrils flared. "Fuck. I should have broken his face."

His voice was low and lethal. My brain yelled at me to run, but my traitorous body responded with blood-boiling lust, not fear. "It's nothing. Just bruises. They'll heal."

He shifted to stand in front of me, his hands lowering to my hips. As if it was something I did every day, I brought mine to rest on his chest, feeling the soft fabric and hard muscles beneath them. We stared at each other for a long while. I let my eyes roam over his face, pausing on his lips before meeting his gaze again.

"Have you... been following me?" I hadn't meant to ask it. I wasn't even aware I'd thought it, but the words came out as if of their own accord.

"Would it bother you if I were?"

"No." The response came out without me even having to think about it.

He leaned forward to press his lips against my ear much like Paul had done, but instead of revulsion, I felt breathless and weak in the knees. "Do you want me to stop?" he asked, his voice low and raspy.

"No," I breathed.

His tongue traced the shell of my ear. "Does it excite you to know I'm watching you?"

"Yes."

He nipped at my earlobe. "Good," he said, taking three steps back, his hands sliding from my waist. The loss of his touch left me feeling hollow and exposed.

"Are you leaving?" I asked, my voice was shaky and weak.

"For now," he replied.

The huskiness of his voice proved he was as affected as I was, and a perverse sense of accomplishment filled me.

"What's your name?" I stepped toward him without realizing it. My hands itched to touch him again, but I folded my arms over my chest instead.

His hands remained at his sides, and he stayed where he was when I stopped only inches in front of him. I was so close I heard it when he softly breathed in my scent.

His jaw twitched once before his lips pulled into a sly grin. "My name is not important right now."

"It is to me."

He tilted his head a little. "Why?"

"I'm tired of thinking of you as 'him' or 'my beautiful stalker.'" *Oh my God, I did not just say that!*

"You think about me?" he asked. When I nodded, his steel-gray eyes darkened with lust, leaving me breathless and wanting. I watched, entranced, as his tongue slipped out to lick his bottom lip. My eyes stayed on his mouth when he spoke again. "What is it you're doing when you think of me?"

I glanced up to my apartment window. "Hmm... I guess you haven't found a way to watch me *all* the time." My own eyes widened in surprise when I realized what I'd said. *Where the hell did that come from?*

The intensity of his stare seared into me, causing a tendril of lust to coil in my core and my pulse to race. "Be careful what you wish for, Sunshine."

Sunshine? I don't know why but the simple nickname had the butterflies in my stomach coming to life again. "If you won't tell me your name, tell me something else. Anything."

He slid his fingers into my pocket and I stopped

breathing. It confused me when he pulled out my phone and held it up to my face to unlock it, and I watched as he did something I couldn't see. When he handed it back to me, our fingers touched, sending a shock of electricity up my arm.

Too curious to wait, I looked down at the screen. A small smile played on my lips when I saw that he'd programmed his number into my contacts under the name Stalker. He had also texted himself from my phone, guaranteeing he had my number as well.

"Are you going to text to me while you stalk me?" I asked, surprised once again by my boldness.

"Goodbye, Sunshine," was his only response before he turned and walked away.

I stood on the sidewalk, staring after him long after I'd lost sight of him. My beautiful stalker had given me a nickname, scared off my asshole ex by threatening to cripple him, and then he'd set every fiber of my being on fire with need. He knew where I worked, where I lived, and had my phone number.

It should have scared the shit out of me. I should have blocked his number and called the police. Instead, I saved his number to my favorites list and eagerly awaited his first actual message.

Chapter Four

Killian

Walking away from her had been one of the hardest things I'd ever done. What I'd wanted to do was toss her over my shoulder, carry her upstairs, and fuck her until my weird obsession with her disappeared. Then that sleazeball approached her, and I wanted to tear him apart with my bare hands. At first, I thought he was her boyfriend, but her reaction had proven otherwise.

I'd almost run across the street to break his neck when he grabbed her arm. Even from my vantage point I could tell he held her too tightly. When she winced in pain, my blood boiled with rage.

I'd kept my cool because I hadn't become who I was by making rash decisions. I sat back, watching her handle the situation until Paul pushed things too far. The instant I saw her flinch again, I stepped in.

The relief in her eyes when she'd seen me made me even angrier. She was so scared of the puny dipshit that she'd willingly accepted the help of a complete stranger.

I wondered if she would have been as relieved if she knew I was a thousand times more dangerous than that skinny junkie could ever be.

When I held her against me, I could feel her trembling. A sense of pride struck me when she spoke up for herself, and then a wave of unadulterated fury washed over me when she'd cringed at his insult about her mother. It had taken all my strength not to kill him where he stood.

Hours later, I still couldn't shake the possessiveness I felt over her. A primal part of me believed she was mine, even if my rational side didn't want her to be. We wouldn't work together. We came from two different worlds. She was pure and clean, and I was too far from being either of those things.

By the end of the night, I decided to watch her from afar without contacting her. I'd make sure she was safe, but that's where it had to end. Then in the morning, after more erotic dreams full of her, I decided to hire someone to watch her for me. The further I stayed away from her, the better. For both of us.

"Good morning, Mr. Asher," Amelia said, looking up from her computer as I entered the office.

"My office," I grumbled as I passed her. She perched herself on a chair in front of my desk and waited patiently for me to speak. "Your guy, the one who got the info on the yoga instructor, I have another job for him."

Her eyes flicked to the envelope holding the information on Skye. It was still sitting where Amelia had left it, untouched. Because the temptation to learn everything I could about her was so strong, I'd withheld it from myself. I could not, would not, let a yoga instructor with barely a penny to her name distract me from what I'd built. I'd worked too hard, sacrificed too much, and crossed too many lines to take my eye off the ball.

Amelia turned her attention back to me and folded her hands in her lap. "Of course. What do you need Leo to do?"

She listened as I gave her the instructions for her guy. "She is not to know he's following her. His job will be to ensure her dipshit ex leaves her alone. If he doesn't stay away, if he gets within ten feet of her…"

Amelia didn't need me to finish the sentence. She'd been around long enough to know what I'd want done. "I'll take care of it." She rose to stand but didn't turn to leave. "I'm taking my assistant hat off for a sec because I need to know… What is it about this woman?"

My teeth clenched. "I don't know," I said firmly. "I just need to know she's safe."

"There are other ways for you to ensure her safety. Why are you choosing to stay away from her? You're clearly interested."

"Watch your step, Amelia," I whispered.

"Mr. Asher—"

"You're prying into my personal life, and you still won't call me Killian?"

She ignored my question and kept going. "I've been with you for nearly a decade, and you've never changed your routine, never canceled appointments, and have never asked me to look into someone who wasn't a target." She leaned forward to rest her hands on my desk, her long brown hair falling forward to curtain her face. "You cannot blame me for being curious about this woman."

I groaned and ran a hand through my hair. She was the only person in the world who could speak to me that way and not end up in the ICU. Amelia was not only the one person who could handle my more sinister requests without blinking, but also ensure their flawless execution.

"She's too tempting," I said.

"I understand." As she reached the door, she paused and turned back to me. "You know, Mr. Asher, it's okay to be distracted sometimes, to give into your temptations, and let someone penetrate that steel wall of yours. It might even be good for you."

I didn't respond, but her words stuck with me. Bringing someone like Skye Larsen into my world could be dangerous for her. I'd made plenty of enemies in my lifetime and some of them would do anything to see me suffer. If I got too close to her... No. It couldn't happen. Ensuring Skye's safety was what mattered, even if it meant I could never touch her.

Days turned into weeks, and I still found myself constantly tormented by thoughts of Skye. The urge to check on her had become unbearable, turning me into an insufferable asshole—even more so than I already was.

My entire life I'd trained myself not to give in to my base desires. I did everything for a purpose, to my advantage, and as I saw it, Skye Larsen held no benefit to me. Work was demanding, and I was too busy for a relationship.

At least that's what I tried to tell myself. Then, as the days went by, I couldn't shake her from my thoughts, no matter how hard I tried. Every time I closed my eyes, I saw her face, felt her touch, and heard her voice.

The craving for her consumed me, keeping me up at night with an insatiable fire that burned deep within. It was a madness, a relentless need that made me ache for her touch, her scent, her taste. I was powerless to resist her pull, and the more I tried to deny it, the more unbearable my longing became. Until one night, alone in my office, I gave in and texted her.

I could no longer fight myself. My lack of judgment could have been because of the half a bottle of scotch I'd had, or the fact that I hadn't slept with anyone since the day I'd spoken to Skye. No one had come even close to enticing me the way she did.

Me: *Have you been thinking about me?*

A full minute went by before the dots appeared telling me she was responding.

Skye: *Ah, so you are alive. You know something? You're the worst stalker ever.*

Me: *Been busy.*

Skye: *Stalking someone new? Should I be jealous?*

I felt my lips curve upward.

Me: *Busy with work.*

Skye: *Oh? What is it you do?*

Me: *Business.*

Skye: *Hmm, okay. You won't tell me your name or what you do for a living. What will you tell me?*

Me: *You first. You never answered my question.*

Skye: *What question?*

Me: *Have you been thinking about me?*

Skye: *Yes.*

My dick sprung to life, straining against my pants.

Me: *What exactly have you been thinking about?*

Skye: *Nope. You need to tell me something about yourself before I answer anything else.*

Me: *My name is Killian.*

Skye: *Killian. I like it, but I'm still going to call you Stalker.*

Me: *That's fine with me.*

Skye: *So, you want to know what I've been thinking about? Is that really what you want to know?*

Me: *Yes.*

Skye: *Hmm, I would have thought you'd want to know what I was doing while I thought about you.*

My dick jumped so hard I thought it might break through my pants. Fuck, this girl was going to drive me insane with wanting her.

Me: *Oh, I do. Except I don't want you to tell me about it.*

Skye: *No?*

Me: *No. I want you to show me.*

The three dots appeared, disappeared, and

reappeared a few times. Three minutes went by before she finally replied. A sick thrill pulsed through me knowing I'd shocked her.

Skye: *You know where I live.*

Fuck me. She'd shocked me right back, sending a jolt of desire right to my cock.

Me: *Don't tempt me, Sunshine.*

Skye: *You started it, Stalker.*

Me: *I think I've already told you once: be careful what you wish for.*

Skye: *Noted. This may sound like a cheesy excuse, but I have an early day tomorrow, so I have to go to bed. Goodnight, Stalker.*

Me: *Goodnight.*

Just as I placed my phone on the desk another text came through.

Skye: *I hope work slows down for you soon, so you'll have more time for your... hobby.*

Damn the woman. She was asking me to stalk her. She was turning out to be way more interesting than I originally thought.

I BARELY SLEPT THAT NIGHT. Dreams of Skye Larsen made it impossible to get a restful sleep. Not even after taking a cold shower and fisting my cock while imagining it was her plump, red lips wrapped around it. I'd come harder than I ever had, but it wasn't enough. It was then that I knew only *she* could quench the all-consuming lust afflicting me. Only her body, her hands, and her pouty red lips would do.

That's why I found myself standing across the street from her place in the rain the next day. I could only see the front desk from where I stood, but every now and again I'd catch a glimpse of her greeting customers or chatting with the gorgeous chick at the front desk. I knew I was in deep when that tall, tan, black-haired beauty held no appeal for me.

After the last class and the front desk chick left for the day, I watched Skye lock the door before disappearing from sight. When the lights turned on in her apartment, I decided it was time for me to go home.

While I berated myself for being pathetic enough to stand in the rain just to catch a glimpse of some girl, my phone alerted me to a text.

Skye: You're going to catch a cold out there.

I looked up to her apartment to find her standing in the window in a bathrobe. *Fuck.* This girl would be the death of me. Every instinct I had told me to run up there, rip that robe off her, and bend her over the couch to fuck her senseless.

Me: Worried about me?

Skye: Something tells me you don't need anyone to worry about you. See you tomorrow?

Me: Maybe.

She turned away from the window and as I watched, she let the robe slide down her body. She stood there in a pair of black lace underwear and nothing else. When she grinned at me over her shoulder, I nearly fell to my knees. Then she was gone. Out of sight, but definitely not out of mind.

My driver pulled up just in time to stop me from making a complete fool of myself. I reluctantly slid into the backseat of the awaiting SUV and slammed the door, cutting off the sounds of the city.

"Home, Mr. Asher?"

"Not yet, Neil. Are you free for a few more hours?" I may be an asshole who has no personal life, but I'm not so bad as to keep my employees from theirs.

"I am, sir." Neil had been my driver for close to twenty-five years. If he had other plans, he'd tell me. Yet even he wouldn't call me by my first name.

"To the office then," I said before settling back against the seat. During the drive I tried to figure out why I was so hung up on a random woman from The Verve. What was it about her that had made me so obsessed?

By the time we pulled up to my office building, I still hadn't figured it out. Neil had barely stopped the vehicle before I jumped out and made a beeline for the elevator. The only people in the building were the security officers and the cleaning crew. Thankfully, my office was empty and dark when I stepped through the door.

I sat behind my desk, flicked on the lamp, and picked up the envelope that had been haunting me for weeks. I'd told myself not to open it because it was invading her privacy. Then I'd told myself not to open it because she wasn't worth my time.

In the end, I needed to know what the white

rectangle held inside, and I hoped that finding out just how uninteresting she was would finally get her out of my head. Besides, I'd never given a fuck about someone's privacy, so why start with Skye 'yoga instructor' Larsen?

As I read through the report, she became more fascinating, not less. Her early years were nothing unusual. She had lived with her parents and older brother in an affluent neighborhood in Connecticut. Her brother was ten years older than her. He had been the star quarterback of his high school's football team. He went on to earn degrees in business, sustainability, and forestry before starting his own maple syrup company. Meadow Maple Farm was now the biggest producer of maple syrup in the States and was creeping into Canada.

When Skye was three, their dad died in a car accident. Her mom held onto the house as long as she could, but ultimately sold it, and they moved to what was now The Verve in lower Manhattan.

Her mother had been an artist with her own art studio, teaching people how to paint. It had gone well for a while until a little over a decade ago when it closed abruptly. When the business failed, she turned to drugs and alcohol. She ended up losing the tiny apartment she'd had. She and Skye were homeless or crashed with her mother's boyfriend of the week. Despite all that, Skye had managed to come out the bubbly, sexy, business owner she was.

There was an addendum on the second page. It was only a few sentences, but it was enough to have my heart stopping and my stomach churning.

"Fuck," I said, pounding my fist on the desk. "Fuck, fuck, fuck."

Those few lines of text made the decision an easy one. My contact with Skye Larsen needed to end. Immediately.

Chapter Five

Skye

It had been over a week since I'd heard from Killian. I'd even tried reaching out to him but he'd never replied. I hadn't felt his eyes on me or seen him at his preferred light pole either. His absence was affecting me way more than it should, and my preoccupation with him was getting on my nerves.

"Focus on your breath. Use it to flow through the movements." Instead of focusing on my own breath, my mind kept wondering why I hadn't heard from him.

The feelings of rejection and frustration clouding my brain were ridiculous. I didn't even know the guy, but it was hard not to wonder why he'd suddenly dropped off the face of the earth. Again. He'd gone nearly a month without texting me or showing up across the street. Then out of nowhere he texted me. We shared what I thought was a cute conversation. Followed by a bit of flirting through my living room window. Then nothing. Radio silence.

I joked with Layla about my stalker finding a new

woman to follow, but I didn't find it funny. I missed him and it made no sense. It was unlike me to be so casual and free with a complete stranger. Especially one who, for all intents and purposes, was stalking me.

There was just something about Killian No-Last-Name. Something I couldn't put my finger on. Something I wanted to figure out. If only he'd stop ghosting me.

Halfway through the class, Layla quietly entered the room. One look at her and I knew what had happened. Without her having to say a word, I stood up straight and made my way to my office. I heard her pick up where I'd left off, but her voice sounded miles away even before the studio door closed.

My phone was on my desk, lit up with a phone call I'd been dreading but expecting. I sat in my chair and with a shaky hand picked it up and greeted whoever was on the other side.

"Skye, it's Tiffany." Her voice was low and heavy with sympathy. "I'm so sorry, but she's gone."

I nodded, the motion quick and frantic. Tiffany couldn't see me, but I still couldn't stop my head from bobbing up and down. The news of my mother's death hit me harder than I thought it would. Even though it had been a long time coming, the reality of it still felt like a brutal shock. She'd been sick for years, in a coma for months. Her death had been inevitable, but that didn't make it any easier. The weight I'd been carrying on my chest should have eased. Instead, it intensified, suffocating me with its heaviness.

She was gone. Meadow Larsen, the brilliant artist

with a beautiful but troubled soul, was gone.

"Are you still there?" Tiffany asked.

"Yeah. Yeah. I'm here."

"Is there anything I can do?"

There was so much to do, so much to plan, and none of it was Tiffany's responsibility. "No. Thank you for offering. Is there something I need to do? Do I need to come down there and..." I let my words trail off because I had no idea how to finish that sentence.

"Yes. I'm sorry. There are some things that you'll have to sign. Um," she paused for a few beats, "we'll also need to know where to send her."

"Okay. All right. I'll be down there as soon as I can."

I ended the call and stared at my phone. I had to call him. It was the last thing I wanted to do. Going to see my mother's lifeless body held more appeal than calling him, but it had to be done. I opened my contacts and scrolled to his name and pressed the call button.

My brother answered the same way he did every time I called him. "Skye, are you okay?"

"Wes? She's gone."

He was silent for a long while, then he cleared his throat. "I'll be there tonight."

"I have to go sign papers at the hospital."

"Wait for me. I'll go with you."

"Okay." It was the first time I didn't bristle at him telling me what to do. It was the first time I was thankful he was taking control of the situation.

The class ended at the same time as my call, and Layla was standing in front of me seconds after the last client left.

"What can I do?" she asked.

"Hold down the fort for the next few days?"

She nodded. "Yeah, of course. Do you need to go to the hospital? I can come with you. Whatever you need, Skye, you know I'm here."

"I didn't think it would hurt this much. I always assumed I'd feel more relieved but..." The tears came then. Warm rivulets flowed down my cheeks as I remembered my mother before everything had turned to shit.

She'd been luminous, intoxicating, and so, so kind. It was that version of her I mourned because I'd always stupidly hoped that one day that version would come back. That hope died along with her, and what's sadder than losing hope?

Layla moved around the desk to wrap her arms around me and rub my back. "I know, sweetie. She was your mother. No matter what darkness she fell into, she was still your mother. It's natural to be sad."

"Wes is coming."

She stiffened but kept rubbing little circles on my back. "He's your brother, I'd expect him to show up. I'm bunking with you, so he has to sleep on the couch."

Wes and Layla had a complicated relationship. They were friends, but Layla didn't like it when Wes tried to run my life. I'd only been three when our dad had died, and mom had to work all the time. Since Wes was ten years older, he'd always felt like he had to look out for me. He'd been in his senior year of high school when Layla and I met, and even at eight years old, she would yell at him for bossing me around.

"One, he wouldn't share a bed with me. He's my brother, weirdo. Two, you know he'll stay at a hotel. And three, you don't need to stay over."

"Well, I am. Wes or no Wes, I'm coming to your place. I just have a few errands to run before I grab a few things from my place."

There was no use fighting her. She'd come back whether I wanted her to or not because that's what best friends do. They don't leave you alone when you're having a shitty day. "Okay. Thanks."

After she left, I went up to my apartment to take a shower and make some tea. It would take Wes at least six hours to drive in from Vermont, so I had time to prepare my nerves for his arrival. He was a good guy, don't get me wrong, but his innate need to take care of me could be overwhelming at times. I groaned as I replayed our last conversation in my head.

Tea wasn't strong enough, so I poured a large glass of wine and took advantage of my time alone by starting a new painting. I had an image in my head that needed to get out and onto the canvas, along with the emotions whirling around inside me.

I took a gulp of wine before placing the glass on the table beside the easel and picking up my palette. After I prepared the palette with the colors I wanted to use, I began. As time went on, my focus narrowed so the world around me melted away, and the only thing I could hear was the sound of my paintbrush stroking the canvas.

As I put the final touches on the painting, the sun had set. I didn't know how long ago it had dipped below the horizon, but the apartment behind me was lit only by the light in the kitchen.

I arched my back to release the tension, then let my gaze sweep over the canvas to fully take in my creation. The left side was bright and vivid. My mother's eye was bright blue and twinkled with joy as her lips parted in a warm smile. The right side was muted and dull. Her eye was sunken in, the white was bloodshot and the iris had lost its brightness. A frown pulled her lips downward as a tear touched the corner.

The painting captured the beauty and tragedy of my mother's life. Of my life. Heartbreaking memories of my mother's addiction and the pain it had caused us both warred with the happy memories of my mother's smile, her laughter, and her joy for life.

The hours I had spent cowering in the corner of a dingy motel room, worrying whether she'd wake up blended with the days full of joy we had felt while dancing in the rain. I realized then tears were streaming down my face, their salty droplets touching the corners of my lips just as they did in the painting of my mother.

My eyes focused more on the dark side of the painting as anger, sorrow, and regret filled me to the point I thought I'd burst.

As I sat staring at my work, I felt a hand on my shoulder. The warmth of their touch brought me back to the room, to the present. When I turned around, I saw it was Layla's hand that had pulled me from my trance, but it was Wes who stood directly behind me.

"It's beautiful," Layla whispered, looking at the painting with tears in her eyes.

"My God, Skye," Wes breathed. He was staring at the dark side of the portrait. His features were tight as his eyes roamed over the side of our mother he rarely saw. "Is that how she…"

I turned back to the painting. "Yeah. That's how she looked the last time I saw her, three days ago."

His jaw tightened as he turned away and moved into the living area. He lowered his tall, broad frame onto the couch. His elbows came to rest on his knees as he slumped forward with his head in his hands. He let out a heavy sigh, but the tension in his shoulders was unmistakable. It was clear he was struggling, and as I watched him from across the room, I couldn't stop my heart from breaking a little.

I sat beside him, placing a hand on his back. "Wes, are you okay?"

"I should have been here. I should have helped more." He turned his head to look at me, his eyes pleading for me to forgive him. "I'm sorry I left it all to you."

"That was my choice. I didn't have to see her. She barely knew who I was most of the time, and when the hospital admitted her, she didn't even know her own name. I chose to keep showing up."

He shook his head. "Why?"

"Because she was once the magnificent and radiant Meadow Larsen. Because whatever she'd become, she'd started as our mom." A pained sound escaped him, and I wrapped my arms around him. "I didn't mean it that way. You did your part. You paid her medical bills, you called me three times a week to ask about her, and if I had asked, you'd have been here in a flash."

"You shouldn't have had to ask. I should have been here."

"I think we need to focus on the present and the future, not the past. We have to go to the hospital to sign things. They want to know where to send the... where to send her."

"We'll go first thing in the morning." He shifted to switch our positions by taking me into his arms. "I love you, Munchkin," he whispered before pressing a kiss to the top of my head.

"I love you too, Ogre."

After one last squeeze, we rose to stand, and he turned to Layla. "Do you want a ride home?"

As she shook her head, I could see her eyes glistening with unshed tears. "No. I'm going to stay here tonight."

He gave her a watery smile and a small nod. "Okay. I'll see you both in the morning. Call me if you need anything before then."

Layla moved in to take his place, wrapping her arms around me. "Are you okay?"

"Yeah. I'm exhausted though."

"Go lie down. I'll join you in a few minutes."

As I climbed into bed, she left the apartment. My curiosity perked up, but my fatigue won out, and I was asleep before she came back from wherever she'd gone.

Chapter Six

Skye

The next day was one of the hardest I'd ever had. Wes and I went to the hospital where he handled everything. He'd insisted on taking care of it, and for once I let him take the lead without arguing. They'd bury her next to my father's grave in Connecticut. There wouldn't be a funeral because it would just be Wes and me attending and neither of us wanted that.

While he made the arrangements, I visited the room I'd been in more times than I could count. It was the place where she'd taken her last breath. The sight of it hurt my heart, but I had to see it one last time. Being there made me feel close to her in some small way.

After a little while, Wes texted telling me he was ready. It was time to go. I hadn't been there when she'd taken her last breath and leaving the room felt like I was abandoning her in some way. Even though it didn't make sense to feel guilty, it still felt suffocating.

After the hospital, Wes took me out to breakfast. It was a nice gesture, but I knew he had an ulterior motive.

As we sat in silence waiting for our food to arrive, he kept his eyes on me.

Then, as if some internal cue had signaled him, he spoke. "Listen, Munchkin. I know we've had this conversation a million times, but I really think you should move in with me, or at least get a place of your own in Vermont. There are plenty of nice, affordable apartments."

"Wes..."

"I know you hate when I bring this up. I can't help it. It's not safe for you here. Paul is here."

I sighed, knowing where this was going. "Wes, I really appreciate your concern, but I'm not leaving everything I've worked for, everything I've built to move to Vermont. I have a home, a business, and friends. I'm not turning my back on all of it because of some jerk I used to date. So please, stop asking me to."

"You think he's just going to leave you alone? Remember, I know about what happened a few months ago." He hit me with a meaningful look to remind me of when Paul had abruptly stormed into my studio during a class. He had forcefully seized my arm and tried to pull me out, but thankfully the class was full, and my incredible students intervened and stopped him. "Paul is still out there, waiting for the perfect moment to strike. I can't stand the thought of him hurting you again." He heaved a sigh. "Is it so wrong for me to want my little sister to be safe? I hate that you're in that apartment alone every night with no security."

I could see the worry etched on his face, but I was resolute. "I'll carry pepper spray and get an alarm system, Wes. The best on the market, and you can even pick it out for me. I can't just uproot my life and leave everything behind. It's not that simple." He clenched his jaw for a second then opened his mouth to say something else, but I pushed on. "Besides, I'm not alone all the time. I have a boyfriend. We've gotten pretty serious recently." *Dammit. Why did I say that? What if he wants to meet him?*

"Really? Why haven't you mentioned him before?"

"Because you're usually too busy lecturing me on how unsafe I am."

He eyed me suspiciously with a wry smile on his lips. "What's his name?"

"Killian." *Holy crap! What am I doing?*

"All right. Does this serious boyfriend have a last name?"

"Of course he does." *I just don't know what it is.* "Why do you need to know it?"

"Because if you're serious about this guy, I want to know more about him. I want to meet him."

Of course you do. "You mean you want to look into him. I don't need you to vet out my boyfriend, Wes. You have to stop trying to make me move to Vermont every time we have a conversation. Can't you just be my big brother without trying to be my father?"

"I'm not trying to be your father, Skye. I just want you to be safe." Though his tone was gentle, I still picked up a tinge of frustration.

"I am safe, Wes. My apartment is in a nice neighborhood. It's not like I'm living in an abandoned building or on the streets." His eyes widened at my comment. I knew I was being snide, but I couldn't help it. The idea of him trying to control my life was infuriating.

"Fine. We'll drop it," he said, narrowing his eyes. "I still want to meet this Killian guy."

We finished our meal in silence, the weight of our conversation hanging heavy in the air. Wes meant well, and I knew he felt guilty about not being there while our mother was dying. I also knew he felt even worse about not being able to keep me safe from Paul's abuse. I loved him for caring so much, but I wouldn't move my entire life because of his guilt.

"I'm going to stay for a few days. If you're free, we can have dinner tonight. Invite Layla and your boyfriend."

"Oh. Um, he may not be able to make it. He's very busy," I said, my voice surprisingly steady.

He studied me for a moment through narrowed eyes. "Skye, I want to meet him. Make it happen." His tone was also steady, but it screamed skepticism.

He wasn't buying my lie, and I needed to figure out how to get him to. "Okay. I'll figure it out."

After breakfast he dropped me off at the studio, which was functioning well in Layla's capable hands. I avoided the front entrance and went up the backstairs to my apartment to run a warm bath. As I relaxed in the lavender scented water, I texted Layla about dinner with my brother. Then I switched to my favorite contacts list where 'Stalker' stared back at me.

"Do I call him or text him?" What I needed to ask him

felt like it deserved a call, so I took a deep breath and touched his name. It went straight to voicemail, and the outgoing message was the one that came with the phone, so I still didn't know his last name. "Fuck."

Disappointment washed over me, along with a little anxiety. If I didn't get him to meet my brother, Wes would figure out I'd lied, and I'd be on the next flight to Vermont.

I needed to get in touch with Killian as soon as I could, so I texted him.

Me: "Hi, I know it's been a while, but there's something important I need to ask you. Can you meet me outside my place in an hour? Or whenever you can, before 6 tonight, please."

As I took another deep breath, I rested my phone on the edge of the tub and settled into my bath. After a while, the water turned chilly, and I still hadn't heard back from him. My stomach churned as I got out of the tub, wrapping a towel around my body. I really didn't want to move to Vermont. The town where my brother lived was beautiful, but it wasn't The Verve.

As I dried off and got dressed, my phone buzzed with a message. My heart skipped a beat when I saw it was from Killian.

Stalker: *Are you safe?*

A blush warmed my cheeks at the thrill that filled me when I read the words on my screen. He cared about my safety. It wasn't lost on me that my brother's concern annoyed me, but when it was my beautiful stalker, I felt... special. I shook my head, trying to ignore the nagging voice inside me that insisted something was wrong with me.

Me: Yes, I'm safe.

Stalker: I can't make it before six. How's tomorrow?

I'd have to come up with a story for my brother, but I'd make it work.

Me: Okay. Tomorrow. In the morning though. Around 8?

Stalker: I'll see you at 8 tomorrow morning. At the light pole.

Me: Okay. See you then.

I couldn't stop the smile from playing on my lips as I re-read our conversation, and that's how Layla found me when she walked through the door.

"What's going on?" She tried to peek at my phone, but I exited the text and switched to text my brother before she could see.

"Nothing." I sent a quick text to Wes asking to postpone dinner until tomorrow then looked up at my best friend. "Dinner is tomorrow instead."

"That works out perfectly then," she said with a mischievous smile. "We're going out tonight."

"We are?"

"Yup. Chelsea put our names on the list at X again. She can't make it, but she figured you might need a night out. Some time to forget about everything going on."

"I love her," I said with a little bounce. "And you."

My phone buzzed, pulling my gaze down to the screen. Layla leaned over to read the text as I did.

Wes: *Tomorrow. Don't postpone it again.*

"What the hell is his problem?" she asked.

I toyed with my phone case and rolled my lips together, embarrassed to tell her what I'd done.

"Out with it, Skye," she said, reading me like a book. "What's going on?"

I heaved a sigh. "I'll tell you while we get ready."

———⌇———

"ARE YOU SURE THIS IS A GOOD IDEA?" Layla asked for the third time on our way to the club. "You're going to ask the guy who is stalking you to pretend to be your boyfriend?"

She'd chosen a gorgeous, backless ivory dress for me to wear. It was short and tight, hugging my curves in a way that made me feel more feminine than ever before. The ivory fabric shimmered when the light hit it, pulling people's eyes to it as I walked down the street. The attention made me uncomfortable, but also made me stand a little taller.

"Yes, I'm going to ask him. No, I'm not sure it's a good idea," I replied as we neared the club. "I just don't know what else to do. If Wes finds out I lied, he'll increase the pressure on me to go back to Vermont with him. He's so scared Paul will come back and do something drastic."

She gave me a look. "He's not wrong to worry about that."

"Yeah, I know. That's why he will eventually wear me down. I'll feel bad about him worrying, and I'll give in."

"Yeah. It's because you're a softie who puts everyone else's needs ahead of yours. You need to learn how to be a coldhearted bitch." She nudged me with her elbow. "I just really don't want you to move."

"You and me both. I hate lying. It's just… if I can pull this off, Wes will leave me alone." My gut clenched as I thought of the fight I'd have with my brother if he found out I'd made it up. "I have to try."

She took my hand and pulled me to a stop. "How can you be sure this guy isn't a crazy asshole? He's been *stalking* you."

"I can't be sure," I said, squeezing her hand. "I just know he would never hurt *me*."

Her eyes widened. "Wow. Okay then. You had better know what you're getting yourself into. I'd like to talk to him."

"We're going to dinner tomorrow night."

"No. I want to talk to him on my own. He needs to pass my psycho radar."

I let out a laugh. If anyone had a malfunctioning psycho radar, it was Layla. Her past was full of narcissistic assholes. In her defense though, none of them had ever raised a hand to her, so maybe letting her vet out Killian a bit wasn't a bad idea.

"Okay. I'll set it up after dinner tomorrow… as long as Killian agrees to play along." I wrapped my arms around her, trying to ignore the unease growing inside me. If Killian refused, I was screwed. "Thank you for not judging me."

She stepped back to straighten her top. The dark purple was stunning against her black hair and tan skin. "Oh, I never said I wasn't judging you."

I laughed and smacked her arm as we moved past the mile-long line to the front door. When we stepped into the club, the music hit me, and my feet took me to the dance floor as if on autopilot.

I was lost in the music, moving my body in time with the beat as I danced with Layla. After a long while, something shifted, and I felt his eyes on me, like a soft caress gliding along the skin of my bare back. The feeling was familiar, and I instinctively knew it was him.

When I turned my head, our eyes locked. The intensity of his gaze made my heart race. As I took a step toward him, he turned and walked away, disappearing down a dark hallway.

"Hey," I yelled to Layla, who was now preoccupied with an admirer of her own. She glanced over at me, and I pointed to the bar. She nodded, and I followed Killian's path.

The hallway was dimly lit by the lights spilling in from the dance floor. I walked slowly down the hall, scanning the area for any sign of him. When I rounded the corner into the little alcove leading to the emergency exit, I saw him leaning against the wall, calmly waiting.

"You're here," I said. I was breathless, but it wasn't from the dancing.

"I am."

"You said you couldn't make it." Without fully realizing what I was doing, I kept taking small steps closer to him.

"I said I couldn't make it before six." He watched me approach, his eyes roaming over my body as I neared him. "I'm free now, and you said it was important."

"It is, but I feel silly—" His last words finally sunk in. "You knew I was here?"

"I did."

"How?"

He smirked. "That's not important." He reached out to take my hand in his and pulled me in to close the distance between us. "I'm here. You're here. Now ask me the question."

"It's more of a favor." I shifted my feet and pulled my bottom lip between my teeth.

"Ask."

"It's a *huge* favor."

"Ask," he repeated, tugging my arm to bring me even closer.

"My mom died yesterday," I said, my voice wavering just a little. I hadn't planned to tell him, but the words came out before I realized I was saying them.

He cupped his hand under my chin, lifting my face until our eyes met. "What do you need me to do?"

His offer to help me with my mom's death made my chest clench.

"Nothing. I'm not sure why I even told you that, but thank you for offering," I said, rambling.

He smoothed his hand up to my cheek, and his touch calmed my nerves, allowing me to take a deep breath. "Before I ask my favor, you need to know I love my brother. Wes is a great guy, but he thinks he knows what's best for me. He has it in his head that I'm not safe living alone in the city. He's been trying to get me to move to Vermont to be closer to him. Nothing I say stops his pestering."

"I haven't heard you ask for a favor yet."

"Eventually, I'll give in. I hate knowing he's home worrying about me all the time. So, I needed to find a way for him to relax."

"Still not hearing it."

A sigh escaped me. I was stalling, frustrating us both. "I told him I have a serious boyfriend, and I can't just pick up and leave. When he asked me for my boyfriend's name, I said your name without even thinking about it." He raised an eyebrow in surprise but didn't speak. "He wants us to have dinner with him tomorrow night at six."

"I'll be there."

My eyebrows flew up at the speed of his response. "You agree that quickly?"

"Yeah, I agree that quickly." He leaned forward, bringing his lips a breath away from mine. "I've tried to stay away from you, to stop watching you, to stop thinking about you. Just the other day I swore to never contact you again. When I got your text, I tried to ignore it, tried to forget about you. I told myself we would never work together, but something about you keeps pulling me back. You draw me in like a moth to a flame."

"Wow." I heaved a sigh. No one had ever said anything like that to me. "Wait a second. Why won't we work together?"

"Because you're a perky yoga instructor, and I'm me."

I tried to pull away from his touch, but he tightened his hold on me, keeping me where I was. "Are you saying I'm not good enough for you?"

"No."

I let out a sarcastic laugh. "It sure sounds that way."

"Sunshine, you have it all wrong." He lowered his hand to the small of my back, pulling me closer until our bodies met. His touch on my exposed skin caused a shiver to course through my body, igniting a fire in my core. "*I'm* not good enough for you. I tried to stay away from you for your protection, not because I don't want to be near you."

"Oh? My protection?" Alarm bells went off in my head, but my body ignored them as it leaned against his rock-hard frame. "Are you in the mob?"

He chuckled. "No. I'm just not a good guy."

I clucked my tongue. "Hmm, I don't believe that at all."

"That's why I'm not worthy of you." As he leaned in, a lock of hair fell to cover one eye. "You try to see the good in everyone. You won't find any in me."

I reached out to brush the stray lock from his face. "Again, I don't believe that."

He leaned in even closer until our noses touched. "You're too good for me." His voice was a whisper.

"You don't know me. Or my past," I said, breathlessly.

His lips brushed mine. Once. Twice. "I know

enough."

"How could—"

He silenced me by running his tongue over my bottom lip before slipping it in to meet mine. The kiss was slow at first, almost tender, until I let out a soft moan. That one tiny sound seemed to awaken something in him, something fierce and dark. The hand that had been on my back slid down to cup my ass possessively, while the other gripped the back of my neck.

With a firm tug, he tilted my head to the side and deepened the kiss. His tongue explored every inch of my mouth until I was dizzy with desire. He slipped his hand under my ass, pulling until I gave a little jump and wrapped my legs around his waist.

The position had his erection pressing against my center, the sensation of it pulled another moan from me. He tightened his hold on my neck, and the bite of his fingers made me shiver with pleasure. I'd have bruises, but they would be worth it because I knew in that moment, as crazy as it was, I was his. There was no turning back for me.

I was lost in him, his kiss, his touch. With the heat of his body pressed against mine, his hands exploring mine, I didn't care about the consequences or the danger I might face. The taste of him was addictive and intoxicating, and I gave myself over to the pleasure, to him.

After Paul, I never thought I'd let myself feel vulnerable or out of control again, but with Killian, my beautiful stalker, I was loving every second of it.

I felt a soft vibration against my left thigh. It took a second for me to realize what it was. "Oh shit, my phone." I wiggled against him, pulling a groan from him. "Sorry, I need to check it."

He released me reluctantly, and I lifted the hem of my dress to reveal the garter belt that held my phone. His gaze moved hungrily along my bare leg, heating my skin. The heat in his eyes had me spellbound, captivated by the intensity of his desire, until my phone buzzed once more, ruining the moment.

A frustrated growl escaped me as I glanced down at my phone. "Shit," I said, tapping out a quick reply. "It's my friend Layla. She's ready to go... I, uh, came here with her."

He took my hand, pulling me back to him. When our bodies touched, I slid my free hand up his back, pressing him closer as our mouths crashed together. He took my lower lip between his teeth, nibbling just enough to make me ache with pleasure.

"Until tomorrow," he whispered against my lips.

"Yeah. Tomorrow," I muttered dumbly and managed to smile as I slowly backed away from him with my pulse racing with desire. I wasn't afraid of what he might do if I turned my back on him, I was more worried he might disappear. He was like a dark dream, an intoxicating illusion that I didn't want to lose.

As I stepped out of the hallway with my eyes still locked on his, I fought the urge to run back into his arms. Ignoring the strange pull urging me to go back, I turned away from him and met Layla by the exit.

"You okay?" she asked, linking her arm with mine.

"Yeah. Thanks for taking me out tonight."

"You're welcome. Sorry to cut it short, but *I* have a yoga class at the crack of dawn." She nudged me to let me know she was messing with me.

As we walked to the subway, I told her about what had happened with Killian, how his kisses had been unlike anything I'd experienced with any other man. How just being near him had made my pulse race.

I didn't, however, tell her I felt the intensity of his gaze on me the entire time we walked. A shiver ran down my spine when I pictured him watching me walk with her, and I couldn't help the smile that pulled at my lips.

Chapter Seven

Killian

That kiss. That fucking kiss had plagued me with the most erotic dreams. They kept me tossing and turning all night, the sheets twisting around my naked body. No matter what I did, I could still taste her lips, still feel her body pressed against mine.

Every time I closed my eyes, I saw her. When I'd finally drift off to sleep, she was there, teasing me, taunting me, driving me crazy with need.

I could even still smell her. Lavender and vanilla, a simple blend that she made enticing, decadent, and irresistible. That one fucking kiss had nearly brought me to my knees, something that had never happened. I had kissed a thousand women, but none had ever affected me like Skye.

I tried to shake the thoughts from my head, but they refused to leave. She consumed my thoughts, my dreams… "Fuck," I groaned into the darkness of the room.

I hadn't planned on kissing her. My intention was to

find out what she wanted, what was so important. Then I saw her dancing again in another dress that hugged every curve of her body. I couldn't help but wonder what those curves would feel like beneath my hands, what her skin would feel like against mine. I wanted to taste her, to explore every inch of her, to bury myself inside her.

Then she turned and nailed me with those big blue eyes and pouty lips, and every thought of staying away, of never contacting her again had disappeared. I wanted her, fucking needed her.

Before I'd realized it, my lips were on hers. The way she kissed me back, with a hunger that matched my own, had me almost tearing her dress off and fucking her against the wall.

"Fuck," I said again as I got out of bed with a massive erection. I'd already taken care of it once, but it kept coming back. It was becoming a nuisance. Skye Larsen was becoming a nuisance.

How was I going to sit next to her at dinner with her brother without touching her? How was I supposed to do anything without imagining her tight little body pinned underneath mine, writhing in ecstasy?

My dick twitched at that thought, and I knew the only way to get her out of my system was to get her into my bed. I wasn't used to feeling this way, so completely consumed by desire. If I didn't have her soon, I would go insane from my constant erection.

Frustration gnawed at me, twisting my insides until I couldn't stand it anymore. Grabbing my phone, I slid back into bed and sent her a text.

Me: You awake? Thinking of me?

Skye: Yes and yes. Why are you still awake?

Me: I could ask you the same thing.

Skye: I just told you. I can't stop thinking about you. About tonight. About those kisses. Your turn.

Fucking hell. My hand tightened on my phone. There was no doubt anymore. She was going to drive me mad with need.

Me: Same.

Skye: Hmm. It's a shame Layla's sleeping over tonight.

A groan escaped me as I shook my head, and my dick grew even harder. She looked innocent and sweet, but there was more to her than met the eye. And I wanted to uncover what she had hidden under the surface.

Skye: Are you still there?

Me: I am.

Skye: Are you always this chatty, or do I bring it out in you?

A laugh escaped me. A genuine laugh, something I hadn't done in what felt like an eternity.

Me: We should get to know more about each other if we're going to pretend like we're in a serious relationship.

Skye: Not a bad idea. Ask me whatever you want.

Me: What's your favorite movie?

Skye: Pulp Fiction. Yours?

My eyebrows shot up. I was not expecting that one.

Me: The Usual Suspects. Favorite color?

Skye: That's a hard one, but I'll go with green. Your turn.

Me: Black. Band?

Skye: Not a band, per se, but Harry Styles and that voice of his... yummm.

As I read her answer, an irrational wave of possessiveness hit me. She'd most likely never meet Harry Styles, let alone fuck him, but I couldn't stop the irritation I felt. My mind reeled with dark thoughts, imagining all the ways I could make her forget every other man alive.

Skye: What about you? I'm trying to imagine what kind of music you listen to. It's Taylor Swift, isn't it? You're a sucker for a good breakup song.

Me: You nailed it.

Skye: Ha ha. I really don't want to end this, but I can't keep my eyes open.

Just texting with her had a sense of calm settling over me, easing the tension that had been building inside me, and it surprised me to find my eyes growing heavy.

A strange feeling settled in my gut, something I couldn't quite name, but I ignored it. For the time being.

Me: Sweet dreams, Sunshine.

Skye: Goodnight, Stalker. See you tomorrow.

AFTER A FEW MORE HOURS OF SLEEP, I woke up feeling lighter than I had ever felt before. I was looking forward to a smooth day, followed by dinner with Skye and her brother, but fate had other plans. When I stepped off the elevator, chaos greeted me. My assistant and the rest of my in-office staff were frantic. When I heard the news, the weight returned as my hands fisted at my sides.

My latest target had a massive stroke and slipped into a coma overnight, and to make matters worse, his idiot son was now the acting CEO. All the efforts I had put into blackmailing Sterling Walsh had disappeared in the blink of an eye. I had to act fast if I wanted to salvage the situation.

As I sat behind my desk, I could feel the weight of the world on my shoulders. I took a deep breath and tried to focus, but my mind was already thinking of the next step.

"I assume you've got someone digging into Chad Walsh," I said to Amelia. The shit we had on Sterling would have toppled him, but there was no way to blackmail a man in a coma.

We needed something on Chad instead.

Things took an upward turn when the door burst open and Chad stormed in. He was arrogant and cocky as he dared me to release the dirt we had on his father. He was an idiot, but he wasn't completely stupid.

Chad knew what we had on his father wouldn't go far anymore. My blood boiled watching the puny prick strut around like he had the upper hand, but I knew better than to let my emotions overwhelm me.

I leaned back in my chair and watched, amused, as he paraded around the room, trying to intimidate me. I knew his type his type well. He'd slip up and give me what I wanted. I waited patiently, biding my time until the perfect opportunity presented itself.

After an hour of him trying to bully me into backing off his family's company, Chad finally made a mistake. Whatever drug he was on seemed to wear off and his shoulders sagged as fatigue took over. That's when he let his guard down.

Chad laughed bitterly as he finally sat down. "What do you want to back off?"

Leaning forward, I gave him a skeptical look. "Come on, Chad, you know the answer to that."

He shook his head, the frantic movement of a man in trouble. "I can't do that."

"Is that so?" I asked. "Why is that, Chad?"

His Adam's apple bobbed as he swallowed hard. For a moment, I thought he was going to start ranting again. Instead, he slumped back in a chair, cupping his face in his hands.

"I'm fucked," he muttered.

The hitch in his voice had a scowl forming on my lips. The little shit was crying. In front of me. He really was an idiot. "How are you fucked, Chad?"

"I'm in so much debt. I'm drowning in it, and there's no way I can pay it back." His hands fisted in his hair. "My dad knew about it, so he rewrote the terms of my inheritance to block me from receiving or taking anything more than the salary assigned to me. I have nothing of my own."

"Debt?" I asked. "What kind of debt?"

He looked up at me then, fear in his eyes. "Gambling debt," he said, his voice barely above a whisper. "I owe some very dangerous people a lot of money. When they find out my dad is in a coma, and unlikely to come out of it, they'll know I'm going to inherit my father's estate... they'll come after me thinking I can pay them back, but I can't." He was crying so hard by then it was difficult to understand him. "They'll torture me."

As I absorbed his words, a shiver of excitement crept down my spine. He was at my mercy, with no way to escape. The rush was intoxicating. I lived for the thrill of gaining the upper hand and getting the leverage I needed to win.

"You might be in luck, Chad," I said smoothly. "Because I happen to know some very dangerous people too. If you play your cards right, I just might be able to help you out of this mess."

He looked up at me, suspicion heavy in his gaze. "How?"

I nodded, a devious smile playing on my lips. "First things first," I said, "there's still something you need to do."

Chad narrowed his eyes. "What? What do I need to do?" His voice was wobbling again.

I leaned back in my chair again. Normally I'd enjoy the power I had over him, but the way he was sniveling and whining disgusted me. I liked my targets to fight back, not cry like a baby.

"You need to get the board to agree to sell," I said. "In exchange, I'll make sure your debts are paid off."

Chad hesitated for a moment, his mind racing. I could see the fear and desperation etched on his face, and I knew he was struggling to make a decision.

"Let me make this easier for you." My voice was low and lethal. "If you say no to me, I'll do things to you that will make you pray you were in the hands of those men you spoke of."

His eyes widened and he gasped, choking on his saliva. "Who the fuck are you?"

I rose to my feet and made my way around the desk, stopping next to his chair. My hand fisted in his hair, pulling his head back to look at me. As I leaned in close to his face, I smiled, an evil twisting of my lips that had him swallowing hard again. "I'm the guy offering you a way out, Chad. But fuck with me and I'll make your life a living hell."

"O-okay. I'll do it. Whatever you want," he sputtered, cowering in fear.

I gave his hair one more pull before shoving him away. "Good choice. Now get the fuck out of my face and make the deal happen. Get it done because if you don't do it, I'll hunt you down and make you suffer in ways you never thought possible," I said.

He nodded frantically, sputtering promises. A grimace formed on my lips as I pushed the button to tell Amelia to come escort him out. There was nothing I hated more than groveling weasels who thought they were better than everyone else, but there was nothing I loved more than taking them down like the worms they were.

After he left, I settled back into my chair, letting the imminent victory sink in. Chad would get it done. With the prospect of being tortured by his bookie's enforcers, or by me, he had no other choice but to ensure I got what I wanted.

At the end of the day, I grabbed a bouquet of flowers and a bottle of wine before heading to Skye's. A strange sense of anticipation filled me when Neil pulled up to the yoga studio. The unfamiliar feeling made me cringe. I wasn't some pimply faced teenager going on his first date. I was a thirty-five-year-old grown-ass man in the process of bringing down a multi-billion-dollar empire.

Then I saw her through the window of her apartment. She was talking to her dark-haired friend while pacing the length of the room. Something had upset her, and I felt a surge of protectiveness.

She turned to glance out the window, and seeing her face full-on had everything around me fading away until she was all that existed.

"Is there anything wrong, sir?"

The sound of Neil's voice pulled me out of my thoughts, and I pushed away the unwanted emotions, reminding myself of the coldhearted man I was. "Not at all. Don't worry about picking me up later. I'll take the train," I said as I got out of the car, ready for the evening ahead.

Chapter Eight

Skye

T he second Layla and I stepped into my apartment, I began to pace, my heart pounding in my chest. She watched me walk the length of the room. The lie I'd told Wes was about to play itself out. If it went south, I'd be in for a hell of a fight. Layla had been right when she said I was a softie. I was, and I would eventually cave and move to freaking Vermont just to make my brother happy.

The thought of leaving everything I'd built and all my friends because of the poor choices I made in men was too much to bear. I shouldn't have to uproot my entire life because Paul was an asshole.

"It'll be okay, Skye," Layla said. "If something happens and Wes finds out, I'll help settle him down."

I nodded, but my nerves continued to get the better of me. I couldn't shake the feeling that something was going to go wrong. Just then, there was a knock at the door, and my heart jumped into my throat.

"It's probably Killian," Layla said, heading for the

door.

As Layla opened the door, Paul shoved it open all the way and pushed her aside.

"Paul, what the hell do you think you're doing?" I asked while trying to get to Layla to help her up, but he grabbed my arm, and held me in place.

"I've already explained this: you belong to me. I let you have your fun, and now it's time for me to come home."

Layla got to her feet and tried prying his hand off me, but he used his free arm to shove her so hard she fell back again, banging her head on the floor.

I could tell he was high on God knew what. This was more than the cocaine he usually preferred. Whatever it was, it had made his eyes bloodshot as they bulged with anger. Panic slammed into me. This was the worst I'd ever seen him, and I knew what he was capable of when he was only half as messed up as he was now. This would be ten times worse.

"You need to leave. Now," I said as I tried to yank my arm from his hold.

He tightened his grip until I flinched in pain. "I'm not going anywhere. This is as much my place as it is yours."

"You're wrong again. This is *my* home. I found it. I pay the rent. You have no right to be here if I don't want you here."

"You belong to me, Skye. You're going to be a good girl, and I'm moving back in. Understood?"

Layla was up again, this time punching and kicking him. He turned on her with a growl, grabbing her by the throat. "Back off, bitch," he said as he squeezed tightly before pushing her away.

"No! Don't you touch her again," I yelled as I struggled against his hold, but it was no use. He was skinnier than he'd been when we were together, yet he was still stronger than me. "Let me go!" I screamed as I stomped on his foot, then kneed him in the groin as hard as I could.

He loosened his hold enough for me to dance backward but I wasn't fast enough. He backhanded me across the face, sending me flying across the room. My back slammed into the window bench, knocking the wind out of me.

As I gasped for air, a noise brought my attention to the front door. There I saw Killian grab Paul by the back of his shirt and pull him out into the hallway. When the door closed again, Layla and I were left alone with a handsome, muscular man in a tailored brown suit. He was about six feet tall with broad shoulders, a thickly muscled chest, and powerful arms.

He stood with his sharp, watchful eyes on me. "Ma'am," he drawled. "My name is Leo. I'm here to protect you, not hurt you."

Because he'd shown up with Killian, I trusted him not to hurt me. I could not for the life of me figure out why I trusted Killian when all I knew about him was that he enjoyed watching me from the street and his kisses left me craving more.

"Okay. Hi, Leo," I muttered as I gently prodded my cheek with my fingers. I hissed when I touched a particularly sensitive spot.

Leo stepped forward and reached out his hand. He was so close I could see a scar on his upper lip and another above his right eye. It was also clear that someone had broken his nose more than once.

"May I?" he asked. I nodded, and he copied my movements, making me hiss again. "Apologies, ma'am. It's bruised pretty good, but it's not broken. I'll get you some ice."

I watched his stocky frame move around my apartment with the ease of someone much smaller. He brought me back a bag of frozen peas. "Thank you," I said, taking the bag and holding it to my cheek. "Can you check my friend too?"

"I'm okay," Layla said with a groan as Leo helped her to her feet. She rubbed at her head but otherwise seemed okay.

"Are you okay?" she asked, sitting beside me on the floor.

"Yeah. I'm so sorry."

She wrapped her arm around me, pulling me against her. "Do not apologize for that asshole."

Nodding, I rested my head on her shoulder as the room fell silent. After a moment, I heard the noises coming from the hall. Flesh hitting flesh mixed with the sickening sounds of bones cracking and grunts and moans coming from Paul. A scream preceded a stomach-churning gurgle. The sounds should have disgusted me. I should have been terrified. Instead, I was more turned on than I'd ever been.

Killian was beating Paul to a pulp, and I was loving

it. I was more frightened by my response to the violence happening in my hallway than the act itself. Someone being beaten shouldn't make me horny, even if it was Paul. It seemed everything about Killian made me want him in a way I'd never wanted anyone else.

The noises stopped and the room fell silent. I held my breath waiting for... I don't know what. I really didn't know what to expect. A moment later, my front door opened, and I released my breath when Killian walked in.

"Take care of the garbage in the hall," he said to Leo. He stayed where he was while the man left and closed the door behind him. Then he was kneeling in front of me in the blink of an eye.

"Are you okay?" he asked, looking at me as if he hadn't realized Layla was in the room.

My back was throbbing in time with my face. After having experienced broken bones, I knew the horrible pain I felt was from bruising not fractures.

"Yeah," I breathed, suddenly not caring about the pain.

"Let me see," Killian said, keeping his voice soft as he covered my hand with his and pulled the bag of peas away from my face. His jaw clenched and his eyes narrowed. "Anywhere else?"

Mesmerized by his eyes, I nodded. "My back hit the bench, but it's just bruised. I'll be okay."

"Show me," he said, his voice thick with emotion.

I twisted, hissing as a jolt of pain shot through me, and lifted my shirt to reveal my back. I knew there'd be the beginning of a bruise, angry and red against my pale skin.

Whatever he saw pulled a deep growling sound from him, and I turned to face him again, lowering my shirt. His eyes were dark, filled with something that I couldn't quite place. Desire or anger, I couldn't tell which, but whatever it was, it sent a shiver of need through me.

He cupped my cheek, keeping his touch featherlight, and met my eyes with his. "I should have killed him."

"You didn't?" I asked, ashamed of the disappointment I felt knowing Paul was still alive.

His lips twitched upward for a millisecond. "No. He's in bad shape, but Leo is taking him to a doctor I know. He'll live. For now." He turned away from me to look at Layla. "How about you? Layla, right?" She nodded. "Are you okay?"

"Yeah, thanks. Just take care of her," she said, and with a mischievous smile, she stood up and walked towards the bathroom.

Killian lowered his hand to my elbow and helped me stand. My eyes never left his as he led me to the couch and helped lower me onto it. As he crouched between my legs, his hands grazed my thighs, which had heat pooling in my core. I longed to wrap my legs around him and pull him close, but I resisted the temptation. Barely.

He must have sensed my arousal because his fingers tightened on my thighs. When I glanced down, I saw how red and swollen his knuckles were.

"Oh! You're hurt." I rose to my feet, taking his hands in mine and pulling him to the kitchen sink.

"It's nothing, I'm fine," he said as I turned on the water. "I can wash my own hands."

"Hush." I dampened a dish towel, gently wiping off the drying blood. The more I washed off, the more I realized it wasn't his blood. His knuckles looked abused, but he had no cuts on them. It was Paul's blood I was cleaning from his powerful hands. I licked my lips as more heat filled my core.

When his hand tensed, I flicked my gaze up to his. My tongue slipped out to moisten my lips, and his eyes lowered to watch the small movement. His head bowed toward mine, and when our lips touched, someone knocked on the door.

"Oh shit," I said, panic replacing my desire. "That's probably Wes."

Layla heard the knocking and came back into the room to answer the door. When she opened it, Wes stood at the door with a gorgeous bouquet of lavender in one hand and a bottle of wine in the other. Layla and I stared at him in shock. He was a great guy, but not the type to think about bringing flowers and wine to dinner with his sister.

"These were in the hallway," he said, sounding just as confused as I felt.

"Those would be mine," Killian said as he took the bouquet of lavender and held it out to me. "This is for you. The wine is for the house."

A sigh escaped me as I took the bouquet from him and buried my nose in it, breathing in the relaxing scent of lavender. "It's beautiful."

He leaned in to press a light kiss on my uninjured cheek. "Lavender always reminds me of you."

My heart skipped a beat, and it took me a few seconds to realize the ruse had begun. We were officially in fake dating mode.

"What the fuck happened?" Wes asked, interrupting the moment. He roughly inserted himself between Killian and me to examine my bruised face.

"Paul." I didn't elaborate because I didn't have to. The only reason I fessed up about Paul was because I knew Wes would assume Killian had hit me.

Layla was the first person I had confided in about Paul's abuse. When I finally mustered up the courage to break up with him, he'd refused to leave, telling me he'd rather kill us both than be apart. I waited until he'd passed out from whatever drugs he'd taken that day and went to Layla's. She had let me crash on her couch and took matters into her own hands by calling my brother to take care of the problem.

Wes had never revealed how he'd dealt with Paul, but I could only imagine the methods he must have used to make him move out.

Wes and Layla still felt guilty for not realizing what I'd been going through sooner. Which was part of why Wes wanted me to move closer to him so badly.

I couldn't blame them for not noticing something was going on. No one would have ever suspected Paul Pratchett of doing anything wrong. Before his addiction, he was always sweet and helpful to everyone. That continued outside our little hell for so long that not even Layla, the person closest to me, had noticed anything wrong. I'd also done a great job hiding it. Long-sleeved shirts, expertly applied makeup, and pretending I had tweaked my back to explain away the occasional limp.

Then Paul broke three of my ribs, my nose, and my right wrist all in one night. There hadn't been enough makeup to hide the swelling on my face and no shirt would have fully hidden a cast on my arm. When the broken ribs got so bad I couldn't stand up, he'd finally taken me to the hospital, and had stayed in the room with me to ensure he looked like the perfect boyfriend after my 'unfortunate fall in the shower.'

He'd really only stayed so he could keep me from telling the truth. When Layla came to visit, he did all the talking. That's when she suspected something wasn't right. He'd been so sleep deprived that when she asked him why he wouldn't let me speak for myself, he slipped up and got angry with her. She finally saw the darkness in Paul's eyes.

"That motherfucker. I'll kick his ass," Wes seethed.

"Already done," Killian said.

Wes finally acknowledged Killian's presence and turned to face him. "You kicked his ass?"

He held up his hands to display his knuckles. "I did."

"You the boyfriend?" Wes asked, eyeing him closely.

"I am," Killian responded in his typical succinct fashion.

Wes grunted his approval and the weight on my chest lifted a little. "How bad did you hurt him?"

"Enough to scare the living shit out of him. He might

need physical therapy if he wants to walk straight again."

My jaw dropped and desire slammed into me so hard, I was certain everyone could sense my arousal. Only Layla seemed to notice anything as she aimed a knowing smile at me. The guys kept talking about the ass-kicking Killian gave Paul.

"Nice job, man," Wes said, clapping Killian on the back.

It was small, almost imperceptible, but I caught Killian's flinch. "You're hurt," I said moving toward him to lift his shirt. A bruise was just starting to form on his left flank. I gently ran my fingers over the mark, his muscles tightening at my touch. "He hurt you."

His hand covered mine. "I let him take the first swing."

"Oh..." I breathed, lost in his eyes. Layla's throat cleared, snapping me out of it and my brother's presence finally hit me.

"Sorry. I guess I should formally introduce you two?" I was so discombobulated it came out as a question. "Killian, this is my brother Wes. Wes, Killian."

"How'd it happen?" Wes asked me, ignoring my needless introduction. He was like a dog with a bone, focused on one thing and one thing only.

"Layla and I were here waiting for you guys. There was a knock at the door. We thought it was one of you, so Layla opened it." I sighed heavily as exhaustion enveloped me. "You can infer the rest. I don't want to talk about it anymore."

Wes narrowed his eyes at me before turning to Killian. "Where is he?"

"With my guy." His tone made it clear Wes should stop asking about Paul, but my brother was not one to let go that easily.

"You should have killed him." Wes said it so matter-of-factly both Layla and I gaped at him in shock.

Killian on the other hand didn't react, and simply said, "The night isn't over."

Wes smirked and nodded. "Well, so far, you're not bad. Don't think I'm not picking up on your vague answers, but you seem like you can look out for Skye."

That was the last straw. "Excuse me? I am right here, and I am a grown woman who doesn't need someone looking out for her. Stop talking about me like I'm some weak little girl who needs a big powerful man to take care of her."

Wes smiled and tousled my hair. "She's adorable when she's angry, isn't she?"

"Stop it," I said, smacking my brother's arm. "Can we just go to dinner now?"

Layla glanced down at herself then at me. We were still in our yoga clothes. "We're not really dressed for dinner, and I think we missed our reservation."

"Dammit." My stomach was growling, and all I had in the fridge was a Diet Coke and a stick of butter.

"I'll cook. Wes and I will go to the store and get what I need," Layla said, taking him by the hand.

My brow furrowed when he left with her without

arguing, but the realization that I was alone with Killian eclipsed my curiosity.

"Thank you again for the lavender and wine," I said after the silence went on too long for me.

"You're welcome."

"Also, thanks for the display of affection for my brother."

He stepped closer to me, and my pulse quickened. "That wasn't a show."

"It wasn't?"

"No. Lavender really reminds me of you." Another step. "You always smell like it. And vanilla."

"Oh, my body wash and lotion." I wasn't sure if what I said made sense because his proximity was making my brain fuzzy.

He took two more steps, leaving him only inches away. "Who is Leo?" I blurted out when the urge to pounce on him became too hard to resist. "Why was he here?"

"Leo works for me. He's been keeping an eye on things when I can't."

"Keeping an eye on things when you can't? Am I *things*?" He nodded. "You have another man stalking me when you're too busy?"

"He's not stalking you. I just need to ensure your safety at all times, and that's where Leo comes in." He reached for my hand, and I backed up. "I won't hurt you." His voice was husky and when he reached for me again, I stayed where I was. "Unless you want me to. I could make you hurt so good, you'll beg me for more." My jaw dropped before I could stop it. His words made my face warm and my core melt. "I'll give you anything you want, Sunshine."

"Stop stalking me." Desire had my voice coming out barely above a whisper.

"Anything but that," he said, taking the last step to close the distance between us. "I'll pretend to be your boyfriend as long as you want. If you want jewels, I'll buy them for you. If you want to fly off to Rome, Paris, New Zealand we'll go right now." He pinned me with a hard, dark look that had my center throbbing. "If you want me to kill your slimy ex, I'll gladly slit his throat from ear to ear."

I gasped. "You'd kill him for me if I asked you to?"

"Without hesitation." He rested his hands on my hips. "If he even thinks about coming near you again, I'll do it anyway.

"Oh," I breathed. I couldn't really believe he'd commit murder for me. He was so close, I could feel the warmth of his body even though he wasn't touching me. I pressed my hands to his chest to push him away but found my hands fisting in his shirt to pull him closer.

He claimed he'd kill a man for me. It wasn't romantic in the traditional sense, but I wasn't a traditional kind of girl.

I shook my head in disbelief or shock... or both. "Why would you do that? You don't even know me."

An emotion I couldn't place flickered in his eyes

before the darkness took over again. "I know more than you think."

"You do?"

He nodded.

"How?"

"I have ways of finding things out."

I was too tired to play his game of keep away with information about him. "I don't think I want Paul to die. It's just... I want to forget he ever lived," I said with a shrug of my shoulders.

His gaze lowered to my lips. "I can make you forget him and any other guy you've ever been with, you only have to ask."

Images of what he was suggesting had my knees turning to jelly. "H-how would you do that?"

A wry grin twisted his lips. "I have my ways. Very effective ways. When you're ready, I'll show you." His lips covered mine in a slow but passionate kiss.

I let out a breathy laugh. "That's a good start."

A cyclone of emotions raged through me. Confusion, desire, anxiety, but the only one missing, the one I knew should be at the top of the list, was fear.

For some reason, I wasn't afraid of the stranger in my house.

Chapter Nine

Killian

We all ate a bizarre concoction Layla called 'spaghetti casserole,' which turned out to be squash, not pasta. Then while we sipped coffee, Wes peppered me with questions, trying to figure me out.

I answered him without giving away too much., but he pushed a little too far. He was Skye's brother but that didn't mean I wouldn't knock him out. For her sake, I maintained my composure, and kept my answers vague. I was all for keeping Skye safe, and helping her out, but Wes went to the extreme. If it were up to him, he'd lock her away on his maple tree farm.

I couldn't risk losing her, so I calmly answered his questions, giving him as little information as possible. There was only one question I couldn't avoid without raising a red flag: my last name.

"Killian Asher," Wes repeated with a furrowed brow. "Why does that sound familiar?"

I pursed my lips and shook my head. "No idea." If he ever figured it out, we'd have a problem. Skye's brother or not, he would not take her away from me, and I knew he'd try if he found out the truth.

When he decided he'd interrogated me enough, he said his goodbyes before taking Skye out into the hallway. Which left Layla sitting across the table staring at me with a shit-eating grin.

"You're enjoying this a little too much," I said.

"Not too much. Just the right amount."

I grunted. "Shouldn't you be concerned that your best friend is playing house with her stalker?"

"Ah, so you admit it. You *are* a pervy stalker," she said with a laugh, before her expression turned serious. "I was worried until you kicked the shit out of Paul. Man..." She let out a low whistle. "I'd have loved to watch you beat the fuck out of that shithead. After doing something like that, I can't imagine you'd turn around and hurt Skye."

"I'll film it next time." Layla thought she was perceptive, but she was naïve if she believed what she was saying. I had no intention of harming Skye, but assuming that was true simply because I kicked Paul's ass was foolish. She didn't know me or what I was capable of.

"See, I like you. I couldn't like you if you were a psycho. Plus, you brought her flowers... or are they technically herbs? Anyway... either you're a real sicko who will eventually kill her and turn her into a skin suit, or you're really into her." She leaned forward, resting her elbows on the table. "Something tells me it's the latter."

"A skin suit?"

"Yeah. Buffalo Bill?" Layla's eyes widened in surprise. "Haven't you seen *Silence of the Lambs*?"

"I have. It's just been a while."

"Ah, man, I watch that movie at least once a month. It's the best," she said before quoting Buffalo Bill's lotion in the basket scene and gave a little shiver at the end. "God, that man scarred me for life. I still can't listen to *American Girl* by Tom Petty if I'm home alone."

"Anyway, I'm getting sidetracked," Layla continued with a little frown. "Skye's never told me what happened to her when she was living on the streets... but I suspect Paul is not the only asshole who has hurt her."

She paused to take a deep breath. "She doesn't like to talk about that time of her life. She always puts on a smiling face and says, 'It's in the past, so why look back.' Even Wes doesn't know anything. I just know she's been through a lot in her short life. *Way* more than anyone should ever have to go through. Please, be careful with her. Don't hurt her."

"I'd never intentionally hurt her."

She pursed her lips and eyed me up. "I guess that's good enough. Just don't ever cheat on her or raise a hand to her."

"Those are two things I can guarantee I'd never do."

"Good because I'd hate to have to kill you."

A small smile pulled at my lips, and I found myself starting to like Layla Montgomery. I rarely enjoyed talking with people. In fact, in all my years, I could count on one hand the number of people I'd called a friend. Most of the guys I knew were business connections, not buddies.

Friendship, like any relationship, requires trust. In my line of work, trust was a weakness, and I'd dropped it a long time ago. Still, there was something about Layla that intrigued me, just like Skye.

When Skye walked back into the apartment, I realized it wasn't the same at all. Despite her beauty, Layla's appeal was not sexual. At least not for me. I felt no attraction toward her whatsoever.

With Skye, there was something about her that drew me in, something I'd never felt for anyone before her. I couldn't put a name to it, but it was deeper, more profound than lust. A primal urge to claim her, to make her mine and never let her go.

"Sorry about that," Skye said as she sat next to me at the table.

In an absent-minded but possessive move, I reached out and placed my hand on the back of her neck. Feeling the tension there, I massaged the knots away.

She sighed in relief and leaned into my touch, and a crack formed in the armor covering my heart.

"What did Wes say?" Layla asked.

"That he approves of Killian. For now." She groaned as she looked at me. "He respects that you kicked Paul's ass, but he wants to know more about you. So... he's staying in town for a while."

The news of Wes staying in town distracted Skye too much to notice her friend's reaction, but I caught it. Layla's lips briefly pulled into a nearly imperceptible smile before she composed herself.

Skye cleared her throat, her vision refocusing on the room. "He said he still blames himself for not stopping Paul the first time. That he'll never let me go through that again."

"Makes sense," I said. Wes clearly cared about his sister. If I were in his shoes, I'd do the same thing, but I hoped he didn't try too hard to find out about me. I'd hate to put Skye's brother in the morgue.

"Yeah, but he didn't know about what was going on because I hid it well. Not even Layla knew, and she saw me every day."

A gasp escaped Layla. "I'm so sorry, Skye," she sobbed, staring at the bruise on her friend's face, her eyes glistening with unshed tears.

"Oh, Lay, you know I don't blame you. It wasn't your fault." She reached across the table and took Layla's hand. "It was mine."

"Fuck that," I said. I tightened my hold on her neck, using it to turn her to face me. "You will not blame yourself for what that asshole did to you." My tone dripped with venom. I hated nothing more than hearing an abuse victim blame themselves. "Is that understood?"

She nodded.

"No." I used my other hand to take her chin between my forefinger and thumb, tilting her face up and forcing her to look at me. "Say it out loud. Let me hear you say you know it wasn't your fault."

"It wasn't my fault." She licked her lips and let out a shaky breath. "I know it wasn't."

"Good." I tilted her head to get a closer look at the bruise. "I should have fucking killed him."

Layla grunted, pulling our attention to her. "I too think you should have killed him. The night's still young, we could go find him." She glanced at her naked wrist. "Oh, but it's not as young as I thought. I should head home, but I gotta pee first."

I watched her stand and walk to the bathroom. "She's... unique," I whispered to Skye.

She let out a strained laugh. "That's the perfect word for her," she said around a yawn.

Layla came out of the bathroom humming *American Girl*. "Before I go, I need more information. You guys are going to pretend to be together, right?"

"Uh-huh," Skye muttered, eyeing her friend warily.

"You're going to go out to dinner. Maybe catch a movie every so often. Stuff like that, right?"

Skye glanced up at me. I kept my expression neutral, letting her take the lead.

"Yeah, I guess so. Stuff like that," Skye said after a beat.

"Sounds like fun." She picked up her purse and walked to the door, seemingly ending the conversation, but then she spun back around with a huge smile on her face. "So, you gonna fuck too?"

"No." Skye and I spoke the word at the same time and then glanced at each other, which Layla found hilarious.

"Oh, this is going to be fun," Layla said, as she stepped into the hallway. "So much fun."

The door closed, leaving Skye and me alone. We stayed where we were for a few moments, my hand still on the back of her neck. Then she yawned again.

"You look like you're about to pass out. Why don't you go take a bath? I'll head home too and check on you a little later."

"You're leaving?" The pouty look she aimed at me had my dick growing hard.

"I probably should."

She adjusted her position in her chair to face me. "Do you really need to?" Her hand reached out to toy with a button on my shirt. I didn't think my erection could get harder, then she looked up at me from under her lashes. That look. That one look did me in. I could no longer deny or fight how much I wanted her.

Fuck that fake dating bullshit. She was mine, and I'd do whatever it took to make sure she knew it.

"I'll stay. Go take that bath, and I'll be right here when you're done."

She eyed me warily but did as I suggested and went into the bathroom. The door shut, and I waited for the sound of a lock clicking into place, but all I heard was the soft gurgle of water filling the tub.

I shook my head. Even after what she'd been through with that scumbag Paul, she was too trusting. That realization solidified my decision to claim her, because as her brother had teased, she needed someone to look out for her, to protect her. I was going to be that person, no matter what it took.

Then the addendum to the report on her flashed through my mind, and I knew I couldn't be with her the way I wanted, the way my dick wanted. Not yet. Not with that information still fresh in my memory. I'd tell her about it eventually, but until then acting on my urge to find out what she felt like, what she looked like when I made her come would be cruel.

I may be a demanding and callous prick, but I'm not heartless. At least not with her.

I needed time to get everything in line first. If I didn't mitigate the inevitable fallout, she'd cut me out of her life and never look back. Waiting for the right time meant I needed a distraction while she was naked and wet only a few feet from me. I glanced around her apartment and appreciated the clever way she'd organized the space, dividing it into separate areas while keeping a natural flow.

Spotting a small bookshelf tucked beside the couch, I strolled over and selected a novel to pass the time while I waited for her.

I lowered myself onto the couch and started reading, but my mind kept wandering back to her, picturing her naked in the tub. The urge to go into the bathroom and bathe her myself was so strong I stood up.

The bathroom door opened, saving me from making a mistake. She stepped out, and I froze, transfixed by her beauty. She looked like a goddess in a sheer robe that revealed the camisole and shorts underneath, as well as the outline of her perky nipples. Her damp curls hung loosely around her face, looking deep bronze instead of golden-blonde, and her skin glowed with a faint pink flush from the hot water.

I wanted to touch her, taste her, possess her. Without realizing I'd moved, I found myself closer to her.

"You stayed," she said as she moved toward me.

We met in the middle, stopping a few inches from each other. "I told you I would."

As she did earlier, she reached out to play with a button on my shirt. "I thought you'd either leave or…"

She looked up at me with those big, blue eyes and I slid my arms around her, pulling her against me. "Or?"

"Or come in."

Fuck. "Did you want me to come in?" She bit her lower lip as she nodded. It was so fucking sexy, I had to stop myself from stripping off her clothes and taking her right where we stood. Instead, I took a step back, breaking our contact. "We should talk."

She aimed a disappointed look my way. "Do we really have to?"

A small smile played on my lips as I took her hand in mine and led her to the couch. "Yes, we do."

She sat with her eyes on her lap, absently twirling the strap of her robe between her fingers. "Do you want to stop pretending?"

"No."

She sighed, finally looking up at me. "Then what do you want to talk about?"

"Ground rules." A laugh escaped me when her face scrunched up in disgust. "I don't like rules either, but I think we should have at least one."

She shifted on the couch to face me, crossing her legs underneath her. "Let me guess, the rule is no sex, am I right?"

"Yes. I don't think it's a good idea."

She tilted her head, examining me for a moment. "Why? You stalk me, kiss me like no one has ever before, agree to pretend to be my boyfriend, but you don't want to fuck me. It makes no sense." Hearing the words 'fuck me' come out of her mouth had my dick springing to life. Her eyes lowered to my crotch and a sexy little smirk formed on her lips. "Hmm… interesting."

I reached out to brush the hair from her face and leaned in until my lips touched her ear. "Trust me, I want to fuck you. I want to rip off those little shorts and fuck you until you scream my name while I make you come. Over and over again. I want to fuck you until you forget every guy who has ever touched you."

Her breath felt warm against my cheek as she released a sigh. "Oh… why don't you?"

I traced the shell of her ear with my tongue, nipping at her lobe before sitting back. "Because you don't know me, and what I want doesn't matter."

"Whose fault is it that I don't know you?" she asked with a sexy little pout.

"There are things about me you can't know, shouldn't know. At least not yet. Until then, I don't think we should act on our urges." I let my eyes linger on her breasts. Her hard nipples seemed to beg for my touch. "No matter how badly we want to."

"You know, if I really wanted to," she began in a sultry whisper, "I could get you to fuck me just as you just described."

"Yes, you could because I'm an asshole, but you won't do that because you are not."

She sat back on a huff, crossing her arms in front of her chest. "Yeah, but it's times like these I wish I was," she said, letting out a pained sigh. I couldn't help but chuckle at her words, and her scowl turned into a small smile. "Can we still get to know each other?" she asked, hesitantly.

"Of course." Because I needed to touch her in some way, I reached over to take her hand in mine. She shifted nervously, and I could see a hint of vulnerability in her eyes.

She fixed her gaze on our intertwined hands. "Have you ever been in love?"

"No, I haven't."

"That was quick," she said with a small laugh.

I shrugged. "It was an easy one. How about you?"

Her smile faded, and she lowered her eyes again. "I thought so, but no." Her voice was barely above a whisper.

"Paul?"

She nodded, her eyes brimming with tears. "Yeah," she said, shaking her head. "In the beginning, things were great. At least I thought they were. I should have known he was an addict. I'd seen enough of it growing up with my mother, but I guess I let myself see what I wanted."

"Or he was good at hiding it."

"Everything changed when we moved in together. At least for me. It started with little things, like insulting my cooking or my choice of clothing or punching a wall. Then one day when I snapped back at him, he slapped me." She shivered, and I slid my arm around her, pulling her up against me. "It escalated, or went downhill, from there until he put me in the hospital with three broken ribs."

My blood boiled with anger as I listened to her. Once again, I regretted not killing the slimy fuck when I'd had the chance. While we were eating dinner, I received a text from Leo informing me that Paul had managed to slip by the guy he had assigned to watch him.

Leo's guy no longer had a job... or a heartbeat.

Paul had dragged his broken leg back into the dregs of the city to get high as quickly as he could. It was easy to disappear into the darkest corners of the city, but Leo had his people looking for him. He assured me they were more competent than their former coworker. Leo knew they had better be, or he'd be my next target.

His people would find him, and once they did, I'd take care of him for good. I had planned on paying him off, making him leave the state, but after hearing Skye's story, that plan had changed.

She must have sensed the shift in my mood because she looked up at me with wide eyes. "I'm sorry. I shouldn't have told you all that. We should learn about each other's favorite foods, not our poor choices in lovers."

"What he did to you was not because you made a

poor choice. What happened has nothing to do with anything you did or didn't do."

She shrugged. "Yeah, I guess. I just should have been more observant —"

Without thinking about it, I grabbed her and pulled her into my lap, lifting a hand to her face and squeezing her jaw to make sure she didn't look away. "I thought we went over this earlier. What he did to you was not your fault. You did nothing to deserve it. He abused you because he's a weak loser who doesn't deserve to breathe the same air as you. Do you understand?"

"Yes."

I released my hold, trailing my fingers over her neck before wrapping her hair around my fist. "Tell me you know it wasn't your fault."

"It wasn't my fault. I know that." Her voice was breathless and shaky, but my instincts told me it wasn't from fear.

I tugged her head back and leaned in to run my tongue up her neck, her cheek, to her ear. "Do not ever blame yourself again. Is that understood?"

She shuddered and her hands gripped my shoulders. "Yes. Never again."

"Good girl," I whispered in her ear, pulling a small moan from her that went straight to my dick. "Fuck, you smell good." Another moan had me grabbing her by the hips and grinding myself against her ass.

"Killian," she said, her voice barely a whisper, "you can't do this. You can't touch me this way and *not* fuck me."

Fuck. I pulled her head to the side and pressed my lips against her ear. "You're right. I'm not going to fuck you. Not yet. When the time is right, I'll fuck you until you beg for me to let you come. Then, you'll come so hard you'll beg me for more."

"Wow..." She shifted to face me but didn't leave my lap. "If I beg you now, will you do it?"

A smirk formed on my lips before I could stop it. "No." I stood, scooping her up into my arms and carrying her to her bed. "Goodnight, Sunshine," I said as I settled her onto the mattress and pressed a kiss to her forehead.

"Goodnight, Stalker."

Chapter Ten

Skye

L ying in bed with Killian on the couch only a few feet away was driving me crazy. His sandalwood scent filled my senses and made my body ache with desire. It was subtle, but every time I inhaled, it made me want to crawl on top of him, to feel his hard body pressed against mine.

My stalker was in my apartment, and I never wanted him to leave. The strange possessiveness I felt for him was unlike anything I'd ever experienced. The thought of him being mine sent a thrill through me.

The cadence of his breathing told me he was also awake, and I wondered if he was thinking of me as I was of him.

"Killian," I whispered into the dark.

"Hmm?"

"It's silly for you to try to fit on that small couch, we can share the bed. I promise not to take advantage of you."

He let out a low chuckle, sending a jolt of warmth to my core. I told myself I was being accommodating, that I really wouldn't try to seduce him. That I just wanted to be closer to him. That I could wait to find out what he felt like inside me.

You're a dirty liar, Skye Larsen, a little voice sang from deep in my mind.

I heard the rustling of movement, then he was there, standing beside the bed. He was looming over me, but instead of scared, I was fascinated and aroused.

He wore only a pair of boxer briefs, and my eyes hungrily took in the taut muscles of his arms, the broad expanse of his chest, and the sculpted ridges of his abs. His tattoos went up both arms from his wrists to his shoulders.

I knew there was a skull with a snake weaving through it on his upper back because I'd watched him undress before he'd settled on the couch.

I hadn't been able to stop myself. The way his muscles rippled under his tan skin as he'd undressed captivated me. I'd never been into tattoos, but on him, they only added to his appeal.

When my gaze returned to his face, his dark eyes fixed on me with an intensity that made my heart flutter. I knew there was a chance I was playing with fire, but I was tired of playing it safe, of being afraid.

Killian brought my body to life in a way I'd never thought possible. I wasn't sure I could keep my promise of not taking advantage of him with him only inches away, peering down at me.

When he slid under the covers, his bare leg brushed against mine and it took all I had not to jump on him. We rolled to our sides to face each other. Despite the darkness of the room, the moonlight shining through the windows allowed me to see him clearly enough.

He lightly ran his fingers over my face, stopping to trace the outline of my lips. "I've seen you before."

I tucked that forever stray lock behind his ear, letting my fingers comb through his hair. "Yeah, I know, that's why I call you Stalker."

As he smoothed his thumb over my bottom lip, he focused his eyes on my mouth. "I mean before that night at the club. It was about two years ago. You were walking down the street with one of those reusable shopping bags."

He remembered. I had always wondered if I'd had the same impact on him as he did on me, and it was clear I had. "I want to show you something," I said, climbing out of bed. When he stood beside me, I took his hand and led him to my art studio.

I lifted the painting and set it on the easel, keeping my gaze trained on him so I didn't miss his reaction when I switched on the light. When his eyes focused on it, his lips parted slightly, and he took a step forward.

"When did you do this?" His voice was low as he traced the portrait with his fingers.

"That day. The day on the street."

He turned to me with a questioning look. "You saw me?"

"Yes. You were burned into my memory, screaming

at me to paint you… so I did."

"The eyes are blank," he said, turning to look at the portrait again.

"I know, I couldn't see them clearly that day. Now I can finally finish it," I said as I slid onto my stool.

He stood behind me as I worked. There was something incredibly sensual about him watching me as I brought his eyes to life in the painting. When I was done, I leaned back until my head rested against his chest. "There. Now it's perfect. Now it's you."

His hands gripped my waist, turning me to face him as his lips crashed into mine. I wrapped my arms around his neck as I opened to him, kissing him back with the same passion I felt from him. Then, just as quickly as it had started, it was over. He took three steps back and held his hands at his sides.

"Fuck. You drive me crazy." He was breathing as heavily as I was.

"I can see that," I said, absently licking my lips as I stared at his erection, straining against his boxer briefs. My body pulsated with need, and I didn't need to touch myself to know I was wet.

"Lift your eyes," he growled.

Right before I tore my eyes from his cock, I saw it twitch, as if it wanted me to touch it. A sick pleasure filled me knowing all I had to do was look at him to make him want me.

"I don't know why you stopped," I said, "but you have my consent, my blessing, my permission. What more do you need?"

"You don't know me."

I stepped toward him. "You don't know me either."

He shook his head. "I know more than you realize."

"Oh? What exactly do you think you know about me?" I rolled my eyes when he didn't respond.

"Don't ever roll your fucking eyes at me again."

"It's hard not to when you're infuriatingly vague. If you think you know so much about me, I should know at least a little about you!"

His eyes narrowed as they filled with sinister heat. For the first time a tiny frisson of fear ran down my spine. The fear disappeared, quickly replaced by fascination at the darkness in his gaze. I pressed my thighs together as I felt myself get even wetter.

"I told you before, I'm not a good guy." He took a step toward me, but I don't think he realized he'd moved. "I've done things, I *do* things. Bad things."

He stopped in front of me, his hands clenched into fists. He was so close, I had to tilt my head back to see his face.

"Tell me," I whispered. He stiffened when I placed my hand over his chest. "I want to know you, Killian. Tell me everything."

"No."

"Fine. We'll just be strangers pretending to be lovers." Frustrated, I huffed out a breath and turned away from him.

He grabbed my arm, twisting it around my back and pulling me to him. My back was to his chest, and I could feel his erection pressing against me.

"Don't be a brat, Sunshine. You're better than that."

His other arm came around my waist, trapping me in his iron grip. I struggled, but his hold only tightened.

A shiver rippled through my body as I felt his lips brush against my ear, his voice dripping with lethal intent. "Stop fighting me. You won't win," he growled.

"You don't have to let me go. Just let me turn around so I can see you." I squirmed against his hold, and another shiver coursed through me when he let out a low moan. "Please, I want to see your face."

"If I let you turn around, will you stop squirming?" he asked in a warning tone.

A wry grin played on my lips when I realized the power I had over him. The way he reacted to my touch made me hungry for more. "Yes, I promise."

He loosened his grip just enough to allow me to turn around. His lips twisted into a lethal smirk that sent a thrill through me.

I lifted my hand to cup his cheek. "That's better," I whispered as I ran my thumb over his lips.

He grabbed my wrist and pulled it away from his face. "Don't fuck with me."

He released his grip on me, though the threat in his eyes remained. I stood before him, unable to ignore the throbbing in my core anymore. His eyes twinkled with a fierce intensity as he watched my hand slip inside my shorts.

A whimper escaped me when my finger glided over

my swollen clit as I tried to find the release I craved. The release I needed.

"What do you think you're doing?" he asked, his voice thick with desire.

"Taking care of myself since you won't." My eyelids grew heavy as I worked myself closer to the edge. "I figured you wouldn't mind... since you like to *watch*," I said, my voice breathless and hitching as I got closer and closer to the release I needed.

I let out a surprised yelp when he scooped me up into his arms. He moved through my dark apartment and dropped me on my bed. His hands moved over my legs to the waistband of my shorts and in one swift motion he pulled them off. A small cry escaped me when he grabbed my legs, spreading them as wide as they'd go.

I watched him, uncertain of what he was going to do next. When all he did was sit back on his haunches, my face scrunched up in confusion.

"What are you doing?" I asked, pressing my legs together.

"No. Keep them spread." He gripped my ankles to push them until my feet were flat on the bed and my knees were bent. The position opened me even more, and his eyes dipped down to take me in. "You're right. I like to watch, and now I have the perfect view." His gaze returned to mine. "Touch yourself. Show me what you do when you're alone thinking about me."

With my eyes on him, I lifted my top over my breasts to cup and squeeze them before pinching my nipples. I slowly lowered one hand between my legs while the other stayed on my breast. His eyes were on the hand on my pussy. With him watching me pleasure myself, it felt more sensual and exhilarating.

"Fuck, look how wet you are just thinking about me," he said in a lethally sexy voice. "I can see you glistening from here." He danced his fingers over my inner thighs, making me writhe. "Mmm, you smell so fucking good."

My breath hitched when my fingers brushed over my clit. It was swollen and sensitive, begging for an orgasm. When I slid a finger inside my opening, Killian licked his lips, and I nearly came right then. My eyes wanted to close, but I forced them to stay open. I needed to see him, see his reaction as I made myself come for him.

He watched me as I watched him, making me writhe under his searing gaze. My hand clenched around my breast and my back arched off the mattress as my climax hit. The way Killian was watching me, with dark eyes and parted lips, made it even more powerful.

"Oh, fuck. Oh, *God*," I moaned, my body writhing as the orgasm went on longer than I thought possible.

When the waves of pleasure began to ebb, my body slumped back onto the mattress. I started pulling my hand from between my legs, but he seized my wrist.

"What…" I forgot what I was about to say when he slipped my fingers into his mouth, licking them clean.

His eyes rolled back a little and a low, deep moan came from him as he pulled my fingers out of his mouth. "That was a mistake," he said with a rasp to his voice.

"What was?" I asked a little too forcefully.

"Tasting you."

"Why?" My face warmed with embarrassment as the possible reasons for his regret screamed through my mind.

"Because now I'll crave it, always wanting another taste."

My jaw parted a little. "Oh..."

When he started getting dressed, I rose to my knees in front of him. "Wait. You're leaving? Just like that?"

"Yes."

"Because you won't be able to control yourself?" I leaned forward and licked his lips, tasting a little of myself on them.

His hand curled around the back of my neck as his lips met mine. "Yes. No fucking, remember."

"Yeah, I remember," I said with a pout as I looked down at his crotch. "Hmm... shouldn't we take care of that? Like you said, it's unfair, and it looks uncomfortable, almost painful."

"Don't worry about me, Sunshine. I'll be fine." I frowned as he covered those tanned muscles with his clothes. "Go to sleep. I'll check in with you tomorrow."

"I don't think I like pretending," I said to his back. He stiffened but didn't turn around. "I want to know you, for this to be real."

He started walking toward the door again and didn't respond or look back as he left.

I lay awake, staring at the ceiling for a long while after he'd left. I'd gotten myself into a fucked situation, and I couldn't see a way out. Because there was no way I was letting Killian Asher slip away.

Just as my eyes were closing, the piercing sound of the fire alarm shattered the peaceful moment. Panic coursed through me as I caught the acrid smell of smoke. Before I could think or move, a crash startled me, and my eyes darted to the left just in time to see Killian emerge through the shattered window.

"What's happening?" I asked as he rushed toward me.

He tossed me my robe. "Put it on, Skye, we need to get out of here. I already called it in," he said.

"My paintings," I muttered as I absently slipped into the robe. "They'll be ruined, all of them."

"I know, baby, but we have to go. Now," he ordered, grabbing my phone from the nightstand before urging me toward the fire escape.

He descended first, and when I reached the bottom of the ladder, he scooped me up in his arms and carried me across the street.

Hysterical sobs wracked my body when I saw my yoga studio full of flames. Killian held me as I cried uncontrollably, my heart breaking as everything I had worked for and built burned before my eyes.

Chapter Eleven

Killian

T he fire department showed up before the blaze had time to spread to Skye's apartment, and while the studio was salvageable, it wasn't safe for her to live there. In her dazed state, it wasn't hard to convince Skye to come back to my place until the restoration was done.

I'd settled her on the couch with a cup of tea. While she sat in a daze, I called Wes and Layla using her phone.

When they arrived, I led them inside to where Skye sat in a trance-like state, fixated on the unlit fireplace across from her. Layla and Wes sat beside her, and even their presence didn't snap her out of her stupor.

Her vacant gaze flickered toward me, that same emptiness still in her eyes. I couldn't tell whether she saw me or was blinded by shock. Nevertheless, I offered her a small smile, hoping to give her some comfort after the chaos that had turned her life inside out.

"Now that she's in good hands, I have some pressing business to attend to," I said to Layla and Wes, my voice revealing none of the turmoil I felt within.

Skye's hollow gaze never left me, and an unfamiliar sensation coiled itself in my gut as I turned away. It physically hurt me to leave her in such a vulnerable state, but I had something to take care of that couldn't wait.

AS I ENTERED MY APARTMENT an hour later, Skye hadn't moved, but her brother and friend were gone. I knelt in front of her, taking in her pallid complexion and the empty look in her eyes.

"Skye," I whispered, brushing a strand of hair from her face, "come back to me." I cupped her face in my hand, and she finally focused on me as tears flowed down her cheeks.

I gently wiped her tears away with my thumb, pulling her closer until our foreheads touched. "Don't cry, baby. It'll be okay. I'll make sure of it, I promise."

Her body shook with silent sobs, making me feel things I'd never felt before. I settled onto the couch, pulling her onto my lap to hold her tightly as she wept.

Compassion wasn't my forte, but I felt the need to comfort *her*. Seeing her in pain made me feel helpless, and that was not something I was used to. I'd do whatever I had to do to take away her pain, to make her feel safe.

I held her until there were no more tears left. She sat in my lap with her face buried in my chest for a long while before she lifted her head to look at me. One look at her face, and I knew I was in too deep.

"Everything is gone. Everything I built. Everything I worked for. Gone," she said, her voice hoarse from crying.

"Not everything," I said as I pulled out my phone and sent a quick text.

Moments later, Neil, Leo, and Amelia entered carrying Skye's paintings and a bag filled with her paints, brushes, and palettes.

"How?" she said, her voice hoarse from crying. "I thought the fire department said it wasn't safe to go back in."

A soft smile tugged at the corners of my lips as I shrugged. "I don't like rules, remember," I said. "There's something I want to show you." I took her hand and led her to the hallway where the bedrooms were.

We stopped in front of a door at the end of the hall. "We can set it all up in here," I said, pushing the door open to reveal an empty room.

In addition to the master suite, I had three guest rooms, but never had guests. One served as my home office, another as a guest room just in case I needed it, and I never got around to doing anything with the third.

Sharing my personal space with someone was unusual for me. I'd grown accustomed to taking my dates to their place, never to mine. In my life, intimacy was fleeting, never lingering long enough to take root. Which is exactly how I liked it. Until now.

Skye made things different. The look on her face as she gazed up at me was all it took to overcome my aversion to having someone in my personal space.

"Are you sure? I don't want to invade your home. I

can stay with Layla or Chelsea."

The thought of her staying with her friends had me irrationally angry. She belonged with *me*, near *me*. I told myself it was so I could keep her safe, protect her if Paul came back.

It was too soon, and she was too vulnerable to let her see the possessive side of me that wanted to keep her all to myself. So I softened my features and leaned down to kiss her lightly.

"I'm sure," I said, pulling her body against mine. "Besides, what would Wes think if you didn't stay with your serious boyfriend?"

She let out a soft laugh. "Okay then, thank you," she said as she snuggled into me, resting her head on my chest.

"You should get some sleep." My voice was strained with the effort of keeping my emotions in check. I'd learned a long time ago that compassion was a liability and ruthlessness was the only way to get anywhere in life.

"I'd rather set up my new, temporary studio." She glanced up at me with a smile that made my heart clench. "If that's okay?"

"Anything you want," I said with a smile. "First, there are two people I want you to meet." I turned back toward the living area, leading her to where the others were waiting. "You've met Leo, but this is Neil and Amelia."

She shook their hands with a warm smile. Only she could smile like that after everything she'd been through. Her resiliency and ability to shine through the darkest times made my chest tighten with an emotion I couldn't name.

"I've programmed their numbers into your phone. Most importantly, if you run into trouble or feel threatened or scared, you call Leo immediately. He will always be close by. Do you understand?" My tone was harsher than I'd meant it to be, but I needed to make my point crystal-clear.

Her eyes were wide, and her bottom lip trembled as she nodded. "I do, yeah."

"Good. Call Neil if you need to go anywhere. If you need anything to make your stay more comfortable, call Amelia."

"Uh…" She stiffened as she turned her gaze back to them.

Amelia stepped forward. "Skye, I know this must all be overwhelming for you," she said. "We're here to help you in any way we can, so please don't hesitate to call us." She shot me a wry smirk. "We *want* to help you; we're not just doing this because our grumpy boss is making us."

Her laughter softened her words, and I felt Skye relax a little. Amelia to the rescue, as usual.

Neil smiled, his grandfatherly demeanor putting her even more at ease. "Ms. Larsen, please don't hesitate to call me," Neil said. "Ms. Reid is correct. I would be honored to help in any way I can, and escort you anywhere you need to go."

Leo being a man of few words simply gave her a

strained half-smile and nodded.

"Wow," Skye breathed. "Okay, thank you."

I stepped in front of her, forcing her to look up at me. "Go get your studio situated," I said before pressing a kiss to her forehead. "I'm going to talk to Leo for a bit and then I'll show you around."

Her eyes flicked briefly to Leo before returning to me. "Sure, okay," she murmured, and then made her way back to her new studio.

When she was out of earshot I turned to Leo. "Has there been any sign of her piece of shit ex?"

"Not yet," he replied. "He couldn't have gotten too far. My guys will find him."

"They know what to do when they have him?" A dangerous twinkle came to his eyes as he nodded. Like me, he had a taste for the dark side, and I couldn't help but like the bastard because of it. "As far as Skye goes, if anything happens to her..."

"I understand."

"Good. Be back here at six Monday morning." It was almost three o'clock on Sunday morning, and I had Skye all to myself all day and night. With that thought fresh in my mind I went to check on her progress. "Looks good," I said, leaning against the doorjamb. "Do you think there will be enough light?"

She chuckled as she placed the painting of me on the side wall before facing me.

"Are you kidding me? There's more light in here now, in the middle of the night, than there was in my closet on the sunniest of days."

She closed the distance between us, her hands resting on my chest as she rose on her tiptoes to kiss me. The moment our lips met, my body responded with a primal hunger, and my arms wrapped around her in a tight embrace.

"Thank you for this. For everything," she said when she settled back on flat feet.

Dark circles had formed under her eyes, and I knew she was practically dead on her feet. "Let me show you the rest of the place." I took her hand and guided her through the rest of the apartment, showing her where everything was, saving the guest bedroom for last. "That's the bathroom, and the closet is through there. My room is down the hall to the right."

"It's beautiful," she said, taking in the mahogany four-poster bed and the silk canopy draped over it.

She pressed a hand to her stomach, a worried look contorting her features.

"What's wrong? Are you in pain?"

"No. Not physically anyway." She took a few deep breaths before continuing. "My mom died then my studio burned down. I—I just..." She shrugged as tears filled her eyes.

I reached out to tuck her hair behind her ear. "It's okay. You lost a lot in a short period of time."

"What am I going to do about my rent? What if my customers don't come back when I reopen? What if they condemn the entire place and I can never return there?" She took another breath, but it was shaky this time. "If I can't afford to stay in New York, I'll have to move with my brother."

That would not happen, no matter what I had to do to stop it. Now that I had her close to me, I wasn't about to let her go.

"Don't worry, baby," I said, pulling her into my arms. "Your insurance should help cover you for a while, but if not, I can help. I have contacts in every type of industry, and I can make sure everything is taken care of. Everything will be okay, I promise."

"You've promised that twice now," she said, her voice a little calmer. "I appreciate it, and I'll take advantage of your contacts, but not your bank account. I won't sit here eating bonbons while you do everything for me."

"Bonbons?" I said with a laugh.

"Shut it, you know what I mean."

"Yes, I do." She wouldn't take my money, and I respected the hell out of her for that, but it didn't mean I couldn't help her in other ways. Looking down into her big blue eyes, I couldn't help but kiss her again as a plan formed in my mind. "We'll figure it out. For now, get some rest. Everything you need is in the bathroom, and Amelia packed some of your clothes in your art bag."

As I turned to leave, she laid a hand on my arm. "Thank you for going back to get my paintings. It means the world to me."

The depth of emotion in her voice poked at my black heart, cracking the armor even more. "They are important to you. When I told you I'll give you anything you want, I meant it. No matter what it takes."

Her eyes shimmered with unshed tears, and I felt a

twinge of guilt at the thought of bringing her into my tainted world.

"You say you're a dangerous man, but then you go and do something like saving my paintings because they mean something to me," she murmured, her voice barely above a whisper. "It makes it hard for me to believe you could ever do anything truly bad."

"All you need to believe is I will never hurt you." I brushed my lips against hers. "Do you believe me?"

"Yes."

"Good." I kissed her long and deep before giving her a gentle shove toward the bathroom. "Go take a bath and get some sleep. I'll see you when you wake up."

While she bathed, I called Amelia explaining the plan I had in mind. By Monday morning, Skye's financial worries would be taken care of in a way that wouldn't bruise her pride.

I'd just settled into bed after a shower of my own when Skye knocked on my door. Her hair was in a messy knot on top of her head, and she wore the thick, terrycloth robe I kept in the guest bathroom. Looking at her made my mouth water.

She stayed just outside the door, playing with the strap of the robe. "How did you know about the fire?"

I folded my arms under my head, propping it up so I could see her better. Satisfaction coursed through me when her gaze hovered on my biceps. "When I left your place, I got to the subway but couldn't get on the train. By the time I turned around to come back the fire was already burning."

"You were coming back?"

I nodded. "Yes."

"Oh," she said, her voice barely a whisper.

Her gaze moved to the empty space beside me, and answering her unspoken question, I patted the mattress in invitation.

She lifted her eyes to mine. "Are you sure? I just don't want to be alone tonight."

"I'm sure, but only for sleeping this time. You're exhausted."

"I promise. As tempting as you are, I really am too tired for anything else."

With a weary sigh, she climbed into bed, settling herself against me. I wrapped my arm around her in a protective embrace, holding her close as she fell asleep.

Sleep didn't come easily. Skye's trust weighed on my mind, as I battled the guilt, threatening to engulf me. I'd done unspeakable things in my life, but I'd never felt guilty about a single one of them. Now, keeping secrets from Skye was tearing me up.

When I finally fell asleep, I dreamt of what life could be like with Skye, a life free from the darkness that had already tainted mine.

Chapter Twelve

Skye

I opened my eyes and found myself in Killian's arms. The scent of sandalwood and the warmth of his body enveloped me, and for a moment, I forgot where I was. Then, reality hit me like a ton of bricks. The fire hadn't been a bad dream. It had really happened.

Panic clawed its way up my throat, making it hard to breathe. I gasped for air, my hands clenching my chest. Killian woke up in an instant and knelt in front of me.

"Skye, look at me," he said, his voice low and calm. I turned my gaze to his gorgeous face, looking into those steel-gray eyes. "There you go. Focus on your breathing. Take a deep breath through your nose and exhale slowly through your mouth."

His touch was soothing as he caressed me, moving his hands up and down my arms. Gradually, my breathing slowed down, and I felt the tension leaving my body.

"Keep breathing," he whispered, his thumbs tracing circles on my arms.

I closed my eyes as I took a few more deep breaths. Killian's touch was my anchor, keeping me from drowning in my fears.

"Ah, there's my girl," he said when I opened my eyes again.

I wrapped my arms around him, burying my face in his chest. "It all came flooding back to me: my mom, Paul, the fire... I'm sorry."

"Do not apologize for having a panic attack," he said firmly. "Do not apologize for your feelings to anyone. Ever."

"I wasn't apologizing for the panic attack, I meant because I woke you up. It came on so quickly I didn't have time to get out of bed," I said, inhaling his scent.

He pulled back, looking at me with a fierce intensity. "I may not be a good guy, but I don't want you to be scared of me. I am not Paul or any of the other assholes from your past. I will never hurt you, never raise a hand to you." His voice grew husky as he continued. "I will never cause you pain unless you ask for it, is that understood?"

I nodded, swallowing hard and pressing my thighs together when his words sunk in. "Mm-hmm... yes. I understand. I'm sor—" I bit my lip, stopping myself from apologizing.

Killian chuckled softly. "Do you feel better?"

I nodded again, feeling more like myself. "I do. Thank you for letting me sleep with you. I think it's the only reason I actually slept."

"No problem. What would you like to do today?" he

asked, his voice gentle.

"Well, I had plans for brunch with Layla and Chelsea at my place, so…" I shrugged. "Guess that means I'm free."

"Call them. Invite them here, and I'll go to the market and get what you need."

I chewed on my bottom lip as I studied him, searching for answers. "Why are you doing all of this for me?"

He leaned in, his breath hot against my skin as he traced the curve of my lips with his tongue. "Because there's something about you, Skye. Something that pulls at me. Something I can't resist."

I shivered at his touch. "Oh," I said on a shaky breath. It was desire, not panic, making my breathing shallow and my heart pound in my chest.

"You feel it too. I know you do." His voice was low and intense.

"I do," I said, turning my head to brush my lips against his cheek before meeting his mouth in a hungry kiss. "If we both feel it, if we can't stay away from each other, why can't we be together?"

He pulled away as if I'd doused him in ice water. "Because I'm not the kind of man you should be with, Skye. Trust me, you don't know what you're asking for."

I shook my head, refusing to believe him. "Then why agree to lie to my brother? Why invite me to stay here? I don't know why you're resisting this, but I know exactly what *I* want," I said, my voice firm. "I want you. You have no idea how badly."

He leaned his forehead against mine. "Fuck, Sunshine, you're killing me. I want you too, more than I've ever wanted anything but it can't happen. Not yet."

I heaved a frustrated sigh. "Okay, but I warn you... I may be a yoga instructor, but I am not a patient person."

He grunted and his eyes darkened. "I'm going to make coffee. Write me a list of what you want," he said, ending our conversation.

TWO HOURS LATER, Layla, Chelsea, and I were on Killian's wrap-around balcony sipping on the best mimosas I'd ever tasted and picking at a charcuterie board unlike any I'd seen before. The meats and cheeses were scrumptious, and the bread was still warm, as if it had just come out of the oven. Every bite was delightful, and I couldn't stop eating the juicy, sweet raspberries, strawberries, and grapes.

"This stuff is way better than what we normally get," Layla said as she smeared brie on a piece of bread followed by fig jam and a slice of prosciutto.

"I can't believe I'm about to say this but forget the food. What about this apartment? It's just... wow." Chelsea gestured around us.

I took a sip of my mimosa, as I looked out at the city skyline. Killian's apartment sat at the top of the tallest residential building in Manhattan. Its height, along with the floor-to-ceiling windows that encased the entire apartment, offered a 360-degree view of the city.

While my friends chatted about gourmet meats and cheeses, my mind wandered to the enigmatic Killian

Asher. A quick Google search had turned up nothing but his company's name: Asher Capital, and there was little information on that as well.

There were also some tabloid photos of him with famous models and actresses, but the articles were more about them than Killian.

The lack of digital footprint in today's world where Google knew everything, should have been a red flag. Instead, it piqued my curiosity even more.

"Are you okay, Skye?" Chelsea reached out to rub my arm, pulling me from my thoughts.

"Yeah," I said. "Just lost in my thoughts."

"We understand," Layla added. "Do you want to talk about what happened?"

I sank back into my chair and let out a long, heavy sigh. The weight of everything suddenly felt too much to bear, the words spewed out of me like a volcano erupting. I couldn't stop them, couldn't contain the flood of emotions simmering under the surface.

"What could I possibly have to talk about? The woman who was supposed to love me and protect me, didn't and now she's dead. Then a fire somehow started in my studio. So, I'm an orphan, and I'm out of a job and a home for the foreseeable future. My brother will not stop texting and calling me."

I slammed my phone onto the table as another one came through. "He'll probably show up here soon to pester me about Vermont. Now I'm living with my stalker. My incredibly sexy, mouthwatering, drop-to-my-knees gorgeous stalker who says he wants me as badly as I want him but refuses to fuck me because… I don't know why! Did I leave anything out?"

My friends had twin looks of surprise on their faces. I couldn't blame them for their shock. Aside from my occasional panic attack, I rarely got upset in front of anyone.

In the three years I'd lived with my mother after she surrendered to addiction, I'd learned quickly to hide my fears under a mask of happiness. The pleasant façade was a survival tactic born out of punishment for displaying vulnerability. It was also my way of faking it 'til I made it. I told myself if I smiled, eventually I'd feel happy again. It hadn't quite worked, but I did a great job at pretending.

Three years may not seem like a long time. However, when you're a preteen, watching the woman you once idolized repeatedly crumble in abandoned buildings, needle in hand, it felt like a never-ending journey through the fiery depths of hell.

"I'm sor—" I stopped myself mid-apology as Killian's words replayed in my head.

Do not apologize for your feelings to anyone. Ever.

"No, don't be sorry," Layla said, reaching across the table for my hand. "You've been through a lot, and you deserve to be angry and scared. So, yell at us, scream out to the city, or cry. Girl, just let it out."

A laugh burst out of me, and I couldn't stop it. I laughed so hard tears came to my eyes, and then I was crying. Body-wracking, ab-clenching, uncontrollable sobs. My friends moved around the table to wrap their arms around me as I cried out all the anger inside me.

Because that's what it was: anger.

I was furious with my mom for giving in to her addiction, for letting those men touch me, for becoming a hollow shell of herself... for dying. I was pissed at Paul for being so narcissistic to think he could treat me the way he had. I was mad at my brother for treating me like a child and thinking he could control my life when he hadn't been there for most of it. I was angry at the universe for punishing me for God knew what reason.

Anger was the one emotion that brought on the worst punishments from my mom and her boyfriends. For over a decade I'd been holding it in, shoving it way down deep, and it felt glorious to let it out. There was a certain power to letting it out, a cathartic release to unleashing your deepest darkest emotions.

The door opened behind us, and my friends stepped to the side as footsteps approached the table.

"Skye?" Killian's tone was intense, but his touch was gentle on my shoulders. "Look at me, baby."

I turned to him, not caring that my makeup was running down my face as I crushed my lips to his. He kissed me back with the same ferocity as me. I clung to him, wrapping my arms and legs around him as I deepened the kiss even more. It was as if I was trying to imprint myself on him, mark him as mine. And I was, because he belonged to me, no matter how much he denied it.

"Well, well, well," an unfamiliar voice said, bringing me back to the real world, "if it isn't the world-famous chef, Chelsea Sinclair."

Still wrapped around Killian, I looked up to see a very tall, very muscular, very handsome stranger. As Killian rose to stand, he patted my ass telling me to unravel myself from him. I reluctantly obliged and moved to stand beside Chelsea who looked as if she'd seen a ghost.

"Lucian? H-how..." Chelsea's mouth hung agape as she stared at the dark stranger.

He was looking at her with a sly grin, as if he was enjoying her discomfort. "It's been a long time, sugar."

Chelsea's cheeks flushed pink at the sound of the nickname. "Why are you here? I thought you were..."

"Hmm. It seems I've left you speechless. That's a first," the man, Lucian, said, stepping closer to her.

His words snapped her out of her stupor and the composed, graceful Chelsea I knew and loved returned. "You couldn't leave me speechless if you were the last man on earth."

"Hi, Lucian, is it?" I said, sticking my hand out. I couldn't help but interject, giving her time to further compose herself.

Lucian's smile grew wider as he took my hand in his impossibly large one. "It is, and you are?"

Killian moved up beside me, slipping his arm around my waist. It was a possessive move I'd normally recoil from, but with him, I welcomed it, reveled in it.

"I'm Skye. What brings you here?" I asked, not missing the way he looked at the arm Killian had wrapped around me.

"I think you're done shaking hands now, Luce." Killian's tone was even but edged with danger.

Lucian slowly slid his hand from mine, licking his lips as he let his eyes roam over me. "Not your usual, Kill, but I like her."

Killian's body tensed, his hand tightening on my hip. He kept his eyes on the other man as he lowered his lips to my ear. "I'm going inside with him." He pressed a kiss to my cheek. "Stay out here, understood?" I nodded. "Good girl, I'll be back soon."

I watched as the two men walked back to the door. Lucian paused before stepping over the threshold and turned back. "It was good to see you again, sugar," he said with a slight bow of his head before disappearing into Killian's apartment.

"Who the hell was that?" Layla asked once the door had closed.

Chelsea took a shaky breath, pressing a hand to her stomach. "He's nobody. Just someone I knew in culinary school."

"Hmm, I don't know about that," I interjected. "You're shaking, he had to be more than *nobody*. Plus, he called you *sugar*." Calling her by a cutesy nickname implied they'd known each other at some point.

"I don't want to talk about it." She stood taller and adjusted her skirt. "Besides, we are here to support you, not talk about culinary school dropouts."

"Oh! Wasn't that a song in *Grease*?" Layla asked.

I let out a laugh. "That was *Beauty School Dropout*."

Layla pointed at me a little too emphatically. "Yes, right! We should watch that movie." She was nervous and when she got nervous, she got goofy. Between all the shit going on with me and Chelsea's weirdness, she was probably about to burst.

In an attempt to put everyone at ease, I changed the subject to the latest addition on Chelsea's menu. As expected, her face lit up as she described the dish and its preparation.

That familiar tingle formed between my shoulder blades, and I turned around to smile at Killian through the window. Even in his own home he was still watching me, and I still found it thrilling.

Chapter Thirteen

Skye

After my friends had left, Killian pulled me aside to tell me he had to go somewhere with Lucian and wouldn't be back until late. He reminded me that Leo was always nearby, and Amelia was only a phone call away if I needed anything.

"What about you? Why can't I call you?" I asked, worry slithering its way into my belly.

His hand curled around the back of my neck, massaging gently as he pulled me in for a light kiss. "I won't be able to answer."

"Why?" I whispered, toying with the collar of his blue t-shirt. It hugged his pecs and showed off his muscular tattooed arms. He looked so delicious I wanted to lick him from head to toe.

His grip tightened, forcing me to look up at him. "It's better if you don't know," he said firmly. "Just stay here. Order dinner in." He leaned in to press his lips to my ear and whispered, "Do not leave the apartment, understood?"

"Yes. I won't leave, I promise." My hands smoothed over his chest to his shoulders. "Will you be in danger?"

"No, baby. Don't worry about me," he said before kissing me. "I'll be back late, so don't wait up."

"Okay." My pulse was racing and my stomach was in knots as I watched him walk to the elevator in the center of the room.

"Do not leave this apartment," he repeated just before stepping on the elevator with tall, dark, and mysterious Lucian.

I roamed the empty penthouse, searching for anything that could tell me more about the enigmatic Killian, but I found nothing. Even in his own home, he was a man full of secrets. I was eager to unravel the mystery behind his dark, brooding gaze.

Feeling restless, I moved to my temporary art studio to paint the image that had been haunting me since the fire.

Hours passed in a blur as I poured my emotions onto the canvas. My stomach growled, but I ignored it, lost in the therapeutic release of painting. When my vision blurred, I realized I hadn't eaten since brunch. A glance at the clock revealed that had been twelve hours earlier.

I lowered myself to the floor, stretching out my tired muscles with a few yoga poses. As I sat up, I looked at the painting I had been working on. It still needed some work, but it was a good start.

When I heard the elevator doors open, I went out to the living area to see Killian. He was doing something on his phone, looking up at me when I moved towards him to greet him. That's when I noticed blood on his shirt, and his bruised and swollen knuckles.

"What happened? Are you hurt?" I asked, my voice barely above a whisper. My gaze traveled up to his cheek, where a fresh bruise was forming.

"I'm okay," he said, slipping his phone into his back pocket. "Why are you still awake?"

I shook my head in disbelief. "You come home covered in blood and bruises and you focus on why I'm not sleeping?"

"Yes."

Not caring about the blood, I grabbed his hand and tugged him towards the bathroom. When he didn't budge, I turned to face him, my eyes narrowed. "You need to clean those cuts," I demanded.

We locked eyes, neither of us willing to back down. When his resistance finally crumbled, I felt a thrill of triumph run through me. I led him into the bathroom, made him sit on the edge of the tub, and slowly lifted his shirt over his head.

My fingers danced over his chest and abdomen, but there were no cuts. The blood on his shirt wasn't his, and the realization sent a shiver down my spine. This wasn't the first time he'd had someone else's blood on him, and it wasn't the first time it made me want to ride him into oblivion. *Yup, there's definitely something wrong with me,* I thought.

I wet a washcloth to clean his wounds. "Are you going to tell me what happened?"

"I won't tell you tonight," he said after a few

moments.

I stopped cleansing his wounds to look up at him. "You will tell me, though?"

He was staring at me with hooded eyes, his tongue slipping out to moisten his lips. "Yes. When the time is right."

"Way to make it even more ominous and mysterious."

He pulled the corner of his mouth into a wry half-smile. "That's me to a T, baby." He slid his hand from mine and brought it to his belt buckle. "Thank you for taking care of me, but I need a shower."

"Uh-huh," I grunted, my eyes glued to his hands as they unfastened the belt then his jeans.

"Are you going to stay?" he asked.

"Uh-huh," I replied. I quickly glanced up at his face and caught him smirking at me, his eyebrow raised in a wicked challenge. "What? No. No. I'll give you privacy."

I turned around just as he was lowering his pants. It took everything I had not to look over my shoulder to see what he'd revealed. I reluctantly stepped out of the bathroom, closing the door behind me and resting my head against it.

My stomach growled, reminding me I was hungry for more than Killian, and I went to the kitchen where I started making scrambled eggs and toast. By the time the food was ready, he was strolling into the room wearing only a pair of light gray cotton sleep pants so thin I could make out the outline of his penis. His thick, long penis. *Holy hell…*

"I... um, I figured you didn't have time to eat," I said, trying not to stare at his crotch while sliding a plate across the island.

He picked up a piece of toast, shooting me a knowing grin. "I didn't. Why haven't you?"

"I started a new painting and lost track of time."

He nodded, chewing slowly with his eyes still on me. "Anything happen while I was gone?"

"Nope. All was quiet."

He grunted, and we fell into a comfortable silence while watching each other eat. We couldn't seem to take our eyes off one another.

"Killian?" I asked after we'd finished eating.

"Hmm?" He was still standing at the island, watching me move around his kitchen as I cleaned the dishes.

"What do you do for a living?"

He studied me for a long while before sighing. "I buy undervalued or poorly run companies that have the potential to thrive. Once under my company's control, we make the necessary changes to drive growth and maximize profits. If we can't save them, we liquidate their assets."

I felt like he was leaving something out, but I got the general idea, and that was enough for me. I'd finally gotten some information out of him. It was a sign of progress in our unusual yet exhilarating relationship, and the thrill of it sent shivers down my spine.

I leaned across the kitchen island, my fingers

tracing over his knuckles. "And these business deals occasionally end in a brawl, or do you belong to some secret fight club?"

He rose from his seat and moved to stand in front of me. He curled his hand around my throat, pulling me in closer to him. "We discussed this already. I'll tell you what happened when the time is right. Don't ask me again."

I knew his roughness should have scared me, but I couldn't bring myself to feel anything other than a perverse fascination. When his lips brushed mine, I opened to him, eagerly welcoming the kiss. He smoothed his free hand down my back to cup my ass, pressing me tightly against his body. My hands slid into his hair to pull him even closer as the kiss deepened.

He moved his hand around to the back of my neck, sliding the other one up my shirt to cup my breast, eliciting a moan from me. My head fell back as his mouth moved to cover my nipple through the thin material.

Wanting to touch him, I slid my hand into his pants, taking his erection in my hand. Our breaths quickened and sweat slicked our skin as our need for each other overwhelmed us.

I tightened my hold and moved my hand over his shaft, letting out a deep moan when his teeth glided along my hardened peak.

"Fuck," he said pulling his head up to look at the island where he'd left his phone. The screen was lit up, showing a blocked number while it lightly vibrated. "I have to answer it."

"Okay," I said with a frown. He lowered his gaze, and I realized I was still holding his cock. "Oh, right, you'll need that back."

He let out a low chuckle as I slipped my hand from his pants. "I've never known anyone like you, Sunshine."

"Back at ya, Stalker."

He took his phone to his bedroom, closing the door behind him. Understanding that he wanted privacy, I went out onto the balcony and leaned against the glass balustrade, looking out over the city. At night, the city turned from noisy and bustling to dark and mysterious. It had always called to me, beckoning for me to explore the shadowed streets, to uncover all its secrets.

It was the same way I felt about Killian: intrigued by something I should fear.

I caught a movement out of the corner of my eye and turned away from the enchanting city below me to face him. He was fully dressed but no less appealing than he was in his penis-revealing pants. As I watched him move toward me with the fluid grace of a jungle predator, I realized the pull I felt towards him was much stronger, more intense than the allure of the city.

Shivers of excitement coursed through my body when his dark, intense gaze met mine. He stood in front of me, placing his hands on the railing to cage me between his arms. His lips covered mine, and I tilted my head to deepen the kiss. My arms went around him to pull him closer, and a soft moan slipped from me when he bit my lower lip before resting his forehead against mine.

"I need to leave again. Leo is still outside. Call him if you need anything." He kissed me again, hard and fast. "Go get some sleep."

AFTER TOSSING AND TURNING FOR A WHILE, I moved to Killian's bed and fell asleep enveloped in his scent. When I woke up the next morning, he had his body pressed against my back and his arm draped over my waist.

Before getting into bed with him, I had slipped into a negligee I found among the things Amelia had packed for me. She must have dug deep in my drawer for the slinky, sexy garment. That she'd include it, made me think she had plans for Killian and me... and I was all for it.

His arm tightened around me when I shifted. "Where do you think you're going?"

"Just rolling over," I said, squirming until he loosened his hold so I could face him. "Good morning."

"Mmm, waking up to this face and body makes it much better than good," he murmured against my lips as his hand slid down to my ass before an unhappy groan escaped him. "I really hate to say it, but I have to go to work."

"Aren't you the boss? Doesn't that allow you some leeway to be late?" I asked, hoping to convince him to stay.

"If I didn't have a meeting, I'd stay in bed with you all day," he replied with a regretful sigh, as he untangled himself from me and began to dress.

I lounged on the bed with one arm behind my head, giving me the perfect view into his massive closet. "At least I get to watch you get ready."

He turned toward me, his pants hanging unfastened. "Now who's the stalker?"

"Call me whatever you want, as long as I get to keep watching," I said, licking my lips as he fastened his pants over his growing erection.

"Fuck, Sunshine."

"That'd be nice, but you said you have to go."

With a smug smile, I flung the covers off and pulled my negligee over my head, leaving me in only my lace panties. My hands moved down my body to my core. Spreading my legs wide, I pulled the strip of lace aside and slid two fingers along my slick folds from my opening to my clit.

He approached the bed with a low, guttural growl, his eyes dark with lust. In one swift motion, he grabbed both of my hands and lifted them above my head, pinning them there with a single hand.

"I'm tired of watching. If you're going to come in my bed, it's going to be me who makes you," he said, lowering his hand to my center and crushing his lips to mine for a fevered kiss.

When his thumb circled my throbbing clit, I moaned, my hips bucking upward. My moans turned to whimpers when he slid two fingers inside me, slowly moving them in and out.

The tingles of my impending climax formed low in my belly, sending tremors of pleasure through me. He quickened the pace, moving his magical fingers faster and faster until my moans and whimpers filled the room.

On a primal growl, he tore his lips from mine. "That's it... fuck, you're gorgeous." His voice was deep and raspy, sending shivers over my skin. "Now come for me like a good girl."

He lowered his lips to my nipple, biting down lightly at the same time he crooked his fingers to hit that deliciously sensitive spot. The orgasm slammed into me like a Mack truck, sending glorious spasms through my body. His hold on my wrists held me in place no matter how much I struggled, making the moment even hotter than it already was.

"Wow," I said. My voice was hoarse and weak as I tried to catch my breath. "Just fucking wow."

He pulled my hands down to cover his cock through his pants. I felt his thick shaft, and my fingers itched to curl around it. "When I get back, I'm going to make you pay for this," he said in a husky voice as he bowed his head to take my bottom lip between his teeth, biting down to cause a sting of pleasurable pain.

"Mmm, I look forward to it," I whispered, moving my hand over his hard length through his pants.

A small yelp escaped me when he tightly squeezed my wrist and pulled my hand away. "Don't leave this apartment unless Leo or Neil is with you."

"Hurry back," I called out as he left the room while buttoning his shirt.

The second I heard the elevator doors slide closed my

phone rang. My face scrunched in confusion when I saw who it was.

"Hi, Amelia," I said into the phone. "Killian just left to come to the office."

"Good morning, Skye. I'm calling because I think I have a job opportunity for you."

"Did Killian put you up to this?"

"No. This is all me."

She said it way too stiffly for me to believe her, but I pushed aside my suspicion. I needed a job, and even if it was Killian's way of giving me money, at least I'd be earning it. "Okay, what is it?"

"I'd prefer you to come into the office. Can you be here around one?"

"Yes," I said a bit too eagerly. I finally had a reason to leave the apartment, and I could see Killian at the office.

"Good, I'll see you then."

PER AMELIA'S INSTRUCTIONS, Neil dropped me off in front of Killian's office building a few minutes before one o'clock. Unable to sit silently, I had struck up a conversation with him. I'd learned Killian's father had hired Neil as a bodyguard and driver for his son over two decades ago. As an ex-Navy SEAL, Neil had extensive experience in security matters. He was also a devoted husband, a father, and a proud grandfather. The ride was over too soon to get any young Killian stories out of him though.

When I stepped into the imposing office building, I had to pass through a security checkpoint before taking the elevator to the top floor and met Amelia at her desk at one o'clock on the dot.

She greeted me with a warm smile and a cup of tea before leading me into a small conference room. After settling into our seats, she pulled up plans for a luxury hotel in the Upper West Side.

The building had once been a popular spot for some of the world's most talented artists and writers but had fallen into disrepair. Killian's company bought it to restore it to its former glory.

Feeling confused, I asked Amelia, "I know nothing about construction or building renovation. What do you want me to do?"

"The artwork," she replied with another smile.

Her request caught me off guard. "I don't understand. My paintings are dark and depressing. I wouldn't think that's the kind of stuff you'd want in a hotel."

"Your work is amazing, Skye. It hit me... hard. I have faith that you can come up with something that would work."

"I've never painted for the public. My work is personal and private," I confessed.

Amelia closed her laptop and faced me. "Take some time to think about it. I'll need to know by tomorrow afternoon."

As I stood up, I glanced through the glass and saw Killian approaching the room. "Did you tell him I was coming?" I asked Amelia.

She smirked. "No. Should I have?"

I hesitated before answering, "No, it's fine."

"Let me know by tomorrow, Skye," she said, exiting the room as Killian entered.

"Amelia had a job opportunity for me. She asked me to come here to talk about it," I explained to Killian.

"I know."

"You do?"

"I know everything that goes on in my company," he said, taking a step closer to me, but a commotion had him turning back to the door. "Fuck. Stay here," he muttered, but before he could leave another man entered.

The man's eyes were bloodshot, his skin was sallow, and his lips were split in multiple places. I knew the signs of an addict well, and this man had fallen deep.

"What are you doing here, Chad?" Killian said in a tone so lethal it had shivers going down my spine.

"I'm out of money," the man said.

My lips pulled into a grimace at his whiny and desperate demeanor. He reminded me too much of Paul toward the end of our relationship, and I instantly disliked him.

"That's not my problem. The deal is done. I don't owe you anything," Killian said.

I felt the tension rise between Killian and the man called Chad, feeling a sense of unease wash over me. Chad was desperate which made him unpredictable and the way he looked at me made my skin crawl.

"This your whore?" Chad said with a sneer and

moving faster than expected, he lunged for me and grabbed my arm.

Killian sprang into action, hitting Chad with a swift blow to the face. The sound of flesh hitting flesh rang through the room, and before Chad could do anything, Lucian entered as if from nowhere.

I watched the two larger men drag a kicking and screaming Chad out of the room. Snapping out of my shocked state, I hurried after them, exiting the conference room just in time to see them enter a door I hadn't noticed before. All the conference rooms and private offices, including Killian's, had glass walls, but this one didn't.

A sick curiosity compelled me to ignore Amelia's warnings as I approached the door. My hand shook as I turned the knob, and as I took in the scene before me, a chill ran down my spine that had nothing to do with fear.

Killian was bent over Chad, his face contorted in rage as he held the already battered and bleeding man's shirt in his hand. Chad was barely conscious, his eyes rolling back as Killian continued pummeling him.

"I should fucking kill you for calling her a whore," Killian said to Chad, his voice so deep, I wouldn't have recognized it as his had I not been looking at him.

Lucian saw me first, his cold and calculating eyes roaming over me as he leaned casually against the wall next to the door. A wicked smile pulled at his lips as he crooned, "Kill, we have company."

Killian froze mid-punch, his eyes focusing on me. "Fucking hell, Luce, why didn't you lock the door?"

Lucian shrugged. "No one's supposed to come in here. *Usually*, people obey that rule."

"She doesn't fucking work here. She doesn't know the rules," Killian growled, his eyes blazing with anger. "Take care of this piece of shit."

Lucian nodded, a sinister glint in his eyes as he stepped forward to deal with the unconscious man. Killian grabbed my arm, pulling me out of the room and through the office to the elevator.

He didn't say a word to me until we were in the backseat of his SUV, and then all he said was, "Do not speak. Do not touch me."

Chapter Fourteen

Skye

K illian didn't say a word on the drive or during the elevator ride up to his apartment, but the second we stepped off it, he threw me over his shoulder, carried me to his room, and tossed me on the bed.

Before I could take a breath, he was ranging himself over me, settling his muscular body between my legs and pinning me beneath him.

"Is this what you want, Sunshine?" His lips brushed mine. "Hmm?"

Unable to speak, I nodded.

"No. Say it." He bit down on my bottom lip, earning a moan from me. "Tell me what you want."

A shudder ran through me when he sucked and licked away the sting of his bite. "I want... I *need* you."

He unbuttoned my shirt, spread it open, and pulled my bra down, freeing my breasts. "What do you need me to do?"

"Fuck me."

His hand circled my neck and his lips went to my ear. "No fucking, so try again."

The harshness of his touch and voice had a surge of heat coiling in my core. "Make me come. *Please.*"

"How?"

"What?" The question came out a little harsher than I'd intended. I was so fucking turned on, I thought I might explode, and he just kept talking.

"How do you want me to make you come?" His hand slid under my skirt to trace the outline of my underwear. "Fingers?" He bent his head and suckled my nipple, pulling a whimper from me. "Or tongue?"

"Both?"

He used his teeth to tug on my nipple, then licked away the pain, turning it into pleasure. "Are you asking me?"

"Use both! Please, use your fingers and tongue to make me come."

"Ah, there's my girl," he said.

His lips pulled into a wicked grin, awakening something primal in me, and when he sat back on his haunches, I let out a low growl.

"Patience, Sunshine," he said with a trace of humor that had me writhing in frustration. His gaze traced the curves of my body, leaving a trail of fire in their wake. "Fuck. You're beautiful."

"Kiss me," I said, holding my arms out to him.

He lowered himself over me, his lips meeting mine in a slow kiss that quickly grew heated and demanding.

A groan came from him as he tore his mouth from mine to nuzzle his head in the crook of my neck. His hand slid between my legs, his finger brushing over my swollen clit to my opening.

Another whimper escaped me when he slowly slid a finger inside me. Everything around me, all my problems and insecurities disappeared. All that mattered, all I could focus on was the aching heat between my legs. My need for him became unbearable, and searching for more, I pressed my hips against his hand.

"You're so fucking wet. So fucking tight," he said, his voice was strained and breathless. A small yelp slipped from my lips when he bit down on my collarbone. "I'm not going to fuck you," he added, more to himself than me. "Not with my cock, anyway."

"Oh… but… *oh my God!*" He slid a second finger inside and curled them until they hit the most sensitive spot, and I lost the ability to think.

He kissed me again, his tongue tangling with mine while his fingers moved in and out of me in a slow, seductive rhythm. I squirmed and moaned as he brought me up to the edge, but not over it. Not yet.

His forehead touched mine, and I could hear his strained breathing as he fought back his urge to take me against his better judgment. "Mmm… You respond so well to my touch."

A long shuddering breath passed through my lips as he kissed and licked his way down my body until his head was between my legs. I nearly sobbed when he pulled his fingers out, but he quickly replaced them with his tongue.

A deep, feral growl rumbled from him after his first lick along my folds. "You taste so good. Too fucking good."

I drove my hands into his hair, holding him against me as I gyrated my hips. He let out a chuckle at my forcefulness but continued licking, sucking, and fingering me until my back arched as my orgasm slammed into me so hard, I saw stars.

"Oh. My. God," I breathed as wave after wave of pleasure pulsated through my body until I sagged onto the mattress, my hands slipping from his hair.

Before I could even register he had moved, Killian's body was covering mine again.

"You good?" he asked.

"Good doesn't even begin to describe how I feel. Thank you." I turned my head to press a kiss to his lips as I slid my hand between us to grip his erection. "We have to keep things fair, remember? So, it's your turn now. On your back, mister."

Once he'd settled, I undressed him then kissed my way down his body. His gorgeous fucking body. When I reached his crotch, my mouth watered when I saw the size of him, and another rush of heat hit my core. He'd just given me the best orgasm of my life, and I was already craving another.

I locked eyes with him as I licked the beads of pre-cum from the head of his cock. He returned my gaze with hooded eyes, folding his arms behind his head to watch me as I took him in my mouth.

My center throbbed, delighted by his groans as I worked him with my mouth and hand. He slipped his fingers into my hair and lifted his hips to push himself even deeper.

"Mmm, that's it. Just like that," he groaned. "Look at you, taking every inch like a good girl." He smoothed his hands over my hair. "You're so fucking beautiful, baby."

His praise, the way he looked at me, and the feel and taste of him was driving me mad with need. My hand drifted between my legs to massage my aching clit, pleasuring us both at the same time. When I felt him tense, I knew he was close to coming, and so was I.

He wrapped my hair around his hand and tried to remove himself from my mouth, but I wouldn't let him. I wanted to taste him, *all* of him. Our climaxes hit at the same time, our bodies shuddering as our moans filled the room.

As the aftershocks still buzzed through me, I sat up, meeting his eyes as I licked my lips.

"Come here," he said in a raspy whisper.

I crawled over the bed until I was next to him again. He curled his hand around the back of my neck, pulling me in for a kiss.

"Killian," I said against his lips.

"Hmm?"

"That was fucking amazing."

"Yeah, it was."

"No. You don't understand. I haven't ever come like that. Not even with my vibrator." I felt my cheeks warm.

Funny how the mention of a sex toy could make me blush after what we'd just done. "I haven't been with anyone since Paul, and even with him, it was never like that."

He kissed me again, tenderly but passionately. "Damn. If I had known that I'd have gone slower."

"No. No, it was perfect," I said, settling beside him on the bed with my head on his chest.

He pressed a kiss on the top of my head. "Did you eat lunch?"

"No," I said. "I was going to grab something on the way back from my meeting with Amelia." The memory of him with Chad flashed through my mind, bringing a flush of warmth to my face. I really didn't want to know why that had turned me on so much.

"I'm going to take a shower, and then take you out to lunch," he said, dancing his fingers down my arm.

I lifted an eyebrow. "Oh? Is that the dating part of our fake relationship?"

His jaw clenched. "I'm not sure we can call this fake anymore."

I gave a half shrug. "Until you put your dick inside me, it's fake."

His laugh rumbled through his chest. "Technically, it was inside you."

"All right, smartass, until you put it in my pussy, it's not real."

His eyebrows shot up. "Such a dirty mouth for a yoga instructor. I like it, say it again."

"Hush. Go take your shower." I let out a yelp when he rolled us over, trapping me under his body.

He lifted my hands over my head, holding them tightly so I couldn't move. "Say it again, Sunshine."

My breath shuddered as he bit my earlobe, then my neck. "Pussy," I said, the word coming out as a moan.

"Mmm..." He bowed his head and licked each of my nipples before getting out of bed, which gave me an excellent view of his gorgeous ass.

Without thinking, I leaned forward and bit his right cheek.

"What the fuck?" he asked, turning to look at me.

I let out a laugh at the shocked expression on his face. "I'm sorry, I couldn't help myself. It's just so perfect."

"Weirdo," he said with a laugh on his way to the bathroom. "Care to join me?"

"I thought you'd never ask," I said, practically skipping to the bathroom.

AFTER A SHOWER AND ANOTHER ORGASM for each of us—mouths and hands only—we were sitting at a sidewalk table at a small café near his apartment. The smell of pastries and coffee had my stomach growling as we placed our orders. The waitress had just walked back inside the café when my phone rang.

"It's Wes. I need to take it," I said before answering it. "Hey, Wes, what's up?"

As usual he skipped the small talk and went right into overbearing brother mode. "Where are you?"

"I'm out to lunch with Killian."

"Where?"

I sighed and rolled my eyes. "The Daily Sift Café."

"I'll be there in twenty minutes."

"Wait, no—" He ended the call, and I sighed as I slid my phone back in my purse. "Wes will be here in twenty."

Killian reached across the table to take my hand in his. "It'll be okay."

"He sounded upset, agitated. This won't be okay."

He squeezed my hand. "Trust me, it'll be okay."

As we waited for Wes to arrive, my mind raced with worries about what could be bothering him. We'd spoken every day about the updates on my yoga studio. Killian had been helping with that and aside from the fire inspector blaming the fire on arson, everything was going smoothly.

They had laid Mom to rest. His business was in good hands. As for my relationship with Killian, he thought we were in love and talking about getting engaged. As far as Wes knew, everything was going well, which left me confused by his angry tone.

When Wes stormed up to the table, his expression full of anger, my confusion turned to concern.

"What's going on, Wes?" I asked tentatively, my heart pounding in my chest.

He glared at Killian with a lethal expression, slamming his phone down on the table with enough force to make me jump.

"What the hell, Wes?" I exclaimed, shocked by his sudden outburst.

"You think you can cheat on my sister and get away with it?" he said, his voice low and menacing.

Killian was eerily calm as he glanced at the photo on Wes's phone. "Are you having me followed, Wes?" he asked in a chillier tone.

"She's my little sister. I need to know she's okay."

Skipping the part where Wes decided he was my caretaker after being absent for years, I picked up Wes' phone to see a photo of Killian with his arms wrapped around a stunning woman. A surge of jealousy slammed into me, and I tightened my grip on the phone, my fingers trembling with a level of anger I'd never allowed myself to feel before.

"Who is she?" I demanded, my voice sounding foreign to my own ears.

Killian turned to me, his gaze softening when it met mine. "She's Lucian's sister. Her name is Elisa Cross." He took Wes' phone from my hand and placed it on the table. His hand then covered mine, instantly calming me. "Someone assaulted her Saturday night. That's why I left you alone."

"Oh... That's why you came back—" He squeezed my hand to stop me from finishing my sentence. I'd almost mentioned him coming back covered in blood. "You were helping her." *By killing the man who hurt her*, I added to myself.

"Yes." He pushed his chair back from the table and tugged my hand. "Come here."

I rose from my seat and moved around the table to sit on his lap. One of his hands wrapped around my waist while the other gripped the back of my neck. He pulled my head down until our lips met.

"I've told you before, I'll never hurt you. You are all I want, all I need, understood?"

"Mm-hmm," I muttered. Part of me was embarrassed at being so turned on with my brother standing right next to me. The other part was torn between believing what Killian was saying and wondering if it was part of our act for Wes.

"What the fuck is going on?" Wes asked. "He was with another woman last night, Skye."

I looked up at my big brother and smiled. "Wes, I appreciate everything you do for me, but I am an adult. I've been taking care of myself for a long time."

"How can you just take his word for it? How do you know he isn't lying?"

Because he came home covered in her rapist's blood. Since I couldn't say that, I said, "Because I just do."

I scooted off Killian's lap and moved to stand in front of my brother, putting my hand on his arm. "Wes, I don't know how to explain it, and I don't expect you to understand, but I trust Killian." As the words came out of my mouth, I realized just how true they were. "I need you to trust me."

He looked down at me with a furrowed brow. "I do trust you."

"No, you don't. You wouldn't have had Killian followed if you did. You're canceling that, by the way.

Immediately."

"I had him followed because I don't trust *him*."

I shook my head. "No. You had Killian followed because you're scared I'll pick another asshole like Paul. You don't trust me to make better choices."

He opened his mouth to argue then slammed it shut again. "When you put it that way... I'm sorry, Skye. I just can't forgive myself for not being there for you when you needed me the most. For not knowing what you were going through. For not protecting you." He pulled me into a tight hug. "With Mom or Paul. I'm so sorry, Munchkin."

I hugged him back, burying my face in his chest. "It's okay, Ogre. You have to stop beating yourself up. What happened is in the past, let's leave it there. You need to realize I'm a big girl. If I need your help, I'll ask for it, so you can take a chill pill for now."

He grunted and gave me a squeeze. "I'll try to remember that."

"You'll call off whoever you have following him," I added since he'd ignored my demand the first time.

"Fine," he ground out through clenched teeth.

"Wes, why don't you join us for lunch," Killian said, waving the waitress over.

Wes and I sat down, he ordered a sandwich, and the three of us talked about the yoga studio restoration. The investigation had delayed the work from starting, but after they'd determined it as arson and had gotten as much evidence as they could, the renovations had resumed.

They hadn't gotten much and weren't confident they'd find the culprit. I had a feeling I knew who it was and had given them Paul's name and his last known address. Though I was sure he'd disappeared into the darkest recesses of the city, and I doubted they'd find him.

I pushed the thoughts of Paul aside. In that moment, as I watched my brother and Killian talk about the latest basketball game, everything was right in the world. All that mattered was sharing the afternoon with the two most important men in my life. I leaned back in my chair, sipping my lemonade and letting the moment outshine the shadows of the past.

Chapter Fifteen

Killian

It had been two long weeks since the lunch with Skye and her brother. The memory of the hurt and anger on her face when she thought I had been with another woman had stuck with me. It made me realize the mistake I had made by letting things get as far as they did.

Between that unfamiliar and unwelcome guilt and my insane hours at work, it had also been two excruciating weeks since I'd let myself touch her or felt her touch me. The need to be with her, to taste her was driving me insane. Sleeping was nearly impossible when I knew she was in the next room with only a wall between us.

When she showered, I imagined her as she lathered her body with soap, gliding her slick hands over her curves, and it took all my willpower not to break down the door and replace her hands with mine. I'd nearly lost control each time she slipped into my bed, thinking I was asleep as she nestled her perfect round ass against me.

Then I came home from work to see her standing in the kitchen, wearing nothing but one of my shirts. It was like she'd stepped straight out of my fantasies. She looked like a goddess with her hair falling in loose waves around her face and her bare, toned legs stretching from the hem of my shirt.

"Your home early today," she said. "I hope you don't mind, I borrowed your shirt. All my clothes are in the washing machine."

Without a word, I crossed the room, closing the distance between us. I drove my hands into her hair, tilting her head back as I crushed my lips to hers. The kiss was full of the hunger and frustration that had been building inside me for the past two weeks and I could no longer ignore it. She melted against me, her fingers digging into my shoulders as she returned the kiss with equal passion.

Our need for each other grew until we tore at each other's clothes, desperate for more contact. Fingers and lips met heated flesh as we explored each other's bodies. She let out a little yelp when I gripped her by the waist and lifted her to set her on the countertop. Before she could react, I dropped to my knees, burying my face between her legs, breathing in her scent as I let myself taste her.

At first, I took my time exploring her slick folds with my tongue. Then her hands fisted in my hair, and her moans and gasps went straight to my dick as she gyrated her hips against me. The erotic way she moved and the sexy moans coming from her drove me wild. My fingers dug into the flesh of her thighs as I feasted on her like a starved man.

Not touching her had left me full of longing with no relief. No woman before her had ever satisfied the burning hunger inside me the way just one taste of her could. Skye Larsen was like manna from heaven, and I was the poor, unworthy soul craving just one drop of her essence.

"Killian," she breathed, her body clenching and quivering as her climax hit.

My name slipping from her lips while she came, triggered something inside me, something primal and possessive. As I rose to stand, my hands roamed over her body, tracing the curve of her hips and the swell of her breasts. She shuddered against me, her nails digging into my shoulders and her legs wrapping around my waist.

There was no resisting her. Not anymore.

Lifting her from the counter, I walked us to my room where I lowered her to the bed before stretching myself over her. She sighed and shimmied her hips until her opening pushed against the head of my cock.

A wicked grin tugged at the corners of my mouth as she released a groan of frustration when I pulled away from her. "Before we do this, you need to know this means you belong to me. There's no one else for either of us. There's no turning back." My hand went to her throat, squeezing lightly. "And if you let another man touch you, you'll be to blame for his slow and torturous death. Is that understood?"

"Yes, yes. I'm yours," she said in a sexy, breathy voice.

"Only yours."

"Yes, you are. I told you before I don't want you to fear me, but you should." My fingers tightened around her neck as I traced the line of her jaw with my nose. "You should be terrified because once I have you, I'm never letting you go."

Her hips lifted off the mattress, pressing herself against me. "I don't want you to let me go."

On a growl, I pressed the head of my cock against her silky opening, holding myself back from slamming into her.

"What? Why are you waiting?" She was practically sobbing. "I'm on the pill and I'm clean. I can show you."

"That's not the problem. I'm clean too." A groan escaped me when she pushed her hips forward, my tip almost penetrating her. "It's just... this won't be gentle."

She pushed her hips up even further, and we both moaned when the tip finally breached her. "I don't want gentle."

"Fuck," I breathed as I thrust my hips until I was buried to the hilt.

So tight. So wet. So perfect. And all mine.

I held still as the sensation of her pussy stretched to accommodate me, and the glorious feeling of finally being inside her overwhelmed me. After spending so long telling myself this would never happen, could never happen, it finally did and just as I had told her, there was no turning back.

She was the light to my darkness, the calm to my storm. She brought purity to my tainted world. She was the answer to everything I never knew I needed.

"Killian, please," she said, her fingers digging into my hips, urging me to move. "Please fuck me!"

"Anything you want, Sunshine," I replied, sliding almost all the way out before thrusting back inside her.

I moved my hips wildly, fucking her like the savage man I was. Her breasts moved in time with my thrusts, and I lowered my head to take her nipple between my teeth. A long moan came from her when I bit down just enough to make it sting before licking away the pain.

"*Fuck,* you take my cock so well, like you were made for it."

"Oh! Killian," she said with a whimper. "I need— ah..."

"Hmm? Tell me what you need." My voice was strained from trying not to end this too soon.

"To come. I need to come," she said, her voice strained and breathy.

My hand clenched around her neck as I watched her cup her breasts and tweak her nipples. Her moans blended with my grunts and the sound of flesh hitting flesh created a wickedly dirty masterpiece.

I slid my hand from her neck down her body to her ass, squeezing hard as I shifted her position so she could take me even deeper. I pounded into her harder and faster, giving myself over to my feral side. She looked more beautiful than ever with her lips parted and her back arched as I drove her up to the edge. When she plummeted over into the abyss, screaming my name, I tumbled in after her.

While we caught our breath, I sealed my fate, *our* fate with a kiss. She was mine. *Only mine.* I was fucking lost to her: heart, body, and soul.

She opened her eyes to meet mine, and I felt myself falling into their deep, blue depths. "That was fucking amazing... mind-blowing," she said with a sexy rasp to her voice. She lifted her head to press her lips to mine for a gentle kiss before I shifted to lie beside her. "This means we're not pretending anymore."

I slipped my arm around her to pull her against me. "No more pretending. I meant what I said, you're mine. No one else touches you. Never again."

"Fine by me."

"Have you decided about the job?" I asked, tracing my fingers over the smooth skin of her stomach.

"Yes, I have," she said, her hand sliding up my arm in a light caress, tracing my tattoos with her fingers. "I told Amelia I'd do it."

"Good."

"I already made some sketches."

"Show me."

She shifted her position so she could see my face. "Really?"

"Yes."

A grin spread across my lips as she let out a squeal and scrambled off the bed. She tugged at my hand; her excitement palpable as she led me through the hallway. As her naked body moved in front of me, I couldn't help admiring the sway of her hips and the curve of her waist.

My dick was growing hard again remembering what she felt like pinned underneath me, how her walls clenched around me when she came. I'd just had her and already needed her again.

Then we stepped into her art room, and a new painting caught my eye. Without thinking, I bypassed her sketches and moved toward it.

It was of her yoga studio engulfed in flames. Shadows shrouded the streets and buildings around her studio, giving the painting a hauntingly dark quality. On the other side of the road, stood a solitary light pole, *my* light pole. It was the only spot of brightness, and beneath its radiant glow, two figures held each other.

The man had his arms wrapped around the woman in a protective and possessive embrace, and as she clung to him, she had her eyes fixed on the burning building.

She stepped up behind me. "I had to paint it," she whispered, staring at the canvas. "It would haunt me until I did." She ran her fingers over the couple then looked up at me. "You saved me that night. In more ways than one."

"How so?"

She gently took the painting from my hands and set it down. When she turned back to me, her eyes were glistening with tears. "Before you came into my life, I felt trapped in a never-ending cycle. Wake up, go to work, paint, sleep. After Paul, I hid myself away from the world. I let go of the hope that I'd ever find true happiness or pleasure in my life. Then you appeared, and everything changed."

She took a shaky breath before she continued. "Part of me died when my mom turned to drugs and alcohol. I died even more with Paul. Then I found you. You brought me back to life."

I looked at her, keeping my expression blank. I had never wanted a relationship, never wanted to feel the things she stirred in me, and no matter how much I wanted to tell her I felt the same, I couldn't let myself be vulnerable.

"Don't get me confused with Prince Charming," I said coldly, trying to ignore the emotions stirring inside me. "It wasn't me that brought you back to life, it was the thrill of someone watching you, someone wanting you."

Her face fell. "That's not true," she whispered. "Paul wanted me and all I felt was revulsion. It was *you*, not your obsession. You. There's something about *you* that pulls to me."

"Just like there's something about you that draws me in whether I want it to or not."

"You don't want it to?"

"No," I lied unable to stop pushing her away. "You're naïve, Skye. Too trusting." I motioned around the room to her paintings. "This darkness inside you is nothing compared to what lurks inside of me."

"You do not know my past," she said, her voice laced with bitterness. "You don't know what I've been through or what I'm capable of." Her deep blue eyes darkened even more when she looked at me. "You are not the only one trying to outrun their demons."

She was right. I wasn't the only one who'd been through hell and back. Her pain was in every stroke of her paintings, it was clear in the way she held back her emotions, and it was in the smile that never truly reached her eyes.

"I know people have hurt you," I said. "I also know you try to pull yourself out of the depths of your past every day, but for me... There's no use for me to even try. There's no climbing my way out of my hell. It's a part of me. I've grown around it, absorbed it. I can't change it. I *won't* change it."

Her jaw set as she glared at me. "You think you're so mysterious and dangerous. You think I should be afraid of you. You *want* me to fear you." She stepped closer to me, narrowing her eyes. "Well, I'm not afraid of you, Killian. No matter how hard you try to scare me."

I grabbed her jaw, squeezing until her eyes widened. "Maybe I'll show you just how scary I can be."

She heaved a frustrated sigh and rolled her eyes. "Try me," she said, her tone shaky but defiant.

On a deep growl, I strengthened my grip, tilting her head back and crushing my lips to hers in a demanding kiss. As the kiss deepened, I moved my hand down to her throat, grasping it tightly.

"You're playing with fire, Skye. You're going to get burned."

"I don't care. I've been numb for so long," she said with a moan. She wrapped her hand around my wrist and pushed it against her neck even harder. "You made me feel again."

Fuck. She stared up at me with wide eyes. Those fucking blue eyes. I should have seen fear in them. Dammit, she was right, I *wanted* to see fear in them. It would have made things easier. Instead, the trust I saw there was undeserved and flipped my entire world upside down.

Using my hold on her neck, I walked her backward until her back hit the wall. "Turn around," I said, a dangerous edge creeping into my voice. When she faced the wall, I pressed my body against hers, caging her in, trapping her. "Lift your arms, press your hands against the wall and stick your ass out."

I stepped back so she could do as I told her. When she was in position, I smacked her right ass cheek, the sound echoing through the room. She moaned, pushing her ass back even more, and I tangled my hand in her hair to pull her head back.

"That was for rolling your eyes at me," I growled in her ear. "I told you before not to do it, don't make me tell you again. Understood?" She moaned again but didn't answer. *Smack.* "Is that understood?"

"Oh, God... Yes."

"Do not take your hands off that wall," I said, wrapping my hands around her waist and yanking her hips back to position my cock against her opening. Sliding one hand up her torso, I pinched her nipple before cupping her breast and squeezing as I thrust myself inside her.

Her moans turned to whimpers as I moved in a punishing rhythm. As her inner walls clamped down on me like a vise, she pushed her hips back, pulling me in even deeper.

"Killian," she sobbed. "I need... ahhh..."

My hand moved to grasp her jaw and turn her head to the side. I curved my body over hers and pressed my lips to hers. "Hmm... Do you want me to make you come?"

"Y-yes... Now. I need to come now."

Her words came out between heaving breaths. I could hear how close she was in her voice, but her punishment wasn't over yet.

I stopped moving and pulled almost all the way out of her. She let out a growl of protest then a moan of pleasure when I smacked her ass again, and a wicked grin formed on my lips. "Is that how you ask for what you want? I didn't hear the magic word."

"Please," she begged. "*Please* make me come."

"That's my good girl," I said, and moved my hand from her throat back to her waist. I held her tightly as I hinged back a little and thrust until I was buried deep inside her.

My control was nearing its breaking point, but I held on to it until she screamed out my name and her body convulsed with her climax. As her moans died down, I let myself go, coming harder than I ever thought possible.

She turned around, rising to her toes to kiss me. "Mmm, that was perfect," she cooed as she reached around and gave my ass a light smack. "Good job."

"Oh? Do you think you're the one in control here? I'll have to change that." Before she could react, I flung her over my shoulder and carried her back to my room to toss her on the bed.

As I looked down at her, her eyes bright and her body still flushed from pleasure, yet another crack formed in the armor around my heart.

Chapter Sixteen

Skye

As I lay beside Killian, my body still humming after two more rounds of mind-altering, earth-shattering sex, I traced the outline of his lips with my finger. A yelp escaped me when he suddenly nipped at it, then rolled me over to pin me against the mattress.

I brushed the hair from his face and let my fingers trace the lines of his jaw. "You mentioned your past, how dark it was." He grunted but said nothing, so I added, "Tell me about it."

When he stiffened, I ran my hands through his hair. "Don't shut down on me, Killian," I whispered. "If this is going to happen, if we're going to be together, I should know more about you."

"I don't talk about my past," he said in a gruff voice as he rolled off me.

Not willing to let it go, I climbed on top of him, straddling him as I trailed my fingers over his chest. "Relax," I whispered, bending forward to press a kiss to his lips. "You can trust me. Tell me what happened."

He drove his hand into my hair, cupping the back

of my head to keep me where I was. "You're pushing it, Skye. Stop before shit gets ugly."

Fisting his hand in my hair he pulled my face away from his. We stared at each other for a long moment, then he released his hold on me.

"You wouldn't hit me," I said, my tone firm and sure.

"You're taking advantage of that by poking at me."

"No. I just want to know more about the man whose house I live in. The man who stalked me, saved me from my ex and a fire." I leaned down again until my lips brushed his ear. "The man who fucked me into oblivion last night."

A ferocious growl erupted from him as I felt him grow hard beneath me. I let out a surprised cry when he flipped us over and pinned me with his body again. "You want to know about my sad childhood? You want to know how my dad beat any emotion other than anger out of me? How he'd reward me for ruthlessness and punish me for showing compassion? How when I cried from his beatings, he'd laugh at me and hit me harder? How my mother was too weak and drunk to give a fuck what happened to her little boy? Is that what you want to know?"

Tears stung my eyes as I nodded. "Yes."

His hand clamped tightly around my throat. "Don't fucking cry over that little boy. Don't you dare fucking cry, Skye." His voice was low and vicious, and his eyes were nearly black with rage, but I knew he wasn't angry with me. He was angry with his parents... and maybe himself.

His gray eyes were stormy and intense as he stared down at me. "Why?" he asked. "Why the fuck does it matter? I'm not that person anymore. That little boy died a long time ago."

I held back my sobs, but the tears fell unbidden from my eyes. "Because all of it made you the man you are today."

A twisted smirk, dripping with bitterness, spread across his lips. "I'll tell you if for no other reason than to shatter your naïve perception of me."

He stayed on top of me as he spoke, keeping me pinned beneath his body. When he told me about the horrors of his past, he did it with a detachment I was all too familiar with. It was like it all happened to someone else, someone he knew many years ago. In a way, it had.

He told me his first memory was when he was around five. He was crying, as children often do, but instead of comfort, his father called him a "pussy" and smacked him across the face. As the years passed, the abuse only intensified. By the time he was thirteen, his father had enlisted one of his enforcers to teach Killian how to 'be a man.' It was clear the enforcer was a sadistic psychopath who treated teenage Killian like an experiment for new ways to torment people.

The things that man did to him caused bile to rise in my throat and made my heart break for the little boy who never knew love or compassion.

His mother knew what was happening, but the father would beat her when she tried to stop it. She'd given up pretty early on and turned to alcohol to numb herself. The violence continued until Killian was fifteen when he'd finally lost it and stabbed the enforcer to death in front of his father.

"Oh my God," I breathed. "What did your dad do?"

"He gave me a cigar, patted me on the back, and told me I did a good job."

"Holy crap." I couldn't imagine what it was like living in a house where murder was rewarded. "Is your dad still alive?"

He grunted and nodded his head. "Barely. His company was the first one I took down. To date, it was the most difficult and most rewarding. It's not easy to intimidate my father, but I found his weakness in the end, and left him penniless and half-insane because of it. He'd always told me nothing else mattered when it came to business, not even family." He sneered. "I showed him how well I learned that lesson. After him, it became my mission to take down any asshole that reminds me of him."

"Do you know where your parents are?"

"Yes. They had to move in with a friend of my mother's. I have no love for them. Not anymore. He'd never allowed love, compassion, or happiness," he said. "He rewarded anger, ruthlessness, and brute strength. He believed to be successful in business you had to be cunning and coldhearted, and business was the only thing that mattered to him."

I couldn't stop the sardonic, almost manic, laugh from escaping me. "I'm sorry, it's just it was the opposite for me."

He lifted a questioning eyebrow. "Tell me."

I sighed. I'd expected to have to share too, but that didn't make it any easier. "My torment only lasted three years, but to me it felt like three hundred. My mom never did anything half-assed, including her addiction." A lump formed in my throat as the memories came back to me.

"When she fell into the fiery pits of hell, she fell hard and fast. After she lost the business, it had only taken her a few weeks to go from the occasional glass of wine to drinking an entire bottle of vodka in a day. Then it was multiple bottles, then it was cocaine, crack, meth, heroine... you get the point."

When I shivered, he shifted to pull the covers over us, keeping me in his arms as I continued. "It wasn't long before we were homeless, bouncing from one junkie's couch to the next," I said in a distant voice. "If I ever spoke up, got cranky, or showed any emotion other than cheerfulness, my mother or one of her boyfriends would hit me until I learned how to be a 'proper young lady.' And I did learn... I learned to keep a smile on my face even during the darkest times. Even when a disgusting, greasy man took an interest in me."

A full-body shudder rocked through me as that memory played out in my mind. "I was fourteen the first time he touched me. He never had sex with me, but he touched me... When he wasn't, he was making me watch while he touched himself. He stayed with my mom to be close to me. If she knew what was going on, she never showed it. When I couldn't take it anymore, I replaced the contents of his little baggie of powder with rat poison. He shot up and... that's when I took off on my own at fifteen."

"Damn," he said, wiping the tears from my face.

"Now we know why we're so drawn to each other," I said as another bitter laugh escaped me. "Two broken souls trying to find their way out of the darkness together."

He leaned in and captured my lips in a kiss that sent a jolt of heat to my core and made my heart flutter. It differed from all our other kisses, there was a tenderness to it that had been missing before. We both seemed to drop our shields for just a moment. It was as if we were seeking solace from our pain—or maybe forgiveness for our sins.

He broke the kiss with a nip to my bottom lip. "You don't have to hide anything from anyone, Skye," he whispered, his voice husky. "From now on, you won't avoid your emotions, and you're free to express whatever it is you're feeling."

"I'll try. After years of hiding behind a smile, it might be hard to change. You can be who you want to be too, you know," I whispered in return.

"I already am," he said.

A moan slipped from me as he slowly slid his thick, hard length inside me, moving his hips in a languid motion that hit secret spots I didn't know I had.

His hands slid down under my thighs, pulling my legs farther apart and sinking himself even deeper inside me.

"You want to be a self-proclaimed bad guy?" I asked, my voice barely audible.

He rose to his knees, pulling my legs up around his

waist so my hips lifted from the bed. "It doesn't matter if I want it or not: I *am* a bad guy." His pace quickened sending a lightning bolt of pleasure through my core. "We're done talking."

"Uh-huh," I moaned, my hands fisting in the sheets and forgetting what we were talking about in the first place.

THAT NIGHT I FELL ASLEEP IN KILLIAN'S ARMS. When I woke up, the sun was just rising, but I was alone in the bed. I found him on the balcony drinking coffee while looking out over the city. Wrapped in his robe, I slid my arms around his and rested my head against his back. It was the most content I'd ever felt.

"Good morning," I said, my voice still raspy from sleep.

He turned in my embrace and pressed a kiss to the top of my head. "Did you sleep well?"

I looked up at him, resting my chin on his chest. "Better than ever. You?"

"Same."

"Look at us, making small talk like we didn't just have sex five times and then share our deepest secrets with each other last night," I said with a huge smile.

He gave me a sly grin. "What are your plans for today?"

I hesitated to tell him, knowing he would insist on having Leo and Neil watch over me. As much as I appreciated the protection, I had hoped for a day alone with my best friend. Though not telling him wasn't an option. Secrets in a relationship, even one of omission, didn't bode well for the future.

"Layla invited me to a picnic in The Verve park."

He let out a little grunt. "Neil will drive you."

"I figured as much," I said with a light laugh. "I assume Leo will also be there." I mentally patted myself on the back for not rolling my eyes... even though memories of what happened when I'd done it the night before had heat pooling in my core.

"Yes." He leaned down for a kiss that had my pulse racing. "Once Paul is out of the picture, Leo will no longer be necessary."

"That'll be nice," I said with a weak smile. "You know I appreciate everything you're doing, right? The always being watched thing is annoying, unless it's you doing the watching, but I'm grateful I don't have to look over my shoulder every time I step outside."

"I know," he replied, his hands trailing down my body. "I'll see you after work. If you need anything—"

"I know, call Amelia or Neil."

He gave me a curt nod and a playful smack on the ass as he walked past me to go back inside. He left for work after we ate breakfast, and I took a shower with my mind full of deliciously erotic thoughts of him.

After I dressed, I settled down to work on the sketches for the hotel until it was time to leave. When I stepped out of the apartment building, Neil was already holding the back door open for me.

A playful smile spread across my lips as I bypassed him and slid into the passenger seat. While he drove,

I peppered him with questions about Killian when he was young. Neil never revealed anything too personal, but I could tell he knew what Killian had gone through as a child.

"You're good for him," he said as we pulled up to the park. "He needs someone who challenges him."

"Yeah? He's good for me too. We both have demons to slay, so I think we kind of understand each other."

As Neil got out of the car to open my door, he gave me a warm smile. Despite my protests, he insisted on doing it every time he took me somewhere, which wasn't very often, but I still felt weird about it.

"Enjoy your afternoon, Ms. Larsen," Neil said, his tone respectful as he gave a slight bow of his head. "I'll be right here when you're ready to leave."

I glanced over at Layla and Wes, who were sitting on a blanket under the shade of a tree. "Thank you, but you don't have to wait here," I told Neil. "I'll be fine with Leo and my brother around. You have other things to attend to."

"Mr. Asher requested I wait for you," was all he said.

I caught the unspoken dismissal and made my way over to Wes and Layla, who greeted me with warm smiles.

"Hey," I said as I settled down on the blanket next to them. "What's up with the picnic? It's a little chilly, isn't it?"

"We have a surprise for you," Layla said, with a little bounce.

Before I could respond, a group of people

approached, all wearing Skye Yoga t-shirts. As the confusion faded, I realized they had all been students of mine before the fire.

"What's going on?" I asked, standing to greet them all.

Layla rose to stand beside me, wrapping her arms around me in a sideways hug. "Wes and I know you miss the studio, and it's going to be awhile before the renovations are complete, so..."

Wes stood on the other side of me. "Layla went online and got Skye Yoga a permit to teach classes here in the park," he said, finishing the explanation.

"Wes and I called all the clients and told them about it," Layla said, gesturing to the smiling people in front of me. "This is everyone who could make it today. There are more. I have a schedule worked up. All we need is for you to say you're in."

"Are you kidding me? Of course I'm in!" I turned to give her a proper hug then threw my arms around Wes' neck. "When's the first day?"

Layla squealed and did a little dance. "You tell us."

"Wow. Thank you, guys," I said with tears blurring my vision.

After a few more hugs from my students and some chit chat, we munched on food that was clearly provided by Chelsea. Two hours later, as Neil drove me back to Killian's apartment, I was full of food and hope, and couldn't wait to tell him the news.

Chapter Seventeen

Skye/Killian

Skye

After my third day of teaching yoga outside in the park, I stayed behind to enjoy the warmth of the sun and crispness in the air. I hadn't been outside much since the fire, so I stayed for a while to sit back and enjoy the peace. It was invigorating to breathe in the fresh air and feel the grass beneath my feet.

A chill ran down my spine, disturbing my tranquility, and I couldn't shake the feeling of someone watching me. It felt nothing like when Killian's eyes were on me. Whoever this was made my stomach churn. I glanced around but saw no one it could be.

Then my phone rang. It was a blocked number, but I answered it in case it was Killian calling me from a secret phone. The second I answered, I knew it was a mistake. It was Paul, and I could tell he was high just from his voice. I'd bet anything he was calling because he knew I had protection who was making sure he couldn't get anywhere near me.

"You can hide behind your scary boyfriend all you want, Skye," he said in a slow, slurred drawl. "I will find a way to get you, because you belong to me."

"That won't happen, Paul." My voice was venomous from the blood-boiling anger inside me. "You have no fucking claim on me. I do not belong to you, and I regret ever being with you."

"You'll regret talking to me that way, that's for sure," he said. "You think they can protect you in a park?" His voice turned weak and shaky at the end, which proved how messed up he was.

"What makes you think you can get to me? You can't even stay awake long enough to finish threatening me. Go back to your hole, and leave me the fuck alone, and you better hope Killian doesn't find you."

I hung up before he could respond, and before I could put my phone back in my bag, Leo stopped in front of me.

"Are you okay?"

"Yeah, it was Paul. He's somewhere around here. He said something about me being in a park, so he must be here."

Leo's expression hardened, and he immediately went into action mode. "We need to get you out of here." He walked me back to where Neil waited, and after telling him to take me straight to Killian's, he returned to the park to search the area with the other guards.

I spent the entire ride seething with anger. For the first time in my life, I didn't push aside the fury, I let it boil. Paul had no right to bully me into being with him. How dare he call and threaten me when I was finally moving on and getting over what he'd done to me. I was done with him, and he needed to leave me alone.

When we got back to Killian's, Neil escorted me upstairs. As graciously as I could, I told him how silly it was for him to go out of his way like that. It wasn't like Paul would be hiding in the elevator waiting for me, but he'd insisted.

When we got to Killian's apartment, he took my hand in his and gave it a squeeze. "Goodbye, Ms. Larsen," he said with a warm smile.

"Goodbye, Neil."

"What happened?" Killian asked as soon as the doors slid closed again.

I cocked my hip and pursed my lips as I looked at him with the anger still churning inside me. "You know damn well what happened. You know what happens in my life before even I know." I walked past him to the bar and poured a glass of his scotch. "What I think you meant to ask is: are you okay?"

His jaw twitched a few times before he took a deep breath. I stifled the smug smile that wanted to pull at my lips. Here I was embracing my anger, and here he was trying to repress his. How quickly the tables had turned.

"Oh, did I upset you?" I asked, purposely poking the bear. Then I took a sip of my drink and choked when it burned my throat. "Oh God, how do you drink this stuff?"

He approached me like the predator he was and took the glass from my hand. "Are you okay" he asked, his tone tight with the annoyance I knew he was holding in.

He tossed back the contents of my glass in one gulp before strolling over to the bar. I watched as he picked up a clean glass and started making a drink.

"Peachy keen. Thanks for asking."

He turned around, handing me a glass with the same amber liquid as the scotch but there was also an orange peel and a maraschino cherry.

"Try this and stop being a brat," he said in a tone and a look that made me swallow my next sarcastic remark.

I took a sip of the drink and while it still burned a bit, it was way better than the straight up liquor. "This is good, thanks."

He took my free hand and led me to the sofa in the living room. "Tell me, in your own words, what happened," he said once we sat in our seats.

I told him everything that happened, from the creepy feeling to me hanging up.

"I'm so angry, I could kill him myself," I said, staring down at the amber liquid as I swirled it around the glass, and surprised to find I meant it. Not that I'd go out of my way to murder Paul, but the idea of it hadn't made me cringe as it would have a few weeks ago. With a sly grin, I flicked my eyes up to him. "I think you might be a bad influence on me, Stalker."

He took the glass from my hand and placed it on the table. "Lean back," he said, lightly curling his fingers around my throat.

When I did as he told me, his hand slid down between my breasts then continued to lift the hem of my shirt. "You think you could kill him? Think you can watch the fear build in his eyes as he realizes he's going to die. Then watch in morbid fascination as he takes his last breath and his eyes glaze over. Hmm? Is that what you think?" His voice was barely a whisper, full of venom yet smooth as silk as he slipped his hand into my yoga pants.

He gave a low hum of approval when he felt how wet I was, and a long moan escaped me as he pushed a finger inside me. Without me even having to think, my body slid even further down on the cushion, and my legs spread wider as he slid another finger inside me. He moved them in and out in a slow, leisurely rhythm that soon had me panting.

A whimper crept from my throat when he pressed his thumb against my clit. My body felt electrified and utterly alive under his sensual ministrations. The flutters of an orgasm built in my lower belly, turning me into a writhing, panting mess.

Then he pressed his lips to my ear and whispered, "The difference between you and me is: you may think about it, but I will do it. I *will* kill him." He spoke that last sentence at the same time he curled his fingers, hitting the spot that made my eyes roll back in my head.

The resulting orgasm rocked through me so hard I saw stars. After the body-wracking tremors eased, I sagged against the sofa.

"Do you feel more relaxed?" he asked, his voice

rumbled against my ear, sending little aftershocks of pleasure over me.

"Yes, thank you." I rose and moved to stand between his legs. "We can't forget about you," I said, lowering to my knees.

I had just unfastened his pants when his phone buzzed. Knowing from experience, he'd check it no matter what we were doing, I sat back on my haunches to wait.

"Fuck. Lucian is here," he said. "We'll continue this later."

Killian

LEAVING SKYE ON HER KNEES in front of me was difficult. The thought of those sweet red lips wrapped around my cock made me want to forget about everything else. I had two rodents to exterminate, then I'd be free to ignore the rest of the world and be with her.

Chad Walsh had made the mistake of hiring a hacker to breach my company's firewalls in an attempt to get leverage over me. Unfortunately for him, Asher Capital was impenetrable, fortified by the best security available in the world.

His attempts to breach my company's security only led to one thing: his hacker's location. Lucian had sent someone to talk to them and find out where Chad was hiding. Until then, I would handle Paul myself.

After weeks of radio silence, he was back to tormenting Skye. Threats against her were more important than some whiny rich kid trying to weasel money from me. If things went as I hoped, Paul would be begging for his life before the end of the day.

From what Skye had told us, we knew he was in the vicinity of The Verve. Both Leo and Lucian had men scouring the area for any sign of him. When they got him, they were to hold him for me.

"In my office," I said to Lucian when he stepped off the elevator.

He greeted Skye with a grin I knew melted the panties off any woman who saw it. When Skye smiled back at him, I wanted to strangle the life out of his body.

"Keep looking at her like that, and I'll have three bodies to hide," I said, my voice full of venom.

Lucian turned to aim that fucking smile at me. "Aww, Kill, you know I wouldn't touch your girl."

As we entered my office, I nailed Lucian with a fierce look. "How has no one found that sniveling fuck Paul yet? He fucking threatened her not even an hour ago. He couldn't have gone far. Your guys should have him by now."

"You don't even ask about Walsh? Just skip to the junkie fucking with your girlfriend." He folded his arms over his chest and pursed his lips. "You're in deep, man," he said, his tone laced with humor.

A low, feral growl escaped me. "Watch your step."

He held up his hands in placation. "Relax. I've just never seen you this into a chick before. She's got you hooked."

I clenched my jaw, choosing not to reply. "Find Paul and stay the fuck out of my private life."

Before he could reply, our phones buzzed.

"We got him," Lucian said.

Adrenaline slammed into me so hard a haze of red clouded my vision. Normally, I only got this amped up when I was already in the thick of it, face to face with my enemy. This time, it consumed me the second I saw the address on my phone screen. The fucker had been lurking in Skye's studio, camping out like a coward. He slipped in at night when the workers left and snuck out before they started their day.

"Let's go," I said in a voice I barely recognized as mine.

"Ah, Killer has come out to play," Lucian said with a dangerous edge to his voice. "I love it when he shows up."

My hands clenched into fists as I walked past him. "Fuck off, Luce."

As I stepped out of the office, I spotted Skye in the hallway, her fingers tight around a paintbrush. Her big, curious blue eyes met mine, and before I could think, I closed the gap between us and crushed my lips to hers. She clung to me, returning the kiss with the same intensity.

I reluctantly broke our embrace with a groan and pressed my forehead to hers. "Stay inside. I'll be back as soon as I can."

"O-okay..." She nibbled on her bottom lip, and I could tell she was debating with herself. "Where are you going?"

"We have some business to take care of," I said,

trying to keep the rage out of my voice. The way her eyes widened even more told me I'd failed. "I'll be back soon."

Before I could turn away, she grabbed my arm to pull me back to her. "Be careful," she whispered, rising to her toes to brush her lips against mine. "If you're going to do what I think you are, be careful. *Please.*"

Her concern for me should have eased the fury within me. Instead, it stoked it, made it grow. The thought of anyone hurting someone so sweet and pure made my blood boil. Paul was as good as dead. "Don't worry about me. I'll be fine," I said, pulling my arm from her grasp and walking away with Lucian trailing behind me.

"The fucker is mine," I said as we got into Lucian's car.

He revved the engine and pulled out into traffic. "No problem."

Chapter Eighteen

Killian

T he sun was just setting as we pulled up to my office building. I had arranged for Paul to be brought there to do the deed. Killing him in Skye's yoga studio probably wouldn't go over well with her, and my office building was already set up for what had to happen.

Lucian drove around the block to park near the back entrance to the building. We entered the backdoor into a dimly lit stairwell and took the steps down to the basement. There sat Paul in the center of the empty room with Leo standing behind him. Even seeing him bound to a chair with tape covering his mouth, my rage bubbled to the surface like molten lava.

A tainted kind of pleasure coiled in my gut when I saw the fear in his eyes. The second he recognized me, his eyes bulged with terror. It was deliciously satisfying to watch the man who had hurt Skye realize his fate.

With a vicious smile, I leaned in closer, savoring the sight of him quivering with fear. He was about to face the consequences of his actions, and I would enjoy making him pay.

"Ah, so, you remember me." I said, keeping my voice low. I'd learned the art of intimidation a long time ago, and I knew a quiet voice was more terrifying than a raised one. "Here's what's going to happen, Paul," I continued, my voice dripping with icy disdain. "I'm going to untie you, and you and I are going to settle this once and for all."

He shook his head frantically, his eyes filling with tears. "No?" I asked, raising an eyebrow in mock surprise. "Interesting. You had no problem beating a woman half your size, but when it comes to facing me, you're suddenly a pacifist, is that it?"

I straightened my back, my muscles coiled tight with anticipation, and motioned to Leo to untie the shithead.

"Well, too fucking bad," I said, "I'm not giving you a choice. Stand up."

He stumbled to his feet, his gaze darting around like a trapped animal. I relished in his terror, knowing he had no escape.

"Why are you doing this? Who the fuck are you?" Each word was more panicked than the one before it, and his pathetic whimpering only fueled my anger.

"You don't get to ask questions," I said, stepping closer. "I'll let you have the first hit, just like last time." He stumbled backward, tripping over the chair and falling on his ass. "Get the fuck up."

He pushed himself up using the chair to stabilize him. "I don't want to fight you, man."

"No? So, you don't like fair fights, you prefer to hit

innocent women, is that it?"

"Innocent? You think Skye is innocent?" He seemed to forget where he was for a moment and let out a laugh. "She's got you fooled, man. Do you know she tried to kill me? She stabbed me! Three times!" He shook his head. "I don't know why you're going through all this for her. She's not worth it. Pussy wasn't even that go—"

"Enough," I bellowed as I lunged forward, my fist connecting with his face and cutting off his words. He crumpled to the ground with blood gushing from his nose. I gripped his shirt, lifting him as I pummeled him with my other hand. The metallic tang of blood filled my nostrils as I unleashed a fury of punches upon him, the red haze of anger blinding me.

Killian Asher no longer existed; the savage figure Lucian had named 'Killer' had taken over. It was as if someone else had control of my body, and I sat watching Killer beat the life out of Paul. The cracking of bones, the sight of blood spilling, and the echo of his screams and grunts fueled the insatiable beast inside me.

"P-please... s-s-stop," Paul said weakly, blood spewing from his mouth.

If he thought he could win my sympathy by begging, he was sorely mistaken. His weak attempt to stop what was coming only made the monster inside me even angrier. His body was so limp, I let it fall to the floor. He was so far gone he didn't even try to protect himself when I started kicking him. I was so blinded by rage, when Lucian pulled me back, I turned on him with my fist raised.

"You don't want to do that," he said, waiting for me

to recognize him. "He's dead. It's over."

I looked back at the unrecognizable heap lying in a pool of crimson. His face was a mess of blood and gore. That same dark, sticky liquid covered my hands, face, and clothes in a gruesome reminder of what the darkness inside me was capable of.

Paul was gone. He'd never bother Skye again, and that made it worth it.

Lucian's dark eyes pierced through mine with a hint of concern etched on his face. "You calm enough to drive?" Lucian asked, snapping my attention back to him.

"Yeah."

"Take my car. Go see your girl. Leo will take me home after we take care of this," he said, tossing me his keys.

I caught them before heading to the bathroom to wash up as much as I could. I'd hate to get blood all over Lucian's souped-up Lotus. His cars and motorcycles were almost as important to him as his dick.

The adrenaline was still pumping through me as I pulled into the garage of my apartment building. Skye wasn't in the living area when I stepped off the elevator. I figured she was sleeping, but as I made my way to my bedroom, I caught a glimpse of light streaming from her art studio. Deciding to wash away the evidence of the night's events before going to her, I headed straight for the shower.

After scrubbing myself clean, I stood under the spray, bracing my hands on the wall in front of me as I leaned forward to savor the way the hot water cascaded over my back. A few moments later, I heard the bathroom door open, and Skye stepped into the shower with me. Her body was soft and warm as she pressed against me, and an electric charge buzzed through me.

She kissed the center of my back, and the feel of her lips and breasts pressed against me had my cock growing hard. As her hands roamed over my abdomen, I couldn't resist any longer, and I spun around to face her, gripping her tightly as I claimed her lips with mine.

The kiss was full of my remaining adrenaline— electric and possessive. She pressed her hot and hungry mouth to mine, and my cock throbbed with a desperate ache for release. Our tongues tangled in a carnal dance as our hands roamed each other's bodies.

A disappointed groan slipped from her when I broke our kiss. "We found Paul." I felt compelled to tell her before we went any further. With what I'd learned from that damned addendum still looming over me, I didn't want to add another secret to the list.

Her eyebrows shot up in surprise, and her lips still plump from our kiss, parted but no words came out.

"Is he...?" she whispered after a few moments.

"He'll never bother you or anyone else again," I replied, my words laced with a dark edge.

A slow grin spread across her face, and a mischievous glint flickered in her eyes. "Thank you," she said, her fingers tracing the contours of my jawline.

I couldn't stop myself from being entranced by her. I'd braced myself for a torrent of tears, or even for her to close herself off, instead she surprised me with her reaction: She was pleased. There was something undeniably sexy about her reaction, the way she seemed to embrace the news.

When she dropped to her knees and slid my cock between those plump, red lips, I was completely lost to her. She'd started out as my obsession, but she was quickly becoming my addiction. She was the one thing I couldn't deny myself, the one thing I craved every second of every day. The one thing I couldn't live without.

I wrapped her hair around my hand as she worked my cock with her tongue and lips, sucking and licking in a way that threatened to make my knees weak. The little whimpers and moans she made sent vibrations through my shaft, driving me crazy. I needed to be inside her, needed to sink myself into her warmth before I lost my mind. Using my hold on her hair, I pulled her head back until my cock slipped from her lips with a little *pop*.

"Stand up, bend over, put your hands on the bench, and spread your legs. As wide as they'll go." She did as I told her to without the slightest hesitation and the resulting view had me thanking a god I didn't believe in. "Fuck. That's it. You obey me so well, and you look so beautiful spread wide for me."

I gave her firm, round ass a slap before fisting my cock and gliding the crown through her wet folds. She moaned and arched her back, pushing herself into me even more. Unable to wait any longer, I drove into her until I was buried to the hilt inside her.

My hands grasped her hips, and my fingers dug into

her soft flesh as I pounded into her. Being inside her was pure bliss, like a salvation I didn't deserve but was selfish enough to take anyway. I fucked her so hard I thought she'd fall apart, but whenever I slowed down, she thrust her hips back, silently begging for more.

My sweet, little yoga instructor was a dirty, wanton slut, and she was all mine. *Mine,* I thought while reaching around to pinch her clit, pulling a raw, feral moan from her.

"Killian," she panted, "I need to see you."

Without a word I spun her around and lifted her until she wrapped her legs around me. Then I slammed her back into the wall and continued driving my cock into her, thrusting my hips in an unforgiving rhythm. Her passion-filled eyes locked on mine, and I watched in awe as the lids fluttered closed and her eyes rolled back as our climaxes ripped through us.

When my head dropped to her shoulder, she whispered my name, and I fell harder than I ever thought possible. I was in so deep there was no turning back. I was drowning in her scent, her taste, her touch, and I had no desire to resurface.

Addiction wasn't a strong enough word to describe the fierce need I had for her. Even *love* was a pitiful description for the powerful emotions that raged inside me.

What I felt for her was all-consuming, a fire that burned hotter and brighter with each passing day. She was my life's breath, the blood that flowed through my veins. Without her, I'd cease to exist.

She didn't fear the darkness inside me. Instead,

she accepted it, maybe even understood it. Love and affection were not my strong suits, but with her, *for* her, I would give them a shot. I'd never bowed to anyone in my life, but for her, I'd gladly drop to my knees. Because Skye Larsen deserved to be worshipped like the radiant fucking goddess she was.

With that thought fresh in my mind, I carried her out of the shower, and set her on her feet. When she moved to grab a towel, I snatched it up instead. "Come here and turn around," I said, the words coming out in a raspy whisper.

When she did as I told her, I dried her glistening body from head to toe before helping her into a robe. I couldn't take my eyes off her. She was radiant with her skin slightly pink from the warm water, her hair hanging in loose curls, and her lips still swollen from our kisses.

"Are you hungry?" I asked, knowing she probably forgot to eat.

"Starving," she said. "I lost track of time while painting the artwork for the hotel."

I wrapped a towel around my waist and pulled her into my arms. "What do you feel like? Anything you want."

A faint flush crept up her cheeks, and her eyes widened as she bit her lower lip. "I'd really love a cheeseburger and fries."

"Done," I said, running my thumb over her lips. A flash of desire hit me when her lips parted, and she sucked it into her mouth. "Go get dressed. I'll call in the order."

Later that night, after we ate, we sat on the balcony enjoying the clear night. There was something about the city after dark that I'd always found appealing. By day, it was a place of chaotic commotion. After the sun set, it transformed into a mysterious labyrinth, its secrets concealed within the shrouded shadows.

"How'd you do it?" Skye asked, breaking the silence.

I knew what she was asking without her having to elaborate. "I won't give you the details, but I'll answer anything else you want to know. Just be sure you really want to know before you ask."

"I want to know." She kept her eyes on her drink but glanced at me from the corner of her eye. "How'd you find him?"

"He made the mistake of calling out his location. When he mentioned the park while on the phone with you, it was clear he was in the area. It didn't take long to find him once we knew that."

She nodded slowly. "Where was he?"

Something in her tone told me she had a hunch. "Your studio."

She looked at me then. "Did you do it there?"

"No."

"Did he tell you why he used to hit me?"

I reached out to tuck her hair behind her ear. "No. There is never a good reason to do what he did to you. Some people are just vicious assholes," I said.

"Did he suffer?"

"Not for long," I said quickly because I knew no

matter how relieved she was that Paul was dead, she wouldn't have wanted him to suffer.

"How do you know you won't get caught?"

"I just know."

She pursed her lips. "Mm-hmm, sure. Have you killed before?"

My jaw clenched. "Why would you ask that?"

She rose from her seat to climb into my lap, wrapping her arms around my neck. "Because I want to know everything about you."

"Fine, but you don't need to know that."

"Hmm... I think you just answered me without answering me." She ran her fingers through my hair, and it felt so good, my eyes grew heavy. "Did you kill the man who assaulted Lucian's sister?"

"He's dead," I replied, not wanting to throw Lucian under the bus. I hadn't killed that scumbag; I'd just helped with the aftermath.

"Again, not an actual answer, but I think I understand what you're saying."

"My turn," I said. "How are you so calm about this?"

She shrugged. "You don't seem like the kind of man who would kill just to kill. There's a purpose behind everything you do. You wouldn't take things into your own hands unless it was necessary." She turned to stare out over the city. "No one knows better than me that our justice system doesn't always work. It failed me more than once. Because of that... I'm not as innocent as you think."

"You killed a child molester who was bound to wind up dead one way or another. That doesn't make you a bad person."

She averted her eyes. "I've done other things, less severe but still not right. I tried to kill Paul once..."

"He told me." I tightened my hold on her when she tried to move. "You were a homeless *child*, whatever you did wasn't your fault. Between that sick fuck from your past and then Paul, you had every right to do what you did. It was self-defense."

She gave me a somber nod, and I felt compelled to answer her earlier question. Maybe if she knew the answer, she wouldn't feel as bad about what she'd done. Still, I hesitated before continuing. "Other than my dad's enforcer and Paul, there were five others. They were corrupt men who had done terrible things."

She visibly relaxed, which was not the reaction you'd expect someone to have after you confessed to murder, but Skye was full of pleasant surprises.

"See. I knew you wouldn't just randomly kill people without a reason," she said with a smug grin.

I didn't want to burst her bubble by telling her there had been others, but I have people on my payroll who usually handle it, so I don't have to.

"Before you guys left, I heard Lucian call you Killer," she whispered. "What did he mean by that?"

I let out a heavy sigh. This was why I never wanted relationships. Telling someone my secrets, letting them see the vulnerable side of me was not something I ever wanted to do. It was different with Skye. Everything was different with her. "When I get angry, it's like I turn into another person. I see red and can't control myself." I felt her tense and slid my hand to the small of her back and began rubbing tiny, soothing circles. "It would never happen with you. That I can promise."

"How do you know that?" She looked out to the city again. "If we stay together, we're bound to have arguments. I'm going to piss you off at some point."

I cupped her face, turning her head to make her look at me again. "It's hard to explain, but I can assure you it won't happen with you. It's a different kind of anger, usually aimed at men who have done something they shouldn't have."

She studied me for a few moments before she nodded and smiled at me. "I believe you. Thank you for telling me all this."

"You're welcome. Now, I think it's time for a change of subject," I said, giving her ass a squeeze.

"I think I have a better idea." She brought her lips to my ear, tugging my hair to tilt my head. "Take me to bed, Stalker," she breathed before trailing her tongue around my ear.

My dick hardened so fast I thought it might punch right through my pants. "With pleasure," I growled, scooping her up and carrying her inside.

Chapter Nineteen

Skye

T he next few days felt surreal, like a dream. With Paul's shadow lifted from our lives, Killian seemed more at ease. We wandered through a bustling farmer's market, caught a movie under the stars in the park, and met up with Layla and Chelsea at the nightclub, X, for a wild night of dancing.

I'd swayed my hips to the music with my girls, while Killian leaned against the bar, brooding and watching me with those intense eyes of his. I didn't care if he was grumpy. We were doing *real* relationship things. Besides, I loved it when his dark eyes followed my every move.

They did so again while I got ready for the surprise date he had planned. His gaze was intense and piercing as he watched me move around the bathroom. He had given me no hints about what we were doing, except for telling me to dress up. I picked an oldie but goodie. A simple yet provocative black dress with a deep neckline that showed off my curves and a thigh-high slit that made me feel sexy and confident.

As I applied my makeup, I couldn't help but notice his eyes roaming over my body, smoldering with desire. I pinned my hair up in a loose bun, letting a few tendrils frame my face, and when his eyes lingered on my neck, shivers ran down my spine.

"You're distracting me," I said with a slow smile. "Per your instructions, we don't have time for distractions."

"Take off your underwear." The deep rumble of his voice moved over me like silk, igniting a fire within me.

If he didn't care about being late to wherever we were going, neither did I. I didn't ask why, I simply turned to face him and slowly pulled open the slit of my dress, revealing even more of my skin.

His eyes followed my every move, smoldering with raw desire. I spread the silky material wider and hooked my thumbs into the straps of my lace thong, slowly lowering the flimsy fabric down my legs until it dropped to my feet.

"I love how you submit to my demands without question," he growled.

"*Submit*, huh? Is that what I've been doing, submitting to you?" I shot him a smug grin as I leaned back against the counter and kicked the small strip of lace toward him. He caught it, inhaling my scent before slipping it into his pocket.

"Yes." He closed the distance between us, curling his fingers around my neck. "You do what I say when I tell you to like a good girl, and I fucking love it." His breath gliding over my skin combined with the words he was saying had a tendril of heat coiling in my core.

That tendril turned into an inferno when he slid his other hand into my dress to run his fingers along my slick folds. "Mmm. Your tight little pussy is already dripping for me." He hummed in approval as he circled my swollen clit with his thumb and my breath hitched at the jolt of pleasure.

My gasps turned to moans as the quivers of an orgasm started in my lower belly. He tightened his hold on my neck, slid two fingers inside me, and pressed his thumb against my clit.

"Now come for me," he whispered, low and husky.

There was no preparing for the tidal wave of pleasure that swept through my body, leaving me gasping and writhing in ecstasy. My moans and cries echoed through the room until his lips descended on mine in a savage, demanding kiss. I sucked in a breath when he withdrew his hand from between my legs, leaving me shaking with aftershocks.

He grinned down at me with a feral glint in his eyes. "See how well you obey me."

"If that's the reward, I'm yours to command anytime," I replied, turning to the mirror to check my makeup.

"You look beautiful, as always," he said, wrapping his arms around my waist and pressing a kiss to the back of my neck. "No one will be able to take their eyes off you, and I'll have to try not to kick their asses."

I leaned back into him, locking eyes with him in the mirror. "Or we can stay in, and I can return the favor."

"We have reservations," he replied, as he strode out of the room, taking my hand and pulling me along with him.

To my surprise he tapped a keycard on a small panel inside the elevator which took us one floor lower than the lobby. We stepped off the elevator into a parking garage I hadn't known existed. The sound of my heels echoed off the cold, concrete walls as Killian led me through the dimly lit space.

When we stopped beside a car unlike any I'd ever seen, my jaw dropped. It was low to the ground, and so sleek and curvy, it looked more like a work of art than a vehicle. The shiny black exterior seemed to glow in the dim light. I knew next to nothing about cars, but even I could tell that it was as rare and valuable as a flawless blue diamond.

Killian opened the passenger side door and gestured for me to get in, but I took a moment to admire the car's interior first. Buttery soft, luxurious black leather covered the seats, and the dashboard was a high-tech display of digital readouts and touchscreens. The car reminded me of Killian, an alluring and calculating predator lurking in the shadows.

As I settled into the passenger seat, I felt a rush of excitement. The car's powerful engine rumbled to life, sending vibrations through the seat, and filling the air with a deep, primal sound. I couldn't help but grin in anticipation, wondering where this incredible machine would take me.

"This... *car* seems too mild of a word... it's a masterpiece," I said, admiring how smoothly it glided over the road despite the immense power it clearly had under the hood. "It's amazing. I've never seen anything like it. What kind is it?"

"It's a custom Bugatti Chiron."

"Huh," I grunted. I'd never heard of a Bugatti, but I quickly fell in love with it. "Why don't you ever drive it?"

"It's not practical to drive around the city. I save it for special occasions," he said, giving the engine a gentle rev as we turned onto a quieter road.

"So this is a special occasion?" I wondered, knowing he wouldn't answer me if I asked where we were going. I'd asked him at least five times already.

"It is. You've been working hard, and you deserve a night out."

A smile formed on my lips when we pulled up to the valet at Chelsea's restaurant, Harvest & Hearth. Killian got out of the car and opened my door before the valet could. As I took his offered hand to help me out of the car, a ribbon of electricity coursed through me.

When we entered the restaurant, there was another surprise. As I looked around the dining area, I caught sight of Layla, Wes, and Lucian seated at a prominent table in the center of the room. The table was a rustic masterpiece, made of solid wood with cushioned benches set atop a raised platform.

The most interesting part of the scene was the way Wes and Layla sat, heads bent toward each other as they spoke in hushed murmurs. It was clear they were engrossed in their conversation, as if they were the only two people in the room. Lucian was looking at his phone but slipped it into his pocket when we approached.

"Hi," I said, cheerfully.

Layla's head snapped up as we entered the restaurant, a slight blush on her cheeks. "Skye!" she exclaimed, jumping up from her seat to wrap me in a tight embrace. "It feels like we never see each other anymore."

"I know," I replied, hugging her back before turning to greet my brother.

The permit to teach yoga in the park only allowed for a few hours a day, leaving Layla with little to do. She could teach a few classes, but it didn't make sense for her to make the trip to teach only three hours of yoga twice a week. Even though she didn't need the money, she'd taken a temporary job at an independent bookstore near her house so she wouldn't have to use her savings.

I'd tried to persuade her to become a co-owner even before the fire, but she had been hesitant. If she agreed, she would share in the profits and decision making. It wouldn't help us see each other more often during the renovations, but it would take our friendship to a whole new level. She helped with so much already, I figured we could make it official.

As I settled in my seat, I nudged Layla with my elbow. "You know what I want to say."

Her face flushed even more. "I know. I'm thinking about it."

"You are?" I asked excitedly, and a little too loudly.

"Oh my God! We can expand into the vacant shop next door, maybe make it a Pilates studio for you."

"Calm down. I haven't agreed to anything," she said, her eyes bright with a mix of excitement and apprehension. "It's a big decision. I think it could be amazing, and I really believe in what you're doing with the business. I just need more time to think about it."

Layla and I had been working together for a while, but the idea of being partners made it more exciting. She was a talented yoga instructor in her own right, with a loyal following of students.

"I think it could be amazing too," I said, reaching around to give her a half hug. "It's a big commitment, so take all the time you need."

We picked up our menus to see what changes Chelsea had made. Her claim to fame in the culinary world was her unique twist of adding bourbon to her recipes. It's not just any bourbon either, it's the most sought-after Copper Oakleaf Distillery bourbons. They were currently the hottest distillery in the Northeast.

As we all perused the menu, my gaze kept landing on Lucian. I knew he was friends with Killian, but I couldn't fathom why he was there. Chelsea clearly knew him too, and she had not been pleased by his presence at Killian's the other day.

"Lucian, have you ever eaten here?" I asked, trying to spark up a conversation.

Although his smile could melt the hearts of everyone around him, it didn't have the same effect on me. Then there was Killian. Without even touching me, a warmth curled low in my belly just because he was close to me.

"No, but I'm familiar with the chef," Lucian answered.

Layla and I exchanged a curious look. "Oh? How do you know Chelsea?" I asked.

Before Lucian could respond, Chelsea approached our table with her usual glowing smile. However, it quickly vanished at the sight of Lucian. Her light green eyes darkened to flaming emeralds, and her peaches and cream complexion flushed almost as red as her hair.

"Why are you here?" she growled.

"Hello to you too, sugar," Lucian replied, the smile never leaving his face.

Chelsea switched tactics and pretended he didn't exist. She greeted everyone else, took a seat next to Wes, and started chatting with the rest of the table as if nothing had happened.

"What would you all like to order?" she asked after a few minutes.

"Why don't you surprise us?" I volunteered for the table. "If that's okay with everyone else."

Everyone nodded, and Chelsea headed back to the kitchen, not sparing Lucian a second glance. I wondered if she would even serve him a dish.

"All right, dude," Layla, the queen of directness, said. "What's up with you and Chelsea?"

Lucian shifted his gaze to her. "We knew each other a long time ago."

His statement ended with a full stop, meaning 'we're

done talking about this,' but my Layla wasn't one to let things go.

"Why does Chelsea hate you? She doesn't hate anyone, so what'd you do to her?"

Killian cleared his throat, pulling my attention to him. He had the slightest of smirks playing on his lips as he looked at his friend. When he noticed me looking at him, he slid his hand to the back of my neck, pulling me in for a light kiss.

That simple touch of lips turned me into a needy mess, but I still wanted to hear where the conversation went. Why *did* Chelsea despise Lucian so much?

"You should ask your friend these questions," Lucian said with an undeniable finality this time.

"Skye, how's the park yoga going?" my brother asked me, breaking the tension by changing the subject.

"It's going well. I still can't thank you two enough for getting it done for me." Since I knew a little more about Lucian than Layla did, I knew changing the subject was a good idea.

I really knew nothing about him, except that Killian had been with him the night he came home covered in blood, *and* Lucian had been with Killian when he'd taken care of Paul. I couldn't shake the feeling that Lucian was not as cheerful as he appeared to be on the surface. Something dark lurked beneath his charming demeanor.

As we munched on rosemary focaccia straight out of the wood-fired oven, we fell into comfortable conversation. When the rest of the table ordered drinks,

Killian ordered me an old fashioned, the same drink he had made for me at his place.

As I excused myself to use the restroom, Layla followed me in, and while I washed my hands, a gorgeous woman entered the restroom, giving me a piercing look before sashaying through the room in my direction. She stood tall and slender, her copper-silk wrap dress clinging to her curves like a second skin.

She moved her long legs with a feline grace in towering stilettos, so thin and fragile, they seemed on the verge of shattering under her weight... what little of it there was. With a flick of her sleek black hair, she stopped only inches from me, her golden-brown eyes smoldering with hate.

She stood in front of me, hip cocked and one eyebrow lifted. "So, you're the one who has him under her spell?" she said, her words laced with venom.

"Excuse me? Do I know you?" I asked. She looked vaguely familiar, but I couldn't place her.

"I'm Claudia Lobos." She said it as though I *should* know who she was. When she didn't see any sign that I recognized her, her perfect heart-shaped lips curled into a sneer. "I should have known you wouldn't know anything about the fashion world." Her gaze raked over me as if I were nothing more than discarded waste, unworthy of being in the same bathroom as her.

I didn't give a damn if she was the queen of England, her lame insults were getting on my nerves. "Do you have something you want to say to me? If not, I'm going to get back to my dinner date."

"Who's this?" Layla asked as she approached the

sink.

"She says her name is Claudia Lobos," I muttered.

Layla squealed in delight, seizing the woman's hand tightly. The bitter part of me enjoyed the fact that Layla hadn't washed her hands yet. "Oh my God, it is! You're Claudia Lobos."

"Seems like your friends have better taste than you," she sneered as she withdrew her hand from Layla's grasp. "I don't know what he sees in you."

I furrowed my brows in confusion. "Who are we talking about?"

Claudia let out a deep, exasperated sigh. She seemed annoyed by me, yet she was the one who approached me. "Killian Asher. You, a yoga instructor," she spat, her tone oozed privilege and disdain. "You're wearing a dress that looks like you plucked it from a bargain bin at Walmart. Your hair is a mess, and your makeup is a disaster. Yet you've somehow managed to snag the most eligible billionaire on the east coast."

Her rudeness completely shocked me. "Wow," I breathed, my eyes wide with disbelief. "Listen, Claire, was it?" I smiled, enjoying the way she bristled at my obvious mistake. "I don't know who the hell you think you are, but you need to back the fuck up."

Layla gasped then chuckled, surprised by my sudden and rare surge of bravado. I'd had enough of Claudia's snobbery and the overpowering scent of her expensive perfume. It probably cost more than the rent for my studio, but it made my head throb.

With an arrogant lift of her chin, Claudia peered

down at me. "It won't be long before he grows tired of you and comes crawling back to me. He always comes back to me," she sneered. "You're not even close to being in his league. There is no way you can satisfy him the way I can."

I plastered my most charming smile on my face and leaned in toward her. "Honey, you said it yourself," I purred. "I'm a *yoga* instructor. Believe me when I tell you, he's more than satisfied." Her flawless features twisted into an ugly scowl, and I reveled in the fact that I'd gotten to her.

I let my features harden and my tone turn to honey and ice. "Now, if you'll excuse me, I'm going to go back to my table."

My cheeks burned, a telltale sign of my rage, but it also revealed how vulnerable I felt standing up to her. Letting my emotions run free was exhilarating, but confronting someone like that was terrifying.

Layla hooked her arm through mine as we walked out of the bathroom. Once we were in the hallway, she pulled me to the side.

"What the hell was that?" she whispered, brushing a lock of hair from my face.

I was starting to shake as the adrenaline wore off. "Killian's ex, I guess."

"He dated Claudia fucking Lobos? She's the top model in the world." She curled her lips around her teeth as she debated saying something else. "She's also known to be quite experimental in the bedroom."

"How the hell do you even know that?"

"It's all over the tabloids," Layla said, a wry chuckle escaping her lips.

As I thought about what Claudia had said, a wave of anxiety washed over me. What if she was right, and Killian grew tired of me?

"So, what kinds of things is she rum—"

"Skye, are you okay?" Killian appeared behind me, his deep voice startling me back to reality.

My eyes widened, and I felt my face flush as I turned to face him. I was still reeling from my encounter with Claudia and embarrassed by my conversation with Layla. I had been about to ask her what kinds of things the model supposedly did in bed, hoping to keep Killian satisfied and prevent him from growing bored with me.

His powerful hands wrapped around my upper arms as he studied me. "What's wrong?" he asked, his voice filled with concern.

Layla playfully smacked Killian's arm. "You never mentioned you dated Claudia Lobos!"

Ignoring her, he cradled my face in his hands, his touch soothing my nerves and sending a current of heat over my body. "Tell me what happened, Skye."

As our eyes met, the restaurant faded away, leaving only the two of us. "Claudia's just upset that you're with me instead of her," I murmured.

His jaw tightened with anger. "What did she say to you? Did she threaten you?"

"No, nothing like that. She's just jealous."

Layla snorted. "Jealous doesn't begin to describe it.

She's pissed that you chose a lowly yoga instructor over her Grade-A ass."

As Killian's eyes lit up with a fierce intensity, the bathroom door swung open, revealing Claudia herself.

"Go back to the table," he whispered to me before touching his lips to mine. "I'll be there soon."

While Killian stayed behind to face Claudia, I grabbed Layla's hand and pulled her along, hurrying back to our table. I looked over my shoulder to see her aim a predatory smile at him, her every move a calculated display of seduction, and my stomach churned with worry.

Chapter Twenty

Skye

"Why didn't we stay? I want to hear what he says to her," Layla whined as we took our seats.

"Who are you talking about? Wes asked, glancing between Layla and me.

"Claudia Lobos," Layla said, smiling from ear to ear. "She used to date Killian, and she confronted Skye in the bathroom."

Lucian, who had appeared disinterested until then, suddenly turned his attention to me. "Killian is with her now?" I nodded, and his jaw tightened. "Excuse me," he said before standing and walking toward the bathroom.

Wes shifted on the bench to look at me. "Are you okay?"

"Yes. I'm fine."

Layla let out a little laugh. "She's more than fine. You should have seen your sister handle that bitch. She was a total badass. I've never seen her like that."

"Lay, you're enjoying this way too much," I said,

picking up my drink and taking a huge gulp, trying to calm my nerves.

Even after emptying my glass, my hands were still shaking when Lucian returned to the table. I turned my head in time to see Claudia step out of the hallway. Her face was red, and her eyes were bright with tears as she strode through the restaurant toward the exit.

"Where's Killian?" I asked Lucian as he sat.

"He'll be back."

Feeling a sudden sense of unease, I stood up and made my way back toward the hallway. I found him pacing in the shadows, his fists clenched tightly at his sides.

"Killian," I whispered.

He spun around, his gaze locked on me but there was something different, something feral about it. As he stalked toward me, his long strides devouring up the space between us, I had a feeling I was dealing with 'Killer' not Killian, and a rush of excitement pulsed through me.

Without a word, he crushed his lips to mine, his hands fisting in my hair as I stumbled backward from the force of his embrace. I wrapped my arms around him, eagerly returning his kiss. When his lips tailed down my neck, I tilted my head to the side to give him better access. His teeth sank into the tender flesh of my neck, eliciting a deep moan from me.

A primal growl rumbled from his chest as he slid his hands under my ass, lifting me up effortlessly. My legs instinctively wrapped around his waist, and I let out a small cry of surprise when my back hit the wall. His hand lowered between us, and I heard his zipper lowering.

"Look down," he growled. A moan slipped from my lips when I saw the head of his cock positioned at my opening.

I watched, mesmerized, as he pressed his hips forward, slowly burying himself deep inside me. There was a tiny voice somewhere in my mind that tried to remind me we were in a public place.

I didn't care. Not when he looked at me, touched me the way he did. We could be in the middle of Times Square, and it wouldn't matter. All I ever wanted, all that ever mattered was him.

He teased us both with slow, shallow thrusts until I was panting and clawing at his shoulders. "Killian, faster. Please," I breathed, begging for the release I so desperately needed.

"Anything you want, Sunshine," he growled.

He moved with long, smooth thrusts, faster and faster until the flutters of an orgasm started and my walls clamped down on his shaft. When my climax slammed into me, I bit down on his shoulder so I wouldn't scream as we came together.

As the waves of pleasure subsided, his body remained pressed against mine, pinning me to the spot as his hand reached up to grasp my jaw.

"She told me what she said to you." The low, raspy timbre of his voice caressed my skin like silk. His fingers dug into my cheeks as he held my face in line with his.

"I'll never get bored with you, Skye."

He pushed himself deep inside me again and my eyelids fluttered when the tip hit that sensitive spot. "I could never tire of the way you respond to my touch, the way you feel clamped around my cock, the way you look when I'm fucking you, or the way you sound when I make you come. Do you hear me?"

"Yes. Yes, I hear you," I said as aftershocks fluttered through me, leaving me breathing in shallow pants. Everything he'd said and did to me made me feel beautiful, sexy, and powerful.

"Good." He stepped back, allowing me to lower my feet to the floor. After we straightened our clothes, he took my hand and led me back to the table.

There was something incredibly erotic about what we'd just done only moments before, only ten feet away from our friends. As we sat sipping our drinks and savoring every bite of Chelsea's delectable creations, I felt delightfully dirty and perfectly sinful.

THAT NIGHT, KILLIAN'S restless movements jolted me awake. He was thrashing about violently in his sleep, tormented by a horror that only he could see. He'd thrown the covers off him, and I could see sweat covering his bronzed skin. His toned, muscular body was rigid, his fists were clenched so tightly that his knuckles turned white, and his jaw was locked in a fierce, unyielding grip.

I pushed myself up and sat with my back against the headboard, peering down at him as he fought an invisible enemy. Even though it was only a nightmare,

I couldn't bear to see him suffer. I slid back under the covers and ran my fingers through his thick, tousled hair while leaning in to whisper soothingly in his ear. He was too lost in this torment for me to break through.

Determined to help him, I brushed my lips over his, kissing him lightly until his movements began to slow and his breathing became even and calm. When he started kissing me back, I knew he was back in the real world with me.

"You were having a nightmare," I whispered against his lips.

"They happen."

"I know." I was far too familiar with the demons that visit in the dead of night, the past traumas that refuse to let us rest. My own nightmares had caused me to lose sleep more times than I could count.

He slid his arm around me, drawing me in close and pressing a kiss to the top of my head. I nestled into him, resting my head on his chest, and lightly trailing my fingers over his abdomen. The rhythm of his heartbeat soon lulled me back to sleep.

When I woke up again, he still had his arms wrapped around me. The sun shimmered through the windows, casting a warm golden glow on his tanned face as he slept. Thick lashes and brows framed his eyes. There was a slight bump on his nose, which hinted at a past injury and only added to his rugged charm.

His well-groomed beard accentuated his strong jawline, adding a touch of wildness to his otherwise refined features. The way it framed his full, inviting lips made them even more enticing.

Unable to stop myself, I kissed him, savoring the taste of him as I nibbled on his bottom lip. As he woke up, I slipped under the sheets and continued to explore his body. I pressed my lips to his chest, and let my tongue trace a path over his muscles. His skin tasted like salt and sin, a decadent treat just for me. I moved lower, trailing open-mouthed kisses down his abdomen until I was nestled between his legs.

The power of being the one in control was intoxicating, and the awareness of having him at my mercy made my pulse race. He tossed the covers off us and looked down at me with sleepy eyes darkened with passion. With a wicked grin, I wrapped my hand around the base of his cock, before sliding my lips around the tip and slowly taking him in until my eyes watered.

A sense of satisfaction blossomed in my chest as his body responded to the way I worked him with my hand and mouth. He fisted his hands in my hair, moving me at the pace he wanted. I moved faster while sucking harder and just when I felt he was about to come, he pulled my hair until his cock slipped from my mouth.

I tried to protest, but he grabbed my arms and flipped us over. His hard, muscular body pressed mine into the mattress, and a cry ripped from my throat when he slammed into me. He didn't wait for me to get used to his length and girth before pumping his hips in an unrelenting rhythm.

He watched me as he fucked me. His eyes were hooded and his lips slightly parted, and the intensity in his gaze made everything feel more electric, more sensual. The pressure built inside me, making my toes curl and my inner walls to flutter around him.

When the orgasm hit me, it was so overwhelming I lost the ability to think or breathe. My back bowed from the force of the pleasure, and I cried out his name while the waves of it continued to wash over me. I was so lost in the hazy aftershocks of my climax that I barely registered his groan and the jerky movements of his hips as he came.

"Fuck, Skye, you're going to be the death of me," he whispered, pressing his lips against mine in a kiss so tender it was a striking contrast to the animalistic way he'd just fucked me.

As he deepened the kiss, a shiver ran down my spine, and I savored the taste of him. His hand on my cheek was warm and gentle, there was a softness to his touch that hadn't been there before.

Until that moment, our relationship had been full of a raw, primal need for each other, a hunger that brought us together. As his lips moved slowly against mine, it felt like there was something more there. Something that went beyond physical desire.

When he broke the kiss, I looked up at him. There was a softness in his gaze that I hadn't seen before, sending a thrill of hope through me. Killian Asher, the man who even the internet knew little about, was showing me a side of him I never dreamed I'd see.

"Good morning," I said with a smile.

He dropped a quick kiss to the tip of my nose before rolling off me. "It has been so far."

"About last night..." I began, hesitantly. "I have a couple of questions."

He shifted to his side, resting his head on his hand as he gazed down at me. His other hand wrapped around my waist to pull me closer to him. "Okay."

"If you dated someone as famous as Claudia, how have I never heard of you? How has Google never heard of you?"

He lifted an eyebrow. "Have you been cyber-stalking me?"

"Maybe. It's only fair since you real-life stalked me."

The faintest of smiles pulled at his lips for a moment. "I have contacts in all the major media outlets. If there's something I don't want published or talked about, it gets buried. In my business, it's best to stay under the radar, but people like Claudia enjoy creating a buzz, and the appearance of dating me does that. I control what the articles say, and I make sure they talk mainly about her."

"So you dated her?"

"Are you jealous, hmm?" He ran a finger around my bellybutton as he spoke.

"No," I lied.

"You have nothing to worry about." His hand slid between my legs, cupping me while gliding his middle finger along my folds. "This is the only pussy I want, the only one I crave. You're mine and I'm yours. End of story."

A deep sigh slipped from my lips when he kept moving his finger back and forth. "Layla said she read something about Claudia being 'experimental' in bed." His finger circled my clit, and I moaned, opening my legs wider. "If there's something more you want… If I'm not—"

He pulled his hand away and slipped his finger between my lips. "Do you taste that?" I nodded, swirling my tongue around and tasting my arousal. "Why the fuck would I want anyone else when I can have this every day?" He slid his finger from my mouth and curled his hand around my neck.

It always surprised me how much I loved the way his hand felt on my throat. Never in my life did I think I'd ever want to be that vulnerable again, but with him, I *wanted* to feel his control over me, to feel his dominance.

His lips grazed my ear, setting my body on fire. "You are more than she could ever be," he whispered.

"I don't want to lose you," I replied so softly I wasn't sure he heard me.

His hand tightened on my throat and his tongue traced the shell of my ear. "You'll never lose me because I'll never let you go. Not even if you want me to." He brought his lips to mine, kissing me, long and deep. "And, Sunshine, when I want to *experiment* with you, I'll tell you… and you'll obey, won't you?"

A rush of desire flooded my veins, imagining what he could do to me, what he could make *me* do. "Y-yes. I will."

"Good girl," he praised, releasing his hold on me and slipping out of bed. "Now, let's get breakfast."

In that moment, I knew I would do anything for Killian… I would surrender myself to him. He made me ache for him with just his words. He made me feel things I'd never felt before, things I didn't even know were possible. There was no one else for me, I was completely and utterly his.

Chapter Twenty-One

Skye/Killian

Skye

"I gotta know, how's the sex?" Layla asked, wiggling her eyebrows suggestively and earning a sharp look from me. "What? He's so dark and brooding, but he's also really fucking hot. I have a feeling he's an animal in bed."

After breakfast, Killian received a call from Amelia and had to go to the office. Since Chelsea had a rare day off, the three of us girls met for lunch to catch up on our lives. I had not planned on having a conversation about my sex life, though, I guess I should have expected it from Layla.

"Lay, that's highly inappropriate," Chelsea scolded before turning to me with one eyebrow lifted. "How *is* the sex?"

I shifted my scowl to her. "Traitor."

Layla laughed and reached across the table to take

my hand. "C'mon Skye, spill it. You moved in with the guy even though he was your stalker."

I glanced down at my plate, feeling a knot form in my stomach. The three of us had always shared *almost* every detail of our lives, but there was something different about talking to them about Killian. It felt like revealing a dark secret, something that belonged only to us.

It wasn't a secret that made me feel guilty or bad. It was just... how could I possibly explain the intensity of our passion, or the way every touch and every kiss sent me reeling into a whirlpool of sensation? Even if I could put it into words, Killian was mine, and I wanted to keep every part of him to myself.

As I looked back at my two best friends, I didn't know if they would understand the way everything about him consumed me. At the same time, I couldn't keep it bottled up any longer. I had to share the truth about the man who had brought me back to life.

"Fine," I began, a chuckle escaping me as Layla danced in her seat. "He's... we're... there just aren't any words to describe it. Killian is everything I never knew I wanted and more. No other man has ever made me feel the way he does. There's no way anyone else ever could come close. He's ruined me for anyone else."

Layla fanned herself dramatically, her eyes wide with excitement. "Oh my, Skye. He sounds amazing."

A flush crept up my neck as I remembered his words from that morning. "Amazing doesn't even come close to describing how he makes me feel."

"Damn," Chelsea said, her voice soft and wistful.

"He's a rare find. Hold on to him tightly."

Her words struck a chord with me, and I couldn't help but wonder what lay behind them. "On that note, Chels," I said. "Who's Lucian?"

Killian's mysterious friend intrigued me, and I couldn't help but notice how he seemed to fluster Chelsea, who was usually unflappable. More than once, I had seen the normally confident woman become unsettled in Lucian's presence. I had to know more.

"He's just someone I used to know."

Layla and I shared a look. "Know as in dated?" Layla asked.

She flung her hands up in the air. "Yes. Okay, yes. I dated him. He was my Killian. He made me feel special and did things to my body..."

She shook her head as if trying to dispel the memories. "We had an intense, amazing three months. He made me feel like I was the only woman in the world, like nothing else mattered. Then, one day, he just... disappeared. No explanation, no goodbye. It was like he had never existed. For weeks, I waited for a text, a call, anything. Nothing ever came. Radio silence."

"Then he showed up out of nowhere and threw you for a loop," I said sympathetically.

"Yeah," Chelsea sighed, pulling out her phone and setting it down on the table. "He's been texting me." Layla and I leaned in, curious, as Chelsea pulled up a thread of messages. They ranged from innocent-sounding 'good morning' texts to more insistent ones like 'stop ignoring me, sugar.'

I could feel the tension in the air, the weight of her unspoken fears and desires. It was clear that Chelsea was conflicted about how to handle the situation.

"You want to talk to him," I said, knowing I was right without her having to tell me.

"I do. I really do, but he broke my heart into a million pieces. It's still shattered. How can I just forget that?"

Layla and I scooted closer to her, wrapping our arms around her and resting our heads on her shoulders.

"You don't have to forget it," I said. "Maybe you'd feel better to tell him how you feel. Tell him what an ass he is."

She gave a weak laugh. "I'd love to, but every time I see him I turn into a blathering moron."

"We know," Layla said with a laugh of her own. "We've witnessed it. Oh! I have an idea. He's friends with Killian, maybe the four of you could have dinner. You'd have Skye there for support and you could tell him off right in the restaurant."

"Or we could have dinner at Killian's place," I offered, knowing Chelsea wouldn't want to make a scene in a public place.

Chelsea was quiet for a long while before she took a deep breath and said, "I'll think about it. Thanks, guys. It feels better to have gotten it out. I love you."

"We love you," I said, giving her a squeeze.

As we settled back into our seats, our conversation turned to the latest rumors about Chelsea's restaurant. There was talk that it was being considered for a coveted Michelin star, and we listened intently as

Chelsea shared her excitement and anxiety about the prospect of being evaluated by the prestigious Michelin Guide.

On my walk back to Killian's apartment, I felt lighter than I had in years. It had been a long time since I had felt truly happy and content with my life, and the realization brought a smile to my face.

I couldn't help but think of my wonderful friends and the new and exciting relationship I had with Killian. It felt like everything was falling into place, and for the first time in a while, I felt truly hopeful about the future.

Then as usual, my thoughts turned to my mother, and a pang of guilt tugged at my heart. I had tried so many times to help her get clean, and each time she had pushed me away. There was nothing for me to feel guilty about, I'd done my best for her, but she hadn't wanted it. I would always love her but it was time to move on.

When I was only a few feet away from Killian's building, something hard pressed against my back. Before I could react, a strong hand wrapped around my arm, holding me firmly in place. Panic shot down my spine, and I instinctively tried to break free.

They evaded my attempts to fight back, and leaned in close, their lips brushing against my ear as they spoke in a low, menacing voice.

"Try that again, and I'll pull the trigger," he warned in a low voice. "Now, we are going to walk into the building, and you're going to act like we're old friends. Got it?"

I swallowed hard, my heart racing in my chest. I couldn't see his face, so I didn't know who he was or what he wanted, but with a gun to my back, I had no choice but to comply. Slowly, I nodded my head, and he led me toward the building.

As we got closer to the entry, my captor pocketed his gun and relaxed his grip on my arm. I thought about signaling Michael, the doorman, that something was wrong, but I was too scared to do anything other than greet him as I normally would. The security guard, Brian, nodded at us, and my stomach clenched with dread. I'd done too good a job of playing it cool, and now I was on my own with a crazy man and his gun until Killian returned.

Inside the elevator, I finally got a good look at him. It was Chad, the man from Killian's office. I was close enough to see that his face still bore the faint bruising and a small scar above his left eye from Killian's fists. I flinched when he leaned in close to me, his hot breath making me gag.

"We're going to wait for your boyfriend to get home, and then you're going to make him give me what I want," he said.

As he spoke, I couldn't help but notice the crazed look in his eyes. It was the same look my mother and Paul used to get when they were high. My stomach lurched as I realized Chad was an addict with nothing to lose.

I knew the best way to deal with him was to remain calm. If I freaked out, it would just rile him up and make him do something stupid... like shoot me. Taking a deep breath, I forced myself to keep my composure.

On the outside, I plastered on my usual mask of happiness. On the inside, my lunch was threatening to make a reappearance.

"Why are you doing this?" I asked. "You know Killian will be back soon."

"Good," Chad replied, his smile taking on a frighteningly maniacal edge. "That's what I'm counting on."

Killian

I'D BEEN IN A MEETING WITH LUCIAN, Leo, and Amelia, discussing Chad Walsh. We were trying to figure out where he'd disappeared to when I got the call from Brian that Skye had returned to my apartment with an unknown man. With Paul dead, I had a sinking feeling I knew where Chad was. Skye was in trouble and I needed to get home as quickly as possible.

"He's at my place," I said, my voice thick with malice. "Luce, let's go."

Neil was a great driver, but Lucian had his Lotus parked just outside. It could get me back to my apartment much faster, and I could count on Lucian to help me take care of Chad Walsh for good.

The thought of that scumbag touching Skye made my blood run cold and brought that red haze back to my vision. Before leaving my office I stopped at my safe and pulled out a gun.

When we pulled up to my building, Michael took the

car to the garage so we could head straight upstairs. My eyes scanned the room for Skye the second we stepped into my apartment. She was sitting on the sofa, staring at Chad standing in front of her. My anger spiked and fear coursed through me when I saw him carelessly brandishing a gun.

Despite the danger, Skye didn't make a move or give away our arrival. Her ability to remain calm allowed Lucian to sneak up behind Chad silently and press his gun to his head. I positioned myself in front of Skye, ready to protect her at any cost.

Chad froze, his hand holding the gun hanging limply at his side. "Make one fucking move, and you'll die right here, right now," I growled.

Killer had taken over and there was no way Chad would leave alive, but I needed to get Skye out of harm's way before I did what needed to be done.

Lucian disarmed Chad with ease as I crouched in front of Skye waiting for her to meet my gaze.

"Did he touch you?" I asked, pointing to Chad. She nodded and my vision went completely red. "Where?"

"My arm," she answered, rubbing her right upper arm.

I pulled her sleeve up to see his finger marks on her skin. She'd have bruises. The anger inside me reached a boiling point, and I nearly shot him right then, but I didn't want her to see that.

"Listen to me," I whispered. "Go to my closet, move aside the suit jackets, and you'll see a panel. Enter the code 545537 followed by the pound symbol. A hidden door will open. Go inside and press the red button to seal yourself in. I'll come for you when this is over."

Skye shook her head defiantly. "No, I want to stay with you."

I loved her bravery and her concern for me, but I needed her safe. I seized her by the jaw and kissed her roughly, my lips hard and demanding. When I pushed her back, I spoke firmly. "Be a good girl and do as I say. Get your ass in that room and don't leave until I come for you."

"He's high, unpredictable."

"I know, baby, but it'll be okay. He no longer has a gun, see?" I gestured to the man cowering in front of an amused Lucian. "You need to go. Now."

She leaned in and kissed me again. "Okay. I'll go," she said, her eyes shifting to Lucian. "If he gets hurt, you'll have to deal with me."

"Understood," Lucian replied with a bow of his head. Even he couldn't resist the allure of a feisty and strong woman, and Skye was all that and more.

I'd lucked out with her. She was tougher than I ever imagined and more passionate than I could have ever hoped for. As she made her way to my bedroom, I couldn't help but appreciate how, even in the face of danger, she carried herself with confidence. My eyes moved lower to admire the soft sway of her hips and the curve of her ass as she walked away.

"Do you want to take care of this piece of shit, or continue to eyefuck your girlfriend?" Lucian said, his tone dripping with humor.

As I straightened to my full height, my phone buzzed. I slid it out of my pocket to read the notification saying my secure chamber had been activated, proving Skye had done as I told her. With her safe, I could focus on the task at hand. Returning the phone to my pocket, I turned to face Chad.

I stood face to face with him, the cold steel of my gun tracing a path from his chin to his forehead. Watching him tremble with fear only added to the dark pleasure inside me. "You made a fatal mistake by touching her," I spoke with a quiet intensity. "No one touches what belongs to me and walks away unscathed."

"I-I didn't t-touch her," he sputtered.

I scoffed, a dangerous glint in my eyes. "On top of everything, you fucking lie to me?"

A fresh wave of fury surged through me, and I seized the front of his shirt, dragging him to the kitchen island. Skye had mentioned he grabbed her right arm, which meant he must have used his left hand. Right or left it didn't matter. Either way, he was going to find out what happens when you fuck with what belongs to me.

"Put your left hand on the counter," I commanded.

When he hesitated, I yanked his arm and slammed his hand onto the cold marble. Knowing my intentions from our years of working together, Lucian handed me a metal meat mallet before moving to stand behind the whimpering moron.

"Not only did you touch her, but you left *marks* on her," I growled, my voice cold and merciless. I couldn't help but relish the terror that flickered in his eyes as I raised the mallet high.

"N-no! No, please," he begged. "I'll disappear. I'll never bother you ag—" His words died on a blood-curdling scream when I slammed the mallet down onto his hand, crushing the bones and leaving it a bloodied mess.

"You're right about one thing, you will disappear," I said, pressing the gun to his forehead. "Get on your knees."

When he didn't do it, Lucian shoved him to the floor. Placing the gun on the kitchen island, I pulled a thin cord from one of the drawers. As I wound the ends around my hands I stalked around him to wrap the cord around his neck, pulling it tightly. He struggled at first, his uninjured hand clawing at his neck, trying to pull the cord away, and I tightened it even more.

His struggles soon stopped, and it wasn't long before his entire body went limp. I released my hold, and as he fell to the floor, I heard a gasp from behind me. Jaw set, I turned to see Skye peering around the corner. Her big, blue eyes were wide, and she held her hand to her mouth.

"Fuck," I growled. "Luce, take care of this for me."

"Sure thing," he said as I strode over to Skye.

"I specifically told you to stay in that room," I snarled, gripping her arm and dragging her towards my bedroom. Slamming the door shut behind us, I pushed her onto the bed before moving to my closet safe to put the gun away.

I returned to find her where I left her, staring straight ahead. "What the hell were you thinking, coming out there?"

She just sat there, those mesmerizing eyes of hers fixed on me. A sickening feeling churned in my gut when she didn't respond. "Say something, Skye," I demanded, lowering to a crouch and bringing me eye-level with her.

Finally, she blinked, licking her lips as she focused on me. "You killed him," she said. Before I could reply, she pressed her fingers to my lips. "You broke his hand for touching me, and then you killed him."

"He hurt you," I said, my voice strained with the anticipation of her response. Skye knew I had killed Paul, but she hadn't seen it happen. This time she'd seen too much of my dark side, and I braced myself for her rejection, for her to say she never wanted to see me again.

"Kiss me," she whispered, her fingers tangling in my hair as she drew me toward her.

Fuck. She had no idea of the power she held over me, the things she did to me. When our lips met, the entire world vanished, and for all I cared, it could burn to ashes as long as I had her by my side. Since that first night in the club, nothing else had mattered but her. My heart beat for her and only her.

"Killian," she breathed against my lips.

"Hmm?"

"I love you."

I love you. Three words I never expected to hear from anyone. Three words I'd been avoiding my entire adult life. Three words that made my heart clench when they passed through her lips. My darkness didn't frighten or disgust her. She didn't want to leave me. *She fucking loved me.*

I kissed her again, fiercely, madly. The words wouldn't come, so I kissed her with every ounce of feeling I had for her. I couldn't tell her I loved her because what I felt for her was so much more than that. She was a part of me, a part of my tainted soul.

We were a perfect match made in hell.

Chapter Twenty-Two

Skye

"Hey, Kill," Lucian called from the hallway.

Killian's kiss had me so worked up, so distracted, I'd completely forgotten about the dead man in his kitchen.

"Stay here," he said as he moved toward the door. "I mean it this time, do not leave this room until I come for you."

He waited for me to slide further onto the bed before wrenching open the door to reveal Lucian leaning against the wall. "What do you want?" he asked him when he just stood there smiling at me over Killian's shoulder.

"The team's on their way. Maybe you want to take your girl out for a drink?" he suggested casually.

Getting out of the house while their 'team' did their thing seemed like a good idea to me. Watching Killian kill someone hadn't affected me the way I would have thought. Hearing about it was one thing, but actually witnessing it should have shaken me, even a little. Instead, a thread of excitement worked its way into my core.

Still, as unaffected as I was, I still didn't like the idea of being there when they disposed of the body.

Killian grunted in response, shutting the door in Lucian's face and turning back to me.

"Should I change?" I asked, gesturing to the yoga pants and sweatshirt I was wearing.

"No, we'll go to the bar around the corner." He held his hand out to me and led me to the elevator.

Lucian had covered Chad's body, so I didn't have to see it, but I still stared at the sheet as we walked by.

"I'll text when it's done," Lucian said, waving at us with a stupid grin on his face.

The guy seemed like a loyal friend to Killian, yet I wondered about his sanity. He seemed to enjoy his work way too much, delighting in the violence and bloodshed more than he probably should. As hypocritical as it sounded, I was rethinking the whole Lucian and Chelsea thing.

Killian and I walked hand-in-hand to an Irish pub close to the apartment where we opted for a small, intimate table outside. The waitress didn't keep us waiting long before taking our order. Moments later, she returned with our drinks: an old fashioned for me and a Jameson 18 for Killian.

"Killian," I said, tentatively.

"Yes."

"You don't have to say you love me too," I rushed out, my words tumbling over each other. "I just wanted to say it, to tell you. What you've done for me, *all* of it, proves to me how you feel."

He kept his gaze lowered as he swirled his drink around the glass. "I'm not good with emotions," he admitted.

"It's okay," I assured him. "I only said it because when you... after... back in your apartment, I was so overwhelmed with gratitude." My brow furrowed at what I'd just said. "What a weird, morbid reason to feel grateful, but it is what it is."

"It's just since I was twelve, I've been dreaming of this." A watery smile played on my lips. "Of finding someone who cared enough about me to keep the bogeyman away. When my mom lost herself to drugs and alcohol, I lost my protector, my sense of security, my idol. I was alone in the dark, with no one to keep me safe. Since you entered my life, I've felt cared for. I've felt like someone finally sees me, like someone finally cares about what happens to me."

He reached across the table to take my hand in his. "You are all that matters to me. I'd give up everything I have if it means keeping you safe. No matter what it takes."

Tears blurred my vision, and I leaned back in my chair, utterly moved by his words. "Wow. That was a million times better than telling me you love me."

His lips pulled into a wry half-smile. "How would you feel about taking a trip with me?"

"I'd love that," I said, excitement bubbling inside me.

"Where should we go? A cabin upstate?"

"I have someplace much better in mind."

"Where?" I asked, my curiosity piqued.

"It's a surprise."

I lifted an eyebrow. "So, you've planned this already?"

"No. When Lucian's team is done and I can safely bring you back to the apartment, I'll have to go into the office to make some calls and rearrange my schedule. We'll leave after that."

Just him thinking of a trip was a wonderful surprise, but I wanted to know where he was taking me. I wasn't giving up that easily. "How will I know what to pack if I don't know where we're going?"

He let out a small chuckle. "Nice try, but I'm not telling you. Just pack a few bikinis, that's all you'll need."

"Ooh! We're going somewhere beachy," I said, wiggling in my seat.

Killian got a text from Lucian then, letting him know the team was done and it was safe to return to the apartment. I'd insisted I could walk myself back to his place, but he made it clear he wasn't leaving my side until I was behind a locked door with the security system armed.

"Killian," I said, tugging my arm against his hold on it when we stepped into the elevator. "I need to go shopping for the trip. You can't lock me up for the rest of my life."

He shot me a wicked, lust-filled gaze and backed me

into the corner, pinning his big, muscular frame against me. "Wanna bet?" he taunted, slapping his hand against the wall beside my head and making me flinch. His other hand slipped under my sweatshirt, his fingertips teasing my stomach with a seductive touch. "I could strip you naked, tie you to my bed, and do things to you that would make you beg to stay."

"Erg…" As that vision passed through my mind, I forgot how to talk, how to think, how to fucking breathe.

He slid his hand inside the front of my leggings and before I even registered what he was doing, he pushed two fingers inside me. "Fuck," he said, his voice low and strained. "I love how you're always wet for me. So fucking wet…"

When the elevator doors opened, he flung me over his shoulder and carried me to his room. He tossed me onto the bed, tore off my shoes and lowered himself on top of me faster than I would have thought possible.

His hands roamed my body, pulling my sweatshirt over my head and hummed in approval when he saw I wasn't wearing a bra. His lips descended on one nipple then the other, nibbling just enough to drive me wild.

"Aren't you supposed to go to the office?" I gasped between moans.

"That can wait. I can't," he growled, rising to his knees to remove his shirt and unfasten his pants.

I only had a moment to admire his chiseled physique before I heard a tearing sound as he tore my leggings open. He used a finger to pull my panties to the side, baring my slick folds to the cool air in the room.

I watched, mesmerized as he stared at what he'd revealed, licking his lips and fisting his cock. A whimper fluttered from my throat when he started moving his hand along his shaft, his eyes still locked on my center.

"You have the prettiest pussy I've ever seen," he said, gliding his thumb along my folds.

My clit was swollen and aching, begging for release. "Mmm... Are you going to stare at it or fuck it?"

I gasped when his eyes flicked up to mine. The fierceness in them had a rush of desire hitting my core, making me even wetter than I already was.

"You keep forgetting who's in charge here, I'll have to remind you," he said with a sinister edge. "I still need to punish you for not obeying me earlier." He spoke in a deep and gravelly tone I'd never heard before.

A new side of Killian had come out to play, and I squirmed with anticipation. My pulse raced as I imagined what he'd do to me. I yelped when he tore what remained of my leggings off, leaving me in a black lace thong.

"Stand up," he ordered, pointing to a spot in front of the bed.

I did as he told me to while watching him walk to his closet. My heart fluttered when he came back holding a necktie.

He stopped in front of me holding the tie taut. "Hold your hands out, wrists together."

Again, I did what I was told, excitement coursing through me as he secured the tie around my wrists. By the time he was done, I was so aroused I could feel the slickness between my legs.

Like a predator circling its prey, he slowly stalked around to stand behind me. He didn't touch me, but I felt the warmth of his body at my back. I took a shaky breath when he leaned forward to align his lips with my ear.

"Next time I tell you to stay put, *you stay*," he growled, sending a thrill down my spine. "When I tell you to do something, you do it. Understood?" I nodded then cried out when his hand landed a hard smack to my ass. "When I ask you a question, you speak your answer."

I was so incredibly turned on I felt dizzy. I couldn't find my voice to respond, and another *smack* echoed through the room.

"*Oh God...* yes," I stammered. "Yes, I understand."

"Very good." He moved to stand in front of me. "Get on your knees."

Without hesitation, I dropped to the floor in front of him. My eyes lowered to his cock, thick and long and begging for me to taste it. I leaned forward to take him into my mouth, but his hand fisted my hair to pull me back.

"Did I tell you to touch my cock?"

"No, but—"

"You're not running the show. I am. Now, be a good girl and open your mouth."

My jaw eagerly hinged open before he'd even finished the sentence. With one hand at the base of his cock and the other still fisted in my hair, he fed the tip between my lips. As I licked the pre-cum from him, a moan escaped me.

When I tried to take more of him in, he pulled my hair, holding me in place, telling me to wait. I looked up at him, pleading with my eyes. With a wicked grin, he pushed his hips forward until he was in as far as I could comfortably take him. When I'd adjusted to that, he pushed in even farther.

He paused, holding himself fully in my mouth for a few seconds before pumping his hips. His hold on my hair kept me from moving my head, muffling my moans and whimpers as he moved faster and faster.

I moaned, pressing my thighs together when the aching in my clit became unbearable. I lowered my joined hands between my legs, but before I could touch myself, he pulled his hips back until he slid out of my mouth.

Killian curled his hand around my neck, pulling me up to my feet. "Did I give you permission to play with yourself?"

"No. I'm sorry, it's just too much. I need you inside me," I said, practically sobbing with need.

He squeezed my neck tightly and crushed his lips to mine. "Kneel on the bed facing the headboard."

I climbed onto the mattress, but with my hands bound I lost my balance and fell forward, landing with my head on the pillows and my bottom in the air. I felt him climb onto the bed behind me, and he gripped my hips tightly, pulling my ass up higher.

"Please, Killian," I begged, my words muffled by the

pillows. "I need you. I need to feel you inside me. *Please*."

He pressed the tip of his cock against my opening but didn't enter me. When I tried to push back into him, his grip on my hip tightened, the bite of his fingers pulling a moan from me.

"Patience, Sunshine," he said, slapping me harder than before, once on each cheek. My cries echoed through the room as he slammed into me so hard, I nearly came right then.

He pounded into me so hard, so fast I couldn't catch my breath. "You don't come until I tell you," he ordered between pumps.

Shudders of pleasure wracked my body as he moved in a punishing rhythm. My breathing became staggered and shallow, and just when I thought I might pass out, he leaned forward to place his lips over my ear, tracing the shell with his tongue. I felt his hand move between my legs, and I held my breath eagerly waiting for his command.

"Come for me," he whispered at the same time he pinched my clit.

My orgasm ripped through me, pulling a moaning scream from my throat and had my body instinctively pulling away from the source of such unyielding pleasure. Killian held me in place, forcing me to ride out the onslaught of sensation. I felt my juices sliding down my thighs, mixing with sweat as he continued pumping inside me until his own climax poured out of him.

"Rise to your knees," he said, helping me up. He reached around to untie my hands, then pressed a kiss to the back of my neck. "Are you okay?"

Turning around to face him, I wrapped my arms around his neck. "I am more than okay. I'm fucking fantastic."

"I'm sorry if I was too rough." His powerful arms slipped around my waist, pulling me in close.

My face scrunched up in confusion. "Why are you apologizing? You said it was my punishment."

"It was. You need to learn when I tell you to do something, it's for your safety, so you need to do it. However, it was my fault that scumbag got anywhere near you."

"How was it your fault?"

"I eased up on your security. I should have kept Leo with you until I had taken care of Chad.

I touched my lips to his for a tender kiss. "You called Leo off because I begged you to."

He shook his head. "I should have known better."

"Shh," I whispered, pressing my lips to his again. "Please don't blame yourself for what happened. That was all Chad's doing. I gotta say, though, your means of punishment don't exactly make me want to behave."

He lifted an eyebrow and let out a soft chuckle. "You're not what I expected when I first saw you."

"Oh? What did you expect?"

"I figured you'd be a quiet, timid little mouse." He lowered his hands to my ass, squeezing tightly. "Instead, I got a seductive, powerful lioness."

"Mmm," I hummed, enjoying the feel of his hands on me. "You bring that out in me. You make me feel strong and sexy, like I don't have to be ashamed or afraid to be me."

"You should never be ashamed of who you are, Skye Larsen. You have the power to bring men to their knees. You're a fucking goddess, and you deserve to be treated like one."

I felt a surge of pride and a swell of emotion at his words. Killian saw me, the real me, and he still wanted me. For the first time in my life, I felt truly seen. He didn't judge me for my past, for the things I'd done to survive. Instead of telling me I was disgusting or broken, he enjoyed it when I touched myself, when I expressed my sexuality.

He wanted *me*. All of me, just the way I was. I had never met anyone like him before, someone who embraced and shared in my darkness and reveled in my sensuality.

After Killian left for his office, I went shopping for the trip. Going off his suggestion, I bought the tiniest bikinis I could find while imagining his reaction when he saw me wearing them. The thought of being alone in a hotel room with Killian had my face flushing and my body pulsing with anticipation. As I was checking out at the last store, he texted me to meet him at the yoga studio.

As I turned the corner, I felt a magnetic pull towards him. He stood there, casually leaning against his light pole, scrolling through his phone, and looking every bit like he belonged on the cover of GQ. His aviators and crisp dark blue suit exuded a dangerous charm that left me longing to touch him. Despite his eyes being concealed behind the dark lenses, I knew the second he spotted me.

As his eyes moved over my body that familiar tingling sensation washed over me. The closer I got, the stronger the sensation became until it was almost overwhelming. Finally, I stood before him, and his lips curled into a small grin.

"You've been shopping," he remarked, glancing at the bags in my hand. His gaze lingered on the telltale pink-striped one.

"I have," I replied with a grin of my own. "For the trip."

He reached out to curl his hand around the back of my neck and pull me in for a kiss. "I have something to show you."

His hand slid down to take mine as we headed across the street to the studio. The workers were busy and barely noticed us when we entered. My brow furrowed in confusion as I looked around the front area.

"It's bigger," I muttered, worried that they'd made an error. If they had made the lobby and my office bigger, that would make the studio smaller, which meant fewer students per class. "Why would they make it bigger?"

"There's more," he said, pulling aside the plastic curtain that led to the studio.

When I crossed the threshold, I stopped dead in my tracks, slowly turning in a circle to look at the space. "I don't understand. How is this possible?"

They had transformed the room from a simple yoga studio to a serene space that transported you to another world. They'd expanded the once roomy area to almost twice the size it had been before.

As I looked around, I couldn't help but fall in love with the beautiful walnut hardwood floors with my logo in the center. The stunning mirrored wall along the back of the room was backlit with a soft blue glow, bathing the entire room in its gentle radiance. A soft sky blue coated the walls, adding to the tranquility.

I kicked off my shoes and walked up to the new raised platform in front of the mirrored wall, feeling the cool wood beneath my feet. As I stood there, I could feel the excitement building within me. This was where I would be, instructing the class and guiding my students on their path. It was all amazing, but I still couldn't understand how it was possible.

"How?" I asked again.

A gnawing sense of frustration simmered just beneath the surface when I realized my insurance wouldn't have covered the expansion, meaning Killian had shelled out the difference.

There was a whirlwind of conflicting emotions churning inside me. I was grateful for the extra space, its beauty, and what it meant for my future, but I'd told Killian I wouldn't accept his financial help.

Chapter Twenty-Three

Killian

"I bought the building and took over the vacant shop next store," I said. "Now you have a bigger studio, which will allow for more students, and there's extra space for you to expand."

"You did what? Expand?"

I nodded, gesturing toward the back of the room. "You can make it a Pilates studio like you mentioned to Layla, or a retail store to sell yoga mats and accessories. Or you can rent it out to another business. It will be here until you decide what to do with it."

As I spoke, she walked toward the clouded glass doors at the back of the room. When she opened them, they revealed a construction site, where workers were busy laying the same walnut flooring.

She turned to face me, her cheeks flushed and eyes ablaze with irritation. "I don't understand why you would do this," she said, barely louder than a whisper. "I told you I didn't want to take advantage of your wealth."

I cupped her face in my hands. "You're not taking advantage of anything. I wanted to do something special for you. It's a gift."

She was silent for a few moments, debating with herself until she finally surrendered, her hands covering mine. "You remembered my conversation with Layla from dinner that night?"

"I did."

"I didn't even know you heard me. Thank you," she said, lifting her lips to meet mine. "I'll find a way to repay you. It might take time but—"

Lowering my hands to her neck, I pressed my thumbs against her skin, feeling the pulse thrum beneath them. "Don't even try to repay me," I growled, sinking my teeth into her lower lip. "At least not monetarily."

She moaned in response, her arms wrapping around my waist. "Mmm, I can think of other ways to thank you," she purred then laughed when a nail gun went off, reminding us of where we were. "Later though." She looked around again. "How did they get all this done so quickly?"

"You're a smart girl," I said. "You can figure that out."

"Ah… money."

I nodded. "It has a way of making things happen. I have more good news," I said, taking her hand and leading her outside to the car.

"Tell me," she said excitedly as we climbed into the backseat.

As Neil started driving, I slid my arm around her,

pulling her close to me. "If you'd like, we can leave for our trip tomorrow."

"Tomorrow?" Her eyes widened. "So soon? That seems quick."

"It pays to have people I can trust taking care of things while I'm gone. Amelia rescheduled most of my meetings, and she'll handle the ones she couldn't. As for the flight, we'll take my private jet so we can leave whenever we want."

Her eyebrows drew together. "You have a private jet."

"I do."

"Is it a small jet?" she asked, her voice wavering a little.

I studied her through narrowed eyes. "Are you afraid of flying, Skye?"

She swallowed hard and shook her head a little too fast. "No. No. Not at all. I just don't enjoy being in a plane... you know, when it's in the air."

A laugh escaped me, and I didn't miss Neil's eyes lifting to peer at me through the rearview mirror. Laughter was something he rarely, if ever, heard from me. Ignoring him and the grin he wore, I pulled Skye onto my lap, tucking her hair behind her ear and caressing her cheek.

"My pilot is one of the best. I promise you'll be safe." She sighed when I nuzzled my head in her neck, placing a light kiss there. "I won't let anything happen to you," I whispered.

Later that night, our passion blazed like a wildfire, consuming us both until it left us panting and spent.

As we lay there, limbs entwined and hearts pounding, I couldn't resist the urge to draw her close. Cuddling had never been my style, but with Skye, it felt like the most natural thing in the world. It felt right.

I molded my body around hers, enjoying the way she fit perfectly against me. It was as if she'd been made just for me, in every way.

I HELD SKYE'S HAND as the jet prepared for takeoff. Her grip was unexpectedly strong and unyielding, as if she was clinging to me for dear life. As the engines roared to life and the plane began to rise, I winced as her nails dug into my skin. She seemed to be scared that the force of our ascent would tear one or both of us out of the plane.

Once we had leveled out at cruising altitude, she relaxed. After the attendant brought us our drinks, she relaxed even more. By the time we were set to land, she was snuggled against me, fast asleep.

She continued to doze during the car ride, but her eyes sparkled with excitement when we boarded the speed boat that would take us to our destination.

"I've never been on a boat," she exclaimed, breathless with anticipation as the vessel cut across the water. "This is amazing!"

I leaned back, taking in the sight of Skye as she reveled in the boat ride. Watching her had become one of my only indulgences in life. She was a force of nature, a woman of extraordinary charisma and kindness. Her infectious energy drew people to her, and I was no exception.

A delighted squeal escaped Skye's lips as our

destination came into view, and the boat began to slow down, pulling up to a private dock that led to a luxurious overwater bungalow.

"Oh my God, Killian! I've always wanted to stay in one of these," she exclaimed, practically bouncing out of the boat and onto the deck. Her eyes were wide with wonder as she took in the stunning view of crystal-clear water stretching out as far as the eye could see.

I couldn't help but smile, watching her bounce in place as she waited for me. As I stepped onto the dock, a wave of contentment washed over me. She centered me, brought me peace, and there was no way I could ever explain to her what she meant to me.

"It's beautiful," she said, as we walked hand-in-hand to the bungalow.

"You haven't seen it yet," I replied.

She looked at me as though I had three heads. "Um, who cares what it looks like on the inside, though from the outside I'm sure it's perfect, but look around! It's amazing, stunning, can't-believe-this-is-real beautiful!" Her expression softened and her eyes sparkled. "Besides, I'm here with you. That makes it perfect no matter what."

I pulled her in for a kiss, letting myself drown in her as she wrapped her arms around my neck. "Thank you for bringing me here," she whispered against my lips, pressing herself even closer to me. "It seems I have more than my studio to repay you for."

"I didn't bring you here expecting anything, but I won't argue if you insist."

She threw her head back in laughter, exposing her neck to me. I took advantage and licked from the hollow to her chin. Her breathy moan was all it took to make my cock as hard as a rock.

The animal inside me wanted to throw her down and fuck her right there on the dock. I knew from the way she was grinding against me, she wouldn't mind, but the staff was still busy unpacking our luggage.

"Let's go inside. I'll show you around," I said, reluctantly stepping away from her.

"You've been here before?"

"Yes. I own it."

She stopped walking and when I turned to look at her, her jaw was hanging open in shock. "I'm sorry, did you just tell me you own this place?"

"Yes."

"Killian, seriously, do you have any idea how weird it is that you're so nonchalant about owning a private bungalow on a private island in the middle of the ocean."

A small smile tugged at my lips. "Sorry, that's not what I meant."

She huffed out a breath and her shoulders relaxed. "Oh, okay."

"I meant I own the island, and everything on it," I clarified, my tone unapologetic as I turned and walked inside, leaving her gaping after me.

I had built my empire from scratch, and nothing I did or bought was to impress anyone else, but there was something satisfying about seeing Skye's shock and speechlessness. As long as people knew not to fuck with me, their opinions of me meant nothing. With Skye, however, I wanted her to know just how much I could provide for her and how much I could protect her.

"Killian," she called as she hurried to catch up to me but she was once again silenced when she stepped over the threshold.

She moved in slow motion, spinning in a circle as she took in her surroundings. As I watched her, I couldn't help but feel a sense of pride.

I had spared no expense in making the villa the ultimate escape from reality. The demands of my job made it necessary for me to find a place where I could disconnect from the world and recharge. When I'd been unable to find a place that worked for me, I designed my own getaway.

From the plush furnishings to the ultramodern entertainment system, every detail was designed with comfort and luxury in mind. I'd never planned to share the space with anyone, but with Skye, everything was different. I was once again surprised by how comfortable I was with her being in my world.

Following her lead, I took off my shoes and followed a few steps behind her as she explored. The wooden floors of the large living area were cool beneath my feet as we meandered around the sofas and an ornate coffee table. Floor-to-ceiling glass doors framed the view of the turquoise sea, teeming with schools of jewel-colored fish. With the push of a button, the doors opened, sliding into the walls and allowing the sounds and scents of the ocean to fill the air. The absence of a wall brought the outside world inside the villa.

The bedroom was a true haven, with a king-sized bed draped in fine linens and an en-suite bathroom with a large soaking tub and a separate walk-in shower. The best part was the private balcony, leading to an infinity pool that seemed to stretch out into the horizon.

There was also an intimate seating area where we could watch the sunset every night, and a dining table where we could share meals together under the stars. Every inch of the villa offered unobstructed views of the ocean. No matter where we were the soothing sounds of the water would reach us, lulling us into a sense of tranquility.

I watched as she walked to the edge of the deck and gazed down into the crystal-clear waters. She turned to me with a seductive smile on her face.

"I'll never be able to fully express how much this means to me, but I'm sure gonna have fun trying." She moved toward me like a magnificent lioness stalking her prey. "I think we can take care of ourselves tonight, don't you?" She stood so close to me, her breasts brushed my chest and I wished we were naked. "Send the staff home, Killian," she purred.

Her voice was throaty, low, and so fucking sexy I'd have chopped off a limb if she asked me to. "Luther," I called out without taking my eyes off her. "You can all go home for the night."

"We haven't prepared your dinner yet, sir," Luther replied.

"Don't worry about it. We'll take care of it tonight."

Skye bit my lower lip and I added, "There's an extra five grand for each of you if you're out of here within the next sixty seconds."

Thirty thousand dollars was nothing when it meant I'd have Skye all to myself. When she stripped off her clothes, I knew I'd have paid ten times that amount if I'd had to.

"Get naked, Stalker," she said with a playful smirk on her lips.

Usually, I was the one in charge, taking control and running the show, but something changed in that moment. As I watched Skye, I found myself unable to take over. Her beauty and confidence overwhelmed me, making me incapable of denying her anything. For the first time in my life, I was content to let someone else lead, to let Skye lead. I'd follow her wherever she wanted to go.

I dropped my shirt to the deck, and she trailed her fingers over my bare chest, looking up at me with those deep blue eyes. Those eyes were far more mystifying than the ocean they resembled. Her touch sent shivers down my spine and made me ache for more, but I didn't want to rush things, so I let her go at her own pace. I surrendered myself to her completely, letting her take the reins.

"Get on the bed," she commanded, following me as I turned back to the room.

From my vantage point on the bed, I watched her disappear into the closet and come back out with one of my ties.

"You are not tying me up, Skye," I said, drawing a

line.

She shot me a mock-pout and cocked her hip to the side, and damn if she didn't look sexy as fuck. "You got to tie *me* up." She climbed onto the bed, crawling her way over my body until she straddled my torso. "Can't I do it just this once?" She leaned forward to slide her tongue along my lips. "I promise I won't hurt you... too much."

"Fucking hell, Skye," I growled. "If you want to do it, do it now before I flip you over and fuck you until you can no longer speak."

A strangled noise slipped from her. "Mmm, that is tempting, but it's my turn."

She aimed a playful smile at me when I held out my hands, letting her tie them together and then to the headboard. I was completely at her mercy. I'd expected to feel ridiculous or frustrated. Instead, I felt more turned on than ever before.

As I lay there, vulnerable and exposed, Skye took her time exploring my body, teasing me with her lips, tongue, and teeth. Every touch felt like it was sending shockwaves through me, and I knew I was completely under her spell.

When she was on her knees between my legs, she looked up and sent me a wicked grin. "You always try to pull me off before you come," she said, licking her lips as she leaned forward to wrap her fingers around my shaft. "This time you won't be able to stop me."

"Skye," I growled in warning.

Her eyebrows rose as she gave me a playfully

innocent look. "Can't talk, I'm busy," she said, meeting my eyes as she slipped my tip between her perfectly plump lips.

She was going to be the death of me. The way she looked with my cock in her mouth, the way her tongue felt as it swirled around my head, everything about her made me all too aware of how much she owned me.

I watched her ass swaying in time with her head as it moved up and down, and a long, deep groan rumbled from my chest. Fuck the ocean, the only view I needed was right in front of me.

Her teeth grazed along my shaft and my hips twitched upward, driving me deeper down her throat. She hummed in approval, and I did it again and again until I felt my balls tighten.

"Get on me, Skye," I groaned, needing to be inside her. "I know you're as worked up as I am, and I want to feel your pussy tighten around me when you come."

She lifted her head, but kept her hand wrapped around my shaft, slowly moving it up and down. "It's hard to say no when you put it like that."

"Get the fuck on me and ride my cock like the greedy slut you are," I ground out when she kept gliding her hand over me.

"Mmm, yes, sir," she purred, crawling until she straddled me.

"Untie me. Now."

"I don't know... if I do, do you promise to be a good boy and not take over?"

"Yes, but I can't promise I won't make you pay for

this later."

"Oooh, I don't want *that* promise." She leaned over me, her breasts hovering over my face just out of reach, as she untied my hands.

The second my hands were free, I grabbed her by the waist then pushed her down onto my cock. I held still, letting her set the pace. She started slowly, her moans filling the room as she rocked her hips against me.

Sweat slicked her skin, making her glow as she let her eyes flutter closed, and I thought I'd never see anything more beautiful. Then her lips parted and her back arched as she rode us both to the edge. Her head fell back on a moan, her body moving harder and faster as her climax hit.

My fingers dug into her soft flesh, holding her against me while pressing my hips upward as my own orgasm slammed into me. As we caught our breath, she melted down onto me, nestling her head in the crook of my neck.

The feeling of her breath against my skin, the softness of her body against mine was pure bliss, and I could have stayed there for the rest of eternity,

Chapter Twenty-Four

Skye

W e stayed like that for a while, with my fingers tracing along Killian's chest, his hands moving up and down my back, and the soft sounds of the ocean floating through the room.

After another few minutes, I lifted my head to look at him. "I need food," I said, sliding off him and padding out of the room.

I heard his soft chuckle and the rustling of the sheets as he got out of bed to follow me.

"How long are we staying?" I asked with my head in the industrial refrigerator. There was so much food I wondered if Killian had invited more people to stay with us.

"A week," he replied. "Why?"

When I turned to face him, I brought a charcuterie board full of gourmet meats, cheeses, and olives with me. "Because there's enough food in here to feed an army."

"The staff always over stocks, but they'll take the leftovers."

I placed the board on the counter and returned to the fridge to get two bottles of sparkling water. Then while I readied some silverware and napkins, he moved to the other end of the kitchen for a jar of fig jam and a fresh baguette.

At my suggestion, we carried everything out to the dining table beside the pool where we ate in companionable silence while watching the sun set. As the sun dipped below the horizon, casting the sky in hues of red and orange, I wandered over to the end of the deck to look out over the water. I couldn't hold myself back from leaning into him when he slipped his arm around my waist.

"Killian?" I asked.

"Hmm?" he hummed.

"Tell me something about yourself no one else knows."

His jaw clenched, a telltale sign I'd hit a nerve. He moved to sit on a chaise lounge designed for two, and I followed suit, sitting at the opposite end with my legs folded underneath me.

"I know you don't enjoy talking about yourself or your past, but I want to know more about you," I said, resting my hand on his shin. Neither of us had gotten dressed and there was something deeply intimate about sitting outside, completely naked, without another soul around to see. It almost felt like we were the only two people left on earth.

"Come here," he said, and I moved to sit beside him. As I settled in, he tucked me against his body, wrapping his arm around me and holding me close. After a moment of silence, he spoke again. "I have a half-sister."

Surprised, I looked up at him. "You do? No one else knows about her?"

"I do, and no. She doesn't even know." I furrowed my brows in confusion.

"I don't understand," I said.

He took a deep breath before explaining. "I started my business the day after I killed my dad's enforcer. I needed to take my dad down, rip away everything he cared about. There was no punishment better than taking away every penny he'd earned or stolen. I was young but because my dad had left a trail of enemies, I had connections a normal teenager wouldn't have. They were just as eager to see my father ruined as I was."

"You were resourceful," I offered.

"Yes. Lucian was a valuable resource for me. He was young too, but he's an expert with technology and uncovering people's secrets. With his help and some financial backing from my dad's enemies, I was able to find plenty of dirt to use against my father. Like the affair he'd had with a housekeeper. When he got her pregnant, he fired her and left her with nothing but a hungry mouth to feed. When I was done with my dad, I ended up with a hefty bank account and it grew from there. So, I financially supported my half-sister from afar. I still do."

"Oh, wow. You've never contacted her?" I asked.

"No. She doesn't need to know me," he said. "I came close once when her mother died. She was too young to live on her own and would have ended up in foster care. So, I worked it out behind the scenes for her to have a live-in caretaker and a bank account that ensured she'd never need for anything as long as she lives."

I thought for a moment before asking, "Where does she think the money came from?"

"I had Lucian pretend to be an estate attorney and tell her that her father, whom she had never met, had left her the money after he died."

"So, Lucian knows about her," I pointed out.

He shook his head. "He may have assumptions, but I never told him who she was."

"Wow," I breathed, lifting my head to look at him. "You're like a superhero."

A deep, rumbling laugh came from his chest. "More like a supervillain."

"Mmm... you sure are intent on labeling yourself a bad guy. Well, I've always preferred the villain anyway."

"Why is that?"

"Because the villain will do everything in their power to keep their love safe. They'd burn the world for them. The hero would sacrifice their love to save everyone else." I shrugged. "Call me selfish, but I want someone who puts me ahead of everyone."

"After everything you've been through, I can understand that." He touched his lips to mine for a kiss. It wasn't exactly tender, but there was something more, something new. Something that told me I'd found my villain.

THE WEEK WITH KILLIAN was undoubtedly the best of my life. As we swam in the ocean and slept under the stars, I felt like I was living in a dream. The delicious food we ate and the endless conversations we had only made it seem more like paradise. We'd grown closer on that trip. He'd dropped his shields and had shown me a little of his playful side.

When we got home to New York, I felt like I was still floating on a cloud. The inspiration I had gained from that trip was immeasurable. I'd finished the paintings for the hotel and scheduled a meeting with Amelia to show her the key pieces.

Since the canvases were large and unwieldy, I had Neil drive me and help me carry them upstairs. As soon as we stepped off the elevator into Killian's office, Amelia greeted me with a warm smile, but then her eyes returned to her computer screen.

"I can set up if you need more time," I said as she typed away.

Amelia shook her head. "No worries, I'm all set." She rose from her seat and led me into a meeting room where eight easels lined the back wall. "Let's see what you've got."

As I unzipped my portfolio case, Neil excused himself and told me he'd wait downstairs until I was ready to leave. I watched Amelia set the paintings on the easels. They were the larger pieces that would be featured on each floor of the hotel, and if Amelia approved of them, I knew she would have no problem

TAINTED DREAMS

with the smaller ones that would go inside the rooms.

"Oh, Skye, these are amazing," she said, strolling down the line, peering closely every so often. "You really captured the tone we wanted. They're perfect."

"Great! I'm so happy you like them. I can send you pictures of the rest, or you can come by to see them." I furrowed my brow. "That is if it's okay with Killian. Sorry, I forgot it's not my place."

She let out a light laugh. "Oh, honey, he wouldn't say no to you. You've got that man wrapped around your little finger."

"Um, I don't know about all that," I said as heat crept up my neck.

"Believe me, he's in deep," she said with conviction. I must have looked skeptical because she continued, "The day we met at his apartment was the first time I'd ever been there, and the same goes for Neil and Leo, who he barely knew and normally wouldn't have even shared his address with. Mr. Asher is incredibly protective of his privacy, and he lets no one, except Lucian, inside his sanctuary. He made an exception for us because he wanted us to help keep you safe and make you feel comfortable. He's letting you *live* in his apartment when he's never even brought a date back there. He prioritized your well-being over his need for privacy."

"Um... I don't really know what to say," I muttered, feeling the heat spread up to my cheeks.

"If that's not enough to convince you, consider this: he's never taken a woman on a trip before, let alone to the private island he purchased as his own secluded getaway spot."

"Why are you telling me this?" I asked, my brain finally catching up to the conversation.

An unreadable expression flitted across her face too quickly for me to decipher. "Because you should know how important you are to him," she said finally. "If you ever find yourself questioning his intentions, remember just how special you are to him."

"Okay. Thank you," I said, but the uncertainty in my voice made it sound more like a question than a statement.

As she clapped her hands together and gestured to the paintings, a smile spread across her face. "Thank you for these. They're perfect," she said, her expression warm and genuine. "I'll have them sent to the framers and schedule something with Mr. Asher to see the others."

"Sounds good," I replied. "Um, I know he's asked you to call him by his first name, so why do you call him Mr. Asher?"

"Because it annoys him," she said with a wry smirk, pulling a laugh from me.

"I think I like you, Amelia."

"That's good, because I have a feeling we're going to be seeing a lot of each other in the future."

As she walked me to the elevator, I caught a glimpse of Killian in his office. He was sitting at his desk, engaged in a heated conversation with Lucian, who was standing in front of him. His anger was clear, even from where I stood, and I wondered what could have caused such a reaction.

When Killian's gaze flicked in my direction, he clenched his jaw, and his expression darkened even more. Confused by his sudden anger, and noting the rare scowl on Lucian's face, I gave a weak wave. If Lucian wasn't leering at me just to annoy Killian, something was definitely wrong.

"Skye? I think Neil's waiting for you," Amelia said, slipping her hand to my lower back and gently guiding me toward the elevator. She'd noticed something was going on, and she wanted me to leave.

"Mr. Asher is having a tough time with his newest business venture," she said in a reassuring tone. "He'll be home around the usual time."

Not wanting to disturb him at his place of work, I stepped into the elevator and met Neil out front. On the drive home, Wes called saying he needed to speak to me right away. We agreed to meet at the Daily Sift Café near Killian's apartment.

Twenty minutes later, I was sitting at an outdoor table sipping an iced coffee when Wes arrived, his features hard and solemn.

"What's going on?" I asked my brother, wishing Killian and I had stayed on that island.

Instead of answering me he placed a folder on the table and slid it toward me. My face scrunched up in confusion as I opened the folder and saw a report from a private investigator.

"I thought you said you called him off?" I asked, anger boiling inside me.

"He stopped following Killian, but I asked him to

keep digging into him." He shook his head and held up his hand before I could respond. "His name was too familiar, Skye. I needed to know why."

I slammed the folder shut. "You found it? You found your answer?"

"I did."

"Fine. Then what does that have to do with me?" My anger turned to fear, and ice crept up my spine as I felt my stomach drop. Whatever was in that folder, I knew it wasn't good, and I didn't want to know. I didn't want anything to ruin what I had with Killian.

"It has everything to do with you. You're dating him, living with him. You should know who he is, what he's done."

I clenched my hands into fists to stop them from shaking. "I do know him," I whispered. "Better than anyone else, and I don't care what's in this folder. It won't change how I feel about him."

"Read the report or I'll tell you what's in it."

That was it. I'd had enough of his overprotective bullshit. "Fuck you," I spat, my voice shaking with rage. "Who the hell are you to tell me what to do? You left me alone with our junkie mother while you went off to make maple fucking syrup. I had to pull myself out of that hellhole, and now you think you can waltz back into my life and start calling the shots? No, Wes. If I don't want to read that report, then I won't. You will not tell me a damn thing."

His eyes were wide as he stared back at me. I had never exploded like that in front of him, nor had I ever told him how much his leaving had hurt me.

It was too late; I couldn't take back my words now. They were out there, raw and honest. It was the truth I'd hidden from myself for too long, and it had finally come to the surface because I was scared the information Wes found would destroy what I had with Killian.

He swallowed and shook his head slowly. "Okay. I get it," he said, his voice cracking. "I'll leave it with you. You can do whatever you want with it. I won't tell you anything unless you ask." With that, he stood up and walked away, leaving me sitting alone at the table staring at the folder.

I sat there, alone and overwhelmed, as I watched him vanish into the chaotic swarm of people flooding the city streets. The pounding of my heart drowned out the blaring horns and clattering footsteps. The full force of what had just happened hit me like a ton of bricks.

My gaze fell to the manila folder in front of me, innocent-looking yet harboring devastating secrets. I hesitated, unsure whether to read it or destroy it, until my curiosity got the best of me. I flipped through the pages, already familiar with most of the information, until my eyes landed on a section highlighted in yellow.

It was like a dagger to my heart, slicing it into a million tiny fragments that pierced me from the inside out. I felt numb, paralyzed by what I'd just read.

It couldn't be true. It was a lie, a way for Wes to get me to move to Vermont. It couldn't be true, it just couldn't.

"Are you okay, miss?" the waiter asked.

I looked up at him realizing he'd been trying to get my attention. "Yeah, I'm fine."

"Can I get you anything else?"

"No. Thank you," I said, pushing my chair back harder than necessary and knocking it over. "Oh, I'm sorry."

He placed his hand on my arm to stop me from bending over. "It's okay. I'll get it, don't worry."

"Thank you," I said, grabbing the folder and heading toward Killian's. The only way to know if it was the truth was to ask him.

Chapter Twenty-Five

Killian/Skye

Killian

When I got home, I found Skye sitting at the dining room table, sipping on a glass of scotch. I knew she hated it straight up, which made her choice unnerving. When her eyes flicked up to me, her expression was indecipherable but the tension in the air was palpable. I'd dreaded this moment since I'd read that damn addendum months ago. It felt like I was walking into my execution.

Wes stopped having me followed and instead had the private investigator look into my past. Lucian's team had hacked the guy and kept me informed of anything they dug up. He hadn't found anything Skye hadn't already known. Then they put the pieces together, and when Lucian had come to the office to fill me in, my entire world had come crumbling down.

It had been too late for Amelia to cancel her meeting with Skye, so she'd made it as quick as possible. When

I saw Skye there, in my office, looking so innocent and pure and radiant, it felt like a hot poker had pierced my heart. Because I knew it'd be the last time she'd smile at me that way.

It'd be the last time she would smile at me, period.

"Join me for a drink," she said, and a knot formed in my stomach.

I moved to the bar to pour myself a scotch before sitting across from her. She slid a seemingly innocuous manila folder toward me and tapped it with her finger.

"*This* was quite fascinating. I wonder if you'll find it as interesting as I did," she said in an icy tone.

I didn't reach for the folder, instead I kept looking at her. "I know what it says."

She lifted an eyebrow. "Do you? I guess that shouldn't surprise me. You seem to know everything before it happens. Exactly how long have you known it was you?" Her voice was getting louder, her cheeks redder.

"I found out not long after we met." Her head jerked back as if I'd hit her, and I figured I may as well continue. "After that first night at the club, I hired a P.I. to look into you and it was included in his report."

"You've known from the beginning and never thought to tell me?"

My jaw clenched as I shook my head. "I've thought about telling you every day, but I couldn't bring myself to do it. I even tried staying away from you, forgetting you, but I couldn't do that either. It's the reason I didn't want to sleep with you."

"Really? Was that your attempt at being noble?" She snorted, shaking her head in disappointment. "What happened, Killian? What made you do it? Did your dick take over your brain and make you fuck me anyway?"

I lifted an eyebrow at her tone, impressed, even though she was directing her anger at me. Despite the situation, I couldn't help feeling a sense of pride in the way she was standing up for herself.

"Tell me why you did it," she said, her voice trembling. "Why her? Why my mom?"

"It had nothing to do with her," I said, my voice hollow.

There was no way around it, she deserved the truth. "The building that housed your mom's art studio had been included in a takedown I'd headed up. The building was in terrible shape." I felt a strange tightness in my chest as I spoke. "It was too far gone to renovate, and the city condemned it shortly after my company gained it. We tore it down and had the property rezoned to residential before rebuilding. That's why your mom lost her business."

She was silent for a few moments, staring into her glass. When her eyes met mine, they were bright with unshed tears and the tightness in my chest grew painful.

"You ruined my life," she said, so low it was barely audible. "Maybe not intentionally, but it was because of you. You're the reason my mom's business closed. You're the reason everything fell apart... the reason those men... *You*."

Her tears fell then, and her body shook with heaving

sobs, making my heart feel like it was in a vise. Seeing her in pain made me physically ill. Knowing I'd caused it made me hate myself more than I ever had.

"I thought you were my hero, saving me from my demons, but you turned out to be the biggest one of all." She let out a cynical laugh. "I did say I prefer the villains, and maybe that was my mistake: overlooking your dark side."

"None of this was your fault," I said, clenching my hand into a fist to stop from reaching for her. "I should have told you from the start."

She took a shaky breath and wrapped her arms around her waist. "Why didn't you?"

"Because I'm a selfish asshole. I wanted you and I'd do anything to have you."

"Including lie to me," she said, a little of her feistiness returning.

"Yes."

She pursed her lips and shook her head. "Why? Did you think you could keep it from me forever?"

"No. I would have told you eventually."

Another humorless laugh escaped her. "When?"

"When I was sure you wouldn't leave me."

She gasped. "Do you know how fucked up you sound?"

Frustration coiled in my gut. I was used to getting what I wanted, used to people agreeing to my every wish. I was not accustomed to people pushing back at me, and she was pushing hard.

"Do you know why I call you Sunshine?" I asked.

"No." Her expression was unreadable, but her eyes were lit with anger.

"Because your eyes are the same deep blue as the ocean. They pull me in like an undercurrent I can't escape. I don't *want* to escape. And because you've never let your past define you. You try every day to pull yourself out of the dark, into the light. You choose to see the good in life and you've made me want to see it too."

Tears fell down her face, and my fingers ached to wipe them away. I wanted to touch her, hold her, make her stay with me. "You bring light to my cold, dark world. I will do whatever it takes to keep you in my life."

Her brow lifted. "Was that a threat?"

I didn't answer her, instead I rose from my seat and moved around the table. She watched me with wide eyes as I knelt in front of her. "When I told you that you have the power to bring men to their knees, I meant it. You are my salvation, the person who made my black heart beat again."

"Those are pretty words, Killian," she said, her tone dripping with venom even as the tears continued to fall. "A few months ago, I would have lapped that shit up, but one thing you have given me is a backbone. You told me you would never hurt me... but keeping that from me hurt more than if you'd punched me in the face. I can't trust you, which means I can't stay with you. I can't be with you anymore."

Her words sliced through me like a knife. "Don't do this, Skye. Don't leave me." It was the first time in my life I'd let myself be completely vulnerable, let myself ask for something I wanted. "I'll make it up to you."

"No. You won't. You can't. What you did was careless. Haven't you ever thought about the repercussions of your actions? The little people that get swept aside while you make billions of dollars?" She pursed her lips. "No, of course not, because you don't have to. Just like your dad never had to think about how his actions affected your mother or the housekeeper or your sister... or you."

Anger slammed into me so quickly I jumped to my feet and clenched my hands into fists. "Do not compare me to my father."

"I just did," she spat, rising to her feet.

"Do you think that will protect you?" I asked, gesturing to the chair she'd put between us. "Do you think you can stop me if I want to touch you?" To prove my point, I stalked toward her, easily moving the chair aside.

As I got closer, she walked backward until her back hit the kitchen island. "You belong with me, Skye. No matter where you are or who you're with, you will always be *mine*."

She paled. "Don't do this, Killian," she said, her voice wavering. "You have to let me go, or you're no better than Paul."

Her words were like a bucket of ice water sending Killer back to hell for the time being. I didn't like or agree with her comparison, but I would not hold her against her will either. "Leave. I won't stop you."

I stood where I was, long after she left, staring at the

spot where she had been. I'd lost the only person who ever meant something to me, leaving me with nothing but tainted dreams of what could have been.

―――――◇―――――

Skye

I MISSED HIS HANDS ON MY BODY, his breath on my neck, and his lips on mine. I missed the sound of his voice first thing in the morning, the soft moans he made when I touched him, the way he looked at me.

I missed *him*.

It had been two weeks since I walked away from Killian. Two weeks since I found out he was the reason for everything bad in my life. Two weeks since he'd started texting me every day with stories from his life, painting pictures of what our future could be like, and pleas for me to return to him. I never replied. I couldn't. The betrayal still felt fresh, raw, and unforgivable.

Leaving him had been the hardest thing I'd ever done, but I had to do it. I needed to get away from him and the truth that had shattered my hope for happiness.

I still felt his eyes on me, watching my every move whenever I left Layla's apartment. I knew he was there, lurking in the shadows, but I never saw him, and I couldn't bring myself to text him to stop.

I wanted him to see me, to remember what he lost. I wanted him to hurt knowing he couldn't touch me. Late at night, I'd lie awake trying to reason with myself, trying to come up with an excuse to call him, but the hurt ran too deep.

I knew Killian didn't set out to hurt my mom or

me, but the shit I'd endured on the streets made it hard for me to even look at him now. He had destroyed everything I'd held dear in my life with a single act of greed.

"Skye, are you listening to me?" Layla's voice brought me back to the present.

I shook my head and forced myself to smile, which wasn't as easy as it had been once upon a time. One good thing I'd taken from my time with Killian was I stopped shoving my feelings aside. I was depressed, and I was wallowing in it.

"Sorry, Layla. I'm just a little distracted," I said, taking the dish she'd just washed and started drying it.

She raised an eyebrow. "What you meant to say is you're still moping around because of Killian?"

"I am not moping, Layla."

She rolled her eyes. "Right, and I'm not obsessed with Henry Cavill."

"Isn't everyone?" I asked, hoping to get her to talk about something else.

"It's enough already with Taylor Swift. I love the girl, but I mean…"

"I haven't been listening to it that much," I lied. Her music had been on a constant loop, but in my defense, I listened to her often regardless of my love life status.

"Skye, you haven't even painted since you've been here. That's the most troubling part of this whole thing."

She was right. Normally when I'm depressed, I paint,

but I couldn't even find the energy to do that.

"What do you want from me? You know what he did, and you know how hurt I am. I can't just bounce back overnight."

She wrapped her arms around me. "I know, babe, but it's been two weeks and you only go outside to teach yoga in the park. Which is why we're going out tonight," she declared, grabbing my hand, and pulling me toward her bedroom. "We're going to X, Chelsea's coming, and you're going to have some fun."

A groan escaped me. I was so not in the mood for a night out, but I knew Layla wouldn't take no for an answer. Not again. "Fine, but just for a little while."

Layla grinned, and I could see the mischief in her eyes. "Oh, we'll see about that. I have a feeling tonight is going to be the night I get you sloppy."

I shook my head and gave a light chuckle, knowing she was planning to ply me with alcohol and force me to dance my worries away. Who knew? Maybe, just maybe, it would help me forget about Killian, even for a little while.

I knew it would make her happy, so I let Layla pick my outfit for our night out. Because if it were up to me, I'd go in sweatpants and a hoodie.

She chose a tiny, sparkly pink crop top, black leather pants, and stiletto knee-high boots. As we walked from her apartment to the subway, I felt Killian watching me, and the petty part of me hoped he was suffering.

When we got to X, Layla, Chelsea, and I went straight to the bar for shots. I hated tequila, but it sure loosened things up quickly. With three shots in me, my balance on the toothpicks Layla called heels was questionable, but I still joined them on the dance floor.

There was something about pulsating music, flashing lights, and gyrating hips that made it easier to forget about your problems. Closing my eyes, I let myself get swept away by the atmosphere as I moved my body in time with the beat.

Someone tapped on my shoulder, pulling me out of my buzzed haze. When I opened my eyes, I was staring at a broad chest covered by a tight black t-shirt. A warm finger slipped under my chin, lifting my head up so I could see his face. Blond wavy hair fell to his shoulders and his light brown eyes sparkled with humor.

"I'm Ethan," he said, leaning down so I could hear him. "Can I buy you a drink?"

I pulled my bottom lip between my teeth as I debated what to do. "One sec," I said, holding up my finger and spinning to grab Layla. "What do I do?"

"What's he want?" she asked, winking at the man named Ethan.

"He says he wants to buy me a drink."

"Go for it. He's pretty yummy, and it's just a drink," she said, smacking my ass before going back to dancing.

I turned to face Ethan, eyeing him up and down. He was hot. His build screamed athlete, but he was nothing compared to Killian. *Ah! Stop it. Stop comparing him to Killian,* I scolded myself.

"All right, Ethan, let's go," I said, linking my arm with his and letting him lead me to the bar. We got two steps before I stopped dead in my tracks.

Killian. I'd felt him watching me dance, but every time I turned to look for him, I couldn't see him. Then there he was leaning against the bar, a drink in his hand just like the first time I'd seen him there. His eyes were on me, making my skin tingle, and making every cell in my body want to go to him.

My chest tightened when I noticed how tired he looked, and I had to fight the urge to go to him, to comfort him, to hold him.

"Are you okay?" Ethan asked, glancing down at me with a concerned look on his face.

"Um... Yeah, yeah. I'm okay," I said, forcing myself to walk the rest of the way.

As we sipped our drinks, I tried to focus on Ethan, but my gaze kept wandering over his shoulder to see Killian's eyes trained on me like a predator. I took a large gulp of my drink and excused myself to the restroom.

I got halfway down the dimly lit hallway when a hand grabbed my wrist and pulled me around the corner to the spot where he'd first kissed me.

"What do you want, Killian?" I asked, trying to free my hand from his grip.

"You know what I want," he replied. "I can't stop thinking about you. I miss you."

It had taken a lot for him to admit that, to say it out loud, but it didn't matter. "No. I don't want to talk to you," I said firmly, my heart pounding in my chest.

He pulled me closer until our bodies met. I tried to pull away from him, but his grip was tight and unyielding.

"Are you with him?" he asked, his voice low and dangerous.

"I just met him five minutes ago," I replied, trying to keep my voice steady. "He offered to buy me a drin — Wait! Why am I explaining this to you? I can be with whoever I want. I need to move on. So do you."

He tightened his hold on my wrist, making me flinch. "No. You don't have to move on, and I never will. We belong together. Remember? We're two broken souls trying to find their way out of the darkness together."

I shook my head, tears burning my eyes. "Don't do that. Don't use my words to try to win me over." My voice cracked with a sob. "It's too late, Killian. You lied to me, you hurt me, and I can't trust you."

"Please, Skye," he whispered, his usually commanding tone replaced by one of vulnerability. "There must be a way we can move past this. Something I can do to prove how much you mean to me and how sorry I am."

He leaned in, his lips brushing against mine, and just like that, I was lost to him. His sandalwood scent washed over me, blurring my thoughts, and I let the kiss linger for a few moments before I pushed him away.

"No," I whispered. "There's nothing you can do." I laid my hand on his chest, pushing him away from me. "You once told me you'd give me anything I wanted... well, I want you to let me go."

"I can't do that."

"You have to," I whispered.

He wrapped his arms around my waist, burying his head in my neck. "I can't sleep, can't eat. I can't *live* without you." His lips brushed against my skin and another sob escaped me. "Without you, I don't exist."

"Please," I begged, my voice as weak as my attempts to push him off me. "Please, let me go."

He fell to his knees, still gripping me. He lifted his head to look at me and the pain I saw in his eyes nearly did me in.

"When you told me you loved me," he began, making me cry harder, "I didn't say it back because 'love' doesn't come close to describing how I feel about you. There are no words that could ever express what I feel for you. You are my light, my hope, my everything."

With sobs wracking through my body, I tried to pry his arms from around my legs. "Killian, please. If you love me, you'll let me go."

"Fuck that," he spat, standing back up. "How can you say *you* love me and not even give me a chance to make things right? I know you went through hell as a kid, and I know you blame me for it, but you can't deny how you felt when we were together. You can't deny you were happier with me."

"It doesn't matter." I gasped in a shaky breath when his fingers traced my jawline. "Knowing what I know... I just can't be with you right now."

He froze, his fingers stopping just under my ear. "Right now," he repeated, his eyes sparkling.

"If you'll leave me alone, give me some space,

maybe… maybe I can forgive you." I told myself I was saying it to get him to go away, but as the words left my mouth, I wanted them to be true.

"I need a time frame, Skye," he said, forever the businessman.

"Give me two more weeks, but I can't promise my answer will be the one you're looking for."

"Two weeks." His features darkened as he leaned in to press his lips to my ear. "You need your space, I'll give it to you, but you are still *mine*. So, go home with him, or any other man in those two weeks, and I'll rip their fucking heart out," he growled possessively.

As I watched him walk away, a shudder ran through my body, but it wasn't fear. I still wasn't afraid of him, though I knew I should be. Despite my heartbreak, I felt a sense of excitement at the realization that, no matter what happened, I would always be his.

Chapter Twenty-Six

Skye

I had asked for space, and he'd given it to me. He hadn't texted or stalked me since our talk at the club. I missed him terribly, every second without him felt like an eternity. Then at five o'clock in the morning on the day those two weeks were up, my phone buzzed with an incoming text.

Killian: *Are you ready to talk?*

My heart raced as I stared at my phone. I'd expected to hear from him. Layla and I had talked out what I wanted to say to him countless times. She'd made some good points, surprisingly most of them were in Killian's favor, and I'd decided to meet with him.

Still, I hesitated when his message came through, feeling like a teenager whose crush had finally noticed her.

"Be a big girl, Skye," I muttered to myself. "Just do it."

Me: *Today, 4:00p.m. at the coffee shop by the yoga studio. It's called Latte Lonnie's.*

Killian: *I'll be there.*

My stomach clenched with the anticipation of our meeting. With no chance of falling back to sleep, I got up, showered, and made coffee. Taking my cup out onto the fire escape, I sat and watched the sun rise over the city while thinking about Killian.

Our relationship had always been unconventional. He started as my stalker, then quickly became my protector, my lover, and the one person I trusted with my deepest secrets.

After learning what he'd been keeping from me, he felt like a stranger. I wasn't sure if I could ever get back to where we were just a few weeks ago. How could I trust someone who destroyed people's lives without a second thought?

Layla interrupted my thoughts with a grumble as she plopped down next to me. "What are you doing up at this ungodly hour?"

"He texted," I replied, taking a sip of coffee.

"Ah," she grunted, leaning against me. "Are you going to see him?"

"Yup. Four o'clock at the coffee shop."

"So, can I just say something?" she asked, tentatively.

I turned to look at her through narrowed eyes. "Can I stop you?"

A sleepy grin spread across her lips. "No. Good point." She turned so she was facing me, her legs tucked underneath her. "Based on what you've told me, it seems like the city would have condemned the building where your mom had her studio even if Killian hadn't been involved."

"Okay…" I'd thought of that already, but for me, it hadn't changed how I felt. It hadn't taken away the feeling of betrayal. "He still hid the truth from me."

"All right, are you upset that it happened because of his company, or are you upset that he didn't tell you right away?"

"Both. I know he does it to ruin the corrupt men who run the companies, but he takes them down without thinking about all the people who work there. He leaves the employees to fend for themselves after losing their livelihood."

She pursed her lips. "Mm-hmm, and why are the employees of an asshole or a poorly run business Killian's responsibility?"

I glared at her. She was my best friend. She was supposed to be on my side even if it wasn't logical. "Lay, I can't make sense of my feelings either, but I know how I feel. I can't just get over it that quickly and act like nothing happened."

"Babe, I am not saying you should pretend like it didn't happen. I'm just saying cut the guy some slack. He's clearly in love with you, and you are so in love with him you can't even see straight. Don't give up on him. Give him a chance to make it right."

"I've made my decision and I'm sticking to it," I said.

"All right. It's your life, Skye, but I just really want you to be happy. You deserve it, more than most people."

"Thank you. I want me to be happy too."

AT FOUR O'CLOCK ON THE DOT, I walked up to *Latte Lonnie's* and saw Killian already there, coffee in hand, sitting at a table outside. There was a second cup sitting in front of the empty chair across from him. A weak smile pulled at my lips as I slid into the chair and took a sip of the chai tea latte he'd ordered me.

"Thank you," I said by way of greeting.

"Are you hungry?" he asked.

I shook my head, losing the ability to speak under his gaze. Despite everything, he still had the power to make me dizzy just by looking at me. As I gazed into his eyes, I noticed the dark circles that marred his handsome face. He looked exhausted, as if the weight of the world was resting on his shoulders.

"How have you been?" I asked, inwardly cringing at how cliché the question sounded.

Not one for small talk, Killian's jaw clenched for a second before he replied, "Fine. What have you decided?"

I hesitated, my resolve faltering as his familiar scent enveloped me. It would be so easy to give in to the pull, to forget everything else and just be with him. I had spent so long pretending, maybe I could do it again. Maybe we could be together again.

I reminded myself of the purpose for our meeting and took a deep breath. "I'm going to Vermont," I said, holding up my hand to stop him from interrupting. "Not permanently, but for a while. The woman who runs Wes' retail store is going on maternity leave, and he needs help. More importantly, I need more time."

Silence stretched between us, and I could feel his eyes on me, searching for any sign of weakness. "You're running away," he finally said, his voice laced with ice.

His words cut deep, and I felt the sting of tears in my eyes because deep down I knew he was right. I was running away from him, from our relationship.

"If that's how you want to see it," I replied, trying to match his coldness. "I need to know... Have you ever thought of all the people you affect?"

His body went rigid with tension. "No. Not until I met you."

"I think that's what upsets me the most. Not that you kept it from me, but that you went on with your life without considering who you may have hurt along the way."

His eyes narrowed, and for a moment, I thought he was going to lash out at me. Instead, he took a deep breath and spoke again. "Until I met you, I never gave a damn about anyone else."

I shook my head, trying to find a way to prove to us both he wasn't completely heartless. "That's not entirely true," I said. "You support your sister and you do it anonymously."

Killian's eyes flicked up to meet mine, his expression cold and unreadable. "When do you leave?" he asked, ignoring my statement.

"Tomorrow," I replied, trying not to show how much his dismissive attitude stung.

A flash of pain crossed his face, but it was gone almost as quickly as it had appeared. I wondered how many other emotions he kept hidden behind that stoic facade.

"What about your business?"

My mouth felt like a desert, so I took a sip of my drink, stalling my response. "Layla will handle everything for me."

"You're giving into your brother so you can run away and leave your friend in charge of your responsibilities."

"And you're deliberately being a dick," I said, my bluntness surprising myself.

"Don't go. Stay here so we can work this out." His voice was low but still had a dangerous undertone. "I made a mistake. After everything we've been through, don't I deserve a chance to make it up to you?"

A knot formed in my stomach. I'd told myself I'd be strong, and I wouldn't let him talk me out of going no matter what he said. Even if sitting in front of him, looking into his eyes, made my resolve waver.

"I'm going to help my brother. I'm going to get away from the city and take the time I need to figure out what I want." There. I'd said it. It wasn't as hard as I expected even if I felt like I was going to throw up.

"Don't do this, Skye. Don't cut me out of your life over something that happened before I knew you," he implored, his eyes intense.

I couldn't let his charm and beguiling eyes sway me. "I have to," I whispered.

Killian grunted, a wicked grin spreading across his lips. "Then why did you come here today, Skye?"

I searched for an answer, but the intensity of his presence clouded my thoughts. "I thought it was only fair to tell you in person," I said, my words coming out weak and unconvincing.

Killian stood up from his chair, towering over me with his imposing figure. He straightened his jacket, giving me a cold, dismissive nod. "Enjoy your trip," he said, his voice devoid of any emotion.

As he walked away, my heart ached with conflicting emotions. I longed to run after him, to forget everything and fall into his arms. I'd made a promise to my brother, and I couldn't go back on my word. Plus, I really needed time away to clear my head and figure out what I truly wanted. Even if it meant leaving him.

"YOU CAN'T COME WITH ME," I said to Layla for the second time. "Who will manage the classes in the park?"

"Sylvia offered to take over," she responded, tossing her hairbrush into her toiletry bag. "She knows the routine, and she'll call me if anything comes up."

Sylvia was a retired yoga instructor who regularly took classes at my studio. She was only twelve years older than me and had only retired because she'd married a wealthy man and no longer needed to work. I wasn't concerned about Sylvia's abilities, but Layla, a self-proclaimed city girl, wanting to join me in Vermont puzzled me.

"You hate anything outside of Manhattan," I said. "I don't understand why you want to come so badly."

Her head jerked back, and her hand went to her chest. "Do you not want me to come?" she asked, dramatically. "Are you trying to get away from me?"

"You should have been an actress," I said with a light chuckle. "You know I don't care if you come, I'm just confused about why you want to."

Layla took my hands and pulled me in for a hug. "Because you're heartbroken and what kind of friend would I be if I let you drive six hours all by yourself."

I stepped out of her embrace and studied her for a few moments. There was something she wasn't telling me, and I'd eventually get it out of her, but in the meantime, I was all for having company on the long drive. Not to mention her support once we got there and Wes started in on me about making it a permanent thing.

"Okay, but if Wes starts, you have to help me," I said, holding out my pinky.

She wrapped her pinky around mine and jiggled our joined hands. "Deal."

Two Months Later

BEING AT WES' WASN'T AS BAD as I'd thought, and Layla's presence had a lot to do with that. The days were full of work, chatting with customers, and spending time with Wes and Layla. Once I was in bed, my dreams wouldn't leave me alone, wouldn't let me forget Killian.

One night when I couldn't take it anymore, I got out of bed and wandered around the house. The bedrooms Layla and I were staying in were spacious and comfortable, with luxurious linens and fluffy pillows. The bathroom was tiled with intricate designs, and had a deep soaking tub, made for long, lazy soaks.

The sweeping staircase descended to the main floor led to a welcoming foyer. The furniture was sleek and modern, with clean lines and understated elegance. A soothing gray coated the walls, framed by bright white crown molding and thick baseboards.

The kitchen was bright and airy, with high ceilings and a ton of enormous windows which allowed plenty of natural light in during the day. A large island dominated the center of the room, and the stainless-steel appliances gleamed under the bright lights.

One glance out those windows, and I couldn't resist the urge to wander the grounds. As I stepped out onto the back porch and into the chilly winter air, the quiet beauty of the landscape struck me. The backyard was a winter wonderland, with the fields and trees coated in a sparkling layer of white. In the distance, I could see the outline of the barn that Wes had transformed into the retail store.

The trees, with their branches silhouetted against the clear night sky, were the real stars of the show. Wes had strung them with twinkling lights for the winter festivities he held for the town. They cast a warm glow over the yard, illuminating the layer of snow that covered the ground.

As I made my way through the snow-covered trees to the frozen pond, the only sound was the crunch of the snow underfoot. I settled into one of the Adirondack chairs, tilting my head back to take in the vast expanse of sky above. Having spent most of my life in the city, the stillness and silence of the Vermont countryside always amazed me. It was a stark contrast to the constant noise and commotion I was accustomed to, and I felt a sense of peace settle over me as I gazed up at the starry night sky.

I was lost in my thoughts, thinking about what life could be like if I gave in to my brother's wish. A small sound to my left shook me from my reverie, and I realized I wasn't alone.

The sound was barely audible, like the rustle of fabric against a tree trunk. I questioned whether it was real or just my imagination, and I held my breath, waiting to hear it again.

"What are you doing out here?" Layla's voice cut through the silence, startling me out of my seat.

I spun to face her, my hand going to my chest. "Dammit, Lay, you scared the crap out of me."

"I'm sorry. Why are you out here in the middle of the night? It's freezing."

"I couldn't sleep."

She frowned. "You haven't slept well since you got here. Why don't you just call him?"

I pulled my bottom lip between my teeth as I considered how to respond. I'd thought about calling Killian every day since we left New York, but fear held me back. Fear of what might happen if we spoke again. Fear of how much I still loved him.

I never thought I'd open my heart to another person after Paul, but it had been so easy with Killian. All it had taken was one look for me to start falling for him. After finding out his secret, my heart sealed itself off, and I was afraid of breaking that seal again.

"What if he has other secrets? What if there's something else he isn't telling me? I don't think I could get over him again," I said then shook my head. "I haven't gotten over him this time."

"There might be other things he hasn't told you, but I doubt there's anything else related to your past." She reached out to take my hand. "You love him, Skye. Isn't that worth exploring? You don't have to commit to anything, just call him."

It was unlike Layla to champion relationships. She was a devout single girl and preached about single life to anyone who'd listen. For her to encourage me to seek out a relationship was strange. That she was urging me to get back together with someone she hardly knew was even weirder.

"Why are you pushing for this? All you know about him is that he's a billionaire who once tore down my mom's building."

"The way he looks at you tells me all I need to know."

I glanced at her, confused. "What? How does he look at me?"

She smiled and a distant look filled her eyes. "Like you're the only person in the world."

"Hmm, if you say so." I brushed off her statement as unbelievable, but Amelia's words floated through my mind.

Because you should know how important you are to

him. If you ever find yourself questioning his intentions, remember just how special you are to him.

"Fine," Layla said, pulling me out of my thoughts. "If you won't call him, will you at least consider going out with Cole?"

Cole worked for Wes, ensuring the boilers turned sap into syrup. He was ruggedly handsome, sweet, and had been asking me out for weeks.

"I'll double with his brother Trent," she added, sweetening the pot.

I stared at her, thinking of ways to say no. She knew my schedule, and she knew when I wasn't working or exercising, I was sitting in my room moping about Killian. So, if I wanted to get out of it, I had to come up with something really good.

"It would just be a casual dinner," she said. "Nothing serious and you don't even have to call it a date."

I knew she wouldn't let it go, and I knew she thought it would help get my mind off Killian, so as usual, I gave in. "Okay. Just dinner. No promises."

Chapter Twenty-Seven

Killian

T he notion of love and what one would do for it was foreign to me. I'd always been a man of logic and practicality, deliberately avoiding matters of the heart. Then Skye Larsen imprinted herself on my soul, and I started doing things I never thought myself capable of.

Like setting aside my corporate responsibilities by handing Amelia and Lucian the reins, then taking a room at a humble bed-and-breakfast in Lilac Grove, Vermont in an effort to win Skye back. I had tried my best to forget her, to numb the ache in my chest, but it didn't take long for me to realize that I couldn't let her go.

Within just a few weeks, I began making the changes to allow Lucian and Amelia to take over the business temporarily. While I could work remotely, I would only do so when necessary.

Once everything was in place, I headed to Vermont. When I arrived, I intended to make my presence known to Skye. I was determined to tell her I wouldn't leave until we worked things out, until she realized we belonged together.

The bed-and-breakfast where I was staying was just down the street from Meadow Maple Farm, and when I couldn't sleep my first night there, I went for a walk. It was late at night, but the moon was bright, and the stars twinkled in the sky.

When I turned the corner, I saw Skye standing in front of Wes's house with another man. My chest tightened, and I felt anger boil inside me as I watched him lean in for a kiss. A red haze crept in from the edges of my vision as his lips got closer to hers. A wicked sense of satisfaction filled me when she rested her hands on his chest and pushed him away.

"I'm sorry, Cole," Skye said, her voice floating through the air. "I've just gotten out of a serious relationship, and I'm not ready for this."

Cole nodded and gave her a soft smile that made me want to punch him in the face. "It's all right, you don't have to apologize." When he tucked her hair behind her ear, I almost lost it. The urge to bash his head in was growing by the second. "How about a movie tomorrow night?"

Skye hesitated for a moment before meeting his gaze. "Um…"

"Just a movie. As friends. Nothing more," he said.

He was slick, using the old 'friends' line, and it made me want to strangle him right there on Wes' front stoop. Especially when it worked on her.

A smile spread across her lips. "Okay. Sounds good, but we buy our own tickets."

"Deal. I'll pick you up at seven."

As Cole drove away, Skye turned toward me, sensing my presence. I stepped out of the shadows and met her eyes.

"Why are you here, Killian?"

"I came to talk to you," I said, my anger barely restrained.

Skye waited a moment before nodding and leading me around to the backyard. We sat on Adirondack chairs in front of the frozen pond.

At first we sat in silence, staring at each other. No matter what had happened between us, our pull was still there. I could see it in her eyes, the want, the need, but also the hesitation and anger.

It took everything I had to stop myself from reaching out for her. "I'm sorry, Skye. If I could go back and change things, I would."

"But you can't," she whispered.

I reached for her this time, cradling her hand between my own. "I can change things now though. I can make it up to you."

Skye's voice trembled with uncertainty as she finally spoke. "Killian, I don't know. I still have feelings for you, but that's not the issue. I can't be sure you're not keeping something else from me or that you won't keep something from me in the future. You didn't tell me the truth from the beginning because you were scared of losing me. How can I trust you not to do the same thing again?"

A mix of hurt and anger filled her eyes, and I knew I had to tread carefully. "I could say I'll never keep anything from you again, but if you don't trust me, it won't mean anything," I said. "I promise you, I'm willing to do whatever it takes to earn your trust again."

I clasped her hand in mine, hoping she could feel the sincerity in my touch. "I love you, Skye. More than anything. I will spend the rest of my life proving that to you."

She tugged her hand free, then wrapped her arms around herself. "I can't stop you from doing what you want, but I'm not ready to think about getting back together with you. You don't understand. I know you had a horrible upbringing, but it wasn't the same for me. Before my mom lost her business, I had a wonderful childhood so filled with love it was almost magical, and to have that happiness and security ripped away is not something you ever get over."

"I'm not asking you to forgive me or forget the past. All I'm asking for is a chance to make things right, to remind you why we fell in love in the first place."

"Like I said, I can't stop you, but I also can't make any promises."

Frustration and what I can only describe as fear had my gut clenching. "We belong together, Skye. You know it. Tell me what I have to do. What can I do to make you give me another chance?"

She shook her head as tears filled her eyes. "I can't tell you that because I don't know. I'm having a hard time getting over what you did." She took a shaky breath.

"Please. I have to go inside. I can't do this anymore."

"We belong together," I repeated. "And I'm going to make you see that. No matter what it takes."

"Go home, Killian. Please." She rose, squaring her shoulders. "If anything happens to Cole, I will never forgive you. Do you understand? Never."

"Understood," I said through clenched teeth.

I struggled to hide my frustration. Skye's insistence on protecting Cole grated on me, but I couldn't deny that it was part of what drew me to her. She had a sense of morality that I didn't.

She had justified the violence against Paul and Chad because they were loathsome assholes, but I knew she wouldn't be okay with an innocent man being hurt just because he was interested in her. It was a line she wouldn't cross, and I respected her for it.

For me, the line was blurrier. I didn't always have a clear sense of right and wrong. It was one reason Skye was so important to me; she anchored me, kept me from going too far.

"Goodnight, Killian," she said before turning and walking to the house.

Once she was safely inside, I turned and made my way back to The Rustic Nest, where I got in my car and navigated through the quiet streets.

It wasn't long before I found a bar. The neon sign flickering above the door read: Whiskey Creek Tavern. When I walked in, the low murmur of conversations and clinking of glasses filled the dimly lit space.

Dark wood paneling lined the walls, and the bar ran

the length of the room. Behind it, shelves of bottles glinted in the soft light, their amber hues promising a night of indulgence. A few locals were scattered around the room, hunched over their drinks or leaning against the bar.

I made my way to an empty stool and ordered a whiskey, half-expecting it to be cheap and harsh. The rich, smooth flavor pleasantly surprised me as I took a sip. The amber liquid slid down my throat like velvet, knocking the chill out of me, but doing little to help ease the tension in my shoulders.

"Well, lookey what the cat dragged in," a familiar voice drawled from behind me. I turned to see Layla standing there, her hip cocked and a wide grin on her face. "Fancy meeting you here, city boy."

I lifted an eyebrow, the tension finally relenting a little. "What are you doing in a place like this, city girl?"

"Touché," she said, sliding onto the stool next to me. "Have you won her back yet?"

My eyes narrowed and my jaw tightened. "Don't be a dick."

"Talk to me," she said, waving the bartender over. "I'll have what he's having and bring him another."

"There's nothing to talk about." I slammed back the rest of my drink and picked up the second one. "I fucked up and she can't forgive me."

"Huh," Layla grunted. "I wouldn't have pegged you as someone who gave up."

I shot her a dark look. "Did I say I was giving up? She belongs to me. We belong together, and I will stop at nothing until she's back in my life."

Layla smacked her hand down on the bar and whistled. "Now there's a declaration every girl dreams about."

"Are you always this annoying?"

She gave a curt nod. "Yes, sir." She chuckled at my threatening growl. "Skye loves you, like to her bones, loves you. She will forgive you. She just needs time. However…"

I held my breath, waiting for her to finish her sentence, but she just sipped her drink and looked around the bar. "For fuck's sake, Layla, spit it out."

Her eyes sparkled with mischief when she turned back to me. "You're fun to mess with, Killian Asher. You're so easy to rile up."

"Only when it comes to Skye," I said, letting the dangerous edge slip into my tone.

"You want to make it up to her, right? You want to win her back, make her forgive you."

My jaw clenched. "You know I do."

"You can't go back and undo what happened with her mom, but you can start fixing things now." She placed her hand on my arm so I'd look at her. "Start helping the people affected by your business dealings. Maybe even try to help some from past deals. I think that's what hurt her the most. That some rich guy took away her mom's livelihood without thinking twice about it."

I knew she was right because that's what Skye had told me. Maybe I should have thought about what happened to all those people, but I hadn't. Layla was on to something, and I had the power to make it happen. I couldn't go back and save Skye's mom, but I could try to prevent it from happening to someone else in the future.

"Go home, get shit done, and show her you heard her," Layla said, squeezing my arm.

I sat there, staring down at the worn wooden bar long after Layla had left. My mind was racing with possibilities, contemplating my first step. I swigged the rest of my drink, feeling the burn of the whiskey in my throat, and left cash on the bar, including a generous tip.

As I walked out of the bar, the cold air hit me like a slap in the face, sobering me up. I got into my car and called Lucian on the drive back to The Rustic Nest. The wheels were in motion before I even made it back to my room.

It would take some time, but I was determined to make it work and prove to Skye I could change. That I could be the man she fell in love with.

THE NEXT MORNING, the sounds of pounding and yelling from the hallway jolted me awake. Confused and disoriented, I stumbled out of bed and flung open the door, ready to confront the person who had disturbed the miserable few hours of sleep I got.

"What the fuck is going—" A fist smashing into my face cut my sentence off.

"I'll do the talking," Wes snarled, barging into the room, and slamming the door behind him. "Leave

Vermont and leave my sister alone."

"I can't do that," I replied stubbornly, bracing myself for the next blow.

Crack. Another punch to the face. And another. And another. Each one landed with a sickening thud, until I was on my hands and knees, gasping for breath.

I didn't fight back. Didn't stop him. I deserved the beating. Skye wasn't the only one whose life had been altered by the downfall of their mother. Wes may not have been around to help his sister, but my callousness had indirectly hurt him as well.

Even if I didn't give a damn about him, I accepted the punishment for how my actions had affected Skye.

Wes continued to rain down blows on me until he was panting with exertion. Finally, he stepped back, breathing heavily.

"You deserved that," he finally said, his voice rough with emotion. "If you ever come near Skye again, I'll do more than just beat the shit out of you."

With that, he turned on his heel and stormed out of the room, leaving me battered and bruised on the floor.

Chapter Twenty-Eight

Skye

"You did what?" I demanded, glaring at my brother.

Wes sat there while Layla bandaged his hands. He'd seen me crying earlier that morning and I had stupidly told him about Killian being in town. He'd stormed out of the house, but I never in a million years expected him to go after him.

As much as I was worried about how badly he'd hurt Killian I was also concerned about the potential for retaliation. If he really felt about me the way he said he did, I highly doubted he'd kill my brother, but he hadn't earned the nickname 'Killer' for being a forgiving man.

"I cannot believe you did this," I seethed at Wes, my anger boiling over. "You had no right. He's my problem and I'll deal with him how I see fit."

Wes looked down at the table, shame etched on his face. I knew his regret was not for hurting Killian but because I was so angry about it.

"I'm sorry," he mumbled. "This time, I had to do something to help you. I just had to."

I sighed, knowing that my brother's intentions were good, but his actions were misguided. "Wes, I'm sorry for blowing up on you that day. I didn't mean what I said... not fully anyway. Regardless of how I feel, I shouldn't have done that." I reached across the table to rest my hand on his arm. "But you cannot keep trying to make up for the past. What's done is done, and I need you to trust me to handle this on my own."

Layla made a small noise, and I aimed a questioning look at her.

"Oh, sorry, don't mind me," she said, taping the gauze around Wes' hand. "It's just... Why should Wes leave his indiscretions in the past but Killian, who didn't even know you back then, should suffer because of his?"

"Layla," he said sternly, a warning in his voice.

Shocked, all I could do was stare at my best friend. "I'm going for a walk," I said, ignoring Wes' attempts to call me back to the table.

I left the house in such a daze, I forgot to grab my jacket. My feet took me toward the Rustic Nest without my brain even realizing it until I turned the corner, and it came into view.

The twinkling lights and evergreen wreaths adorning the facade made it look like something out of a holiday postcard. It definitely didn't seem like the type of place where a fist-fight would go down.

As I stepped inside, a fire crackled in the stone

fireplace, welcoming visitors with its warmth. The air was heavy with the scent of spiced cider and fresh-baked cookies, and I couldn't help but be charmed by the coziness of the inn.

I stepped up to the front desk, and a plump older woman greeted me with a warm smile. Her eyes crinkled at the corners, and I couldn't help but return the infectious grin. "Well, hello there," she said cheerfully. "How may I help you today?"

My nerves were on edge, but I tried to keep my voice steady as I replied, "I'm here to see one of your guests. Killian Asher."

Recognition dawned on her face, and her smile brightened even further. "Oh, yes," she said with a twinkle in her eye. "Such a handsome young man."

"He is. Do you know what room he's in?"

"He's in room 401," she replied. "You go on up, dear. I'm sure he'd be pleased to see such a pretty face this early in the morning."

With a grateful nod, I made my way to the stairs, my heart racing with each step. The anticipation was almost too much to bear, but I couldn't help the fluttering feeling in my chest as I ascended to the fourth floor.

I stood in front of his door, my hand trembling as I mustered the courage to knock. When there was no answer, I hesitated for a moment before slowly turning the knob and pushing the door open.

A gasp escaped me when I saw Killian slumped against the bed, his face battered and bruised, his breathing shallow. Even in his weakened state, I couldn't help but think he was beautiful.

"Killian," I breathed, my heart breaking at the sight of him. "Why did you let him do this?"

Wes hadn't had a mark on him, other than his fists, which meant Killian hadn't fought back. He'd accepted the beating without trying to stop it.

He groaned softly, his swollen, bruised eyes fluttering open to meet mine. "I deserved it," he rasped, his voice thick with pain.

Tears stung my eyes as I took in his injuries. I couldn't bear to see him like this, to think of the pain he must have endured. A fierce protectiveness stirred inside me, making me want to hold him close and keep him safe from harm.

As gently as I could, I rested my hand on his cheek. "Shh. You didn't deserve this."

He lifted his hand to cover mine. "I did. You were right. I should have thought about how I affected other people." He struggled to speak, and it clearly hurt, but he kept going. "All I cared about was taking down assholes like my father, but in doing so, I became one of them."

I wanted to reassure him, to tell him he was nothing like his father, but the words got caught in my throat. I couldn't forgive him so easily for what he had done, even if seeing him in pain tore me apart.

No matter how upset I was with him, I couldn't stop the ache in my heart as I looked at him. "You are not your father. Though, if you don't like something about yourself, you can change it. It's never too late."

His battered eyes lit up, and I realized what I'd said. "Does that mean it's not too late for us?" he asked.

My stomach twisted with apprehension. "I don't know, Killian," I replied, shifting to sit beside him. Our bodies pressed together, and I felt his warmth envelope me. "It still hurts."

I couldn't give him false hope, so I took a deep breath, preparing myself for the painful conversation that was to come. "I need to be honest with you," I said, my voice steady but tinged with sadness. "I'm not ready to get back together, and I'm not sure I ever will be."

His eyes darkened with anger, and I knew it was going to be difficult to stay firm. "What happened between us, it's not something that can be fixed easily," I continued. "I'm not sure how much time I'll need or if I'll ever be able to get over it."

"Why are you here, Skye?" he asked, irritation clear in his voice.

"Because no matter what, I will always care about you. Wes had no right to do this, and I'm sorry he did."

A knock at the door interrupted whatever he was going to say. Killian called for the person to enter, and Lucian strode into the room. His eyes lit up with a menacing fire as soon as he saw Killian's injuries. "Who did this?" he demanded, his voice harsh and unforgiving.

Killian groaned in pain as he tried to turn around. "Don't worry about it, Lucian," he said through gritted teeth. "Skye was just leaving."

I raised my eyebrows in surprise at his dismissal but didn't argue. "Yeah, okay." I stood up and headed toward the door. "I'm sorry, Killian," I added, turning back to him.

He didn't even try to look at me. "Didn't I tell you never to apologize for your feelings?" he asked bitterly. "Goodbye, Skye."

As I stepped out of the room, my heart broke again, and I knew that the pain would never truly go away. Every time I looked at him, I remembered what he'd done, and it hurt even more. It was time for me to walk away, to find a fresh path, even if it meant leaving him behind.

Three Weeks Later

"I DON'T UNDERSTAND," I said into the phone. I'd been setting up a display of fresh apple cider in the store when my phone rang. It was a woman named Madeline Hearst from a boutique art gallery in Manhattan offering me an art show for my work. "How is this possible?"

"I attended the grand opening gala at the Blue Sky Veranda Hotel and Spa. The artwork blew me away, and I inquired about the artist. The manager gave me your name and number. I'd love to see your other pieces."

"Did Killian Asher put you up to this?" I asked, my stomach clenching.

"No. He wasn't at the gala, and I can assure you this was all my idea. You are very talented, and I'd love to be a part of your journey,"

I nearly laughed at her choice of words. "It's not a journey. The pieces in the hotel are the only ones I've done for the public. The rest of my work is extremely personal."

"Ah, yes. Passion, turmoil, love, hate. They all make for exceptional art." She sighed heavily. "Listen, Skye, I won't force you into anything you don't want to do. Please just think about it. You have some time. The first slot I have available isn't for six months."

"Uh-huh," I muttered, too shocked to come up with anything better. "I'll think about it."

"Great. Call me if you decide you want to do it." She paused. "I really hope you do," she added before hanging up.

As I slid my phone into my pocket, I couldn't help but feel conflicted. On one hand, the opportunity to showcase my work was thrilling, but the thought of exposing myself to the public was terrifying. If Killian really had nothing to do with it that would mean the offer was based purely on my work. It would mean I did it on my own.

"Who was that?" Layla asked, pushing a cart full of more cider toward me.

"A woman from an art gallery in New York," I said slowly, still trying to wrap my head around the situation. "She's interested in seeing my work and even offered to have a show for it."

Layla gasped, clearly excited for me. "Skye, that's incredible! Which gallery is it?"

"The Hearst Gallery," I said, the name finally sinking

in. "Oh my God, I just spoke with Madeline Hearst. *The* Madeline Hearst."

She squealed and bounced up and down. "Damn, Skye, this is big. Like huge!"

"I know," I said to Layla, my voice tinged with uncertainty. "I don't know what to do. Part of me wants to go ahead with it, but another part is afraid to put myself and my work out there. You've seen my art, Layla. It's personal, it's intimate, it's *mine*. How can I sell it to strangers who have no connection to it? They'll have portraits of my mom hanging on their walls and they won't know the pain, the heartbreak, the darkness that went into creating them."

I paused, my mind racing with conflicting thoughts and emotions. "Yet, I'm so incredibly tempted to say yes. To have my art displayed in a prestigious gallery in Manhattan. It's a dream come true, but it's also a nightmare. What if they don't understand it? What if they don't like it? What if it's all for nothing?"

"Skye, you're spiraling. Take a deep breath," she said. "Now listen to me. You're an incredible artist, and your work reflects your soul. The emotions you pour into your paintings are clear, even to someone who knows nothing about art. Trust me when I say that anyone who sees your work will know the depth of feeling that went into creating it. They will love it because it will speak to them."

I smiled at her words. Layla had always been my biggest cheerleader, and her support meant the world to me. I took a deep breath and nodded. She was right. It was time to take a leap of faith.

"Layla," I whispered, "I think I'm going to do it."

A smile spread across Layla's face as she wrapped her arms around me. "Of course you are," she said, her voice brimming with confidence. "That means we get to go home."

A laugh bubbled up from my throat as I hugged her back, feeling a sense of relief and excitement wash over me.

Chapter Twenty-Nine

Skye

Six Months Later

The Hearst Gallery was sleek and modern with strategically placed spotlights, casting a warm glow on the white walls and polished concrete floors. The minimalist design created an air of sophistication and elegance, with towering concrete pillars and large glass windows showcasing the bustling city beyond.

As I gazed upon my artwork, hanging on those very walls, and illuminated by the same radiant spotlights, my heart swelled with joy and my stomach clenched with fear. Agreeing to the show was the most exciting and terrifying experience of my life.

A sea of elegantly dressed attendees milled around my work, their voices hushed as they pointed out different aspects of the pieces with nods of approval. Oblivious to the turmoil churning inside me, they sipped champagne and nibbled on hors d'oeuvres, enjoying the glitz and glamour of the exhibition.

Despite Madeline's encouragement to mingle and answer questions, fear had me frozen in place for the ten minutes since the doors had opened. Then, to my relief, Layla and Wes walked in. The tension in my shoulders eased as they made their way over to me, beaming with pride.

"Skye! This is amazing," Layla exclaimed, enveloping me in a tight hug.

Wes hugged me next. "I'm so proud of you, Munchkin."

Feeling a renewed sense of confidence, I chuckled nervously and replied, "Thanks, but I'm so nervous, I could puke."

Madeline approached us with a mischievous twinkle in her dark brown eyes. She moved through the gallery with effortless grace in a backless black silk jumpsuit that perfectly complemented her lithe figure. Her silvery gray hair cascaded down her back in loose waves, adding an air of elegance to her appearance.

"Do you feel like throwing up yet?" she asked with a soft laugh.

I pressed a hand to my stomach. "Definitely."

She aimed a warm smile at me. "Have a glass of champagne and mingle. These are potential buyers, and you want to let them see you."

"Okay," I said, nodding my head a little too much.

Taking a deep breath, I picked up a glass of champagne from the table and made my way through the crowd. I stopped to chat with interested buyers and art enthusiasts. The more I spoke about my pieces, the more comfortable I became, and my nerves slowly dissipated.

After a while, I noticed Layla and Wes standing in the corner, their heads close together as they whispered heatedly. Their argument came to a halt when they saw me headed their way. They replaced their frowns with bright smiles, but their stances still showed the tension between them.

"What's going on?" I asked, my gaze moving between them.

"We were just discussing which piece was our favorite," Layla offered in explanation.

Although I was suspicious of their sudden change in demeanor, I let it go and made a mental note to revisit the topic with Layla later.

"How's it going?" Wes asked, slipping his arm around my waist.

"It's all so surreal, but amazing," I replied, taking a sip of champagne as I surveyed the gallery. Everyone I had spoken to had praised my pieces, and some of them even had little red dots next to them, indicating someone had purchased them.

"I'm still a little freaked out by the idea of these paintings hanging in someone's house. I mean, it's Mom..." I trailed off, feeling a twinge of unease.

Wes slipped his arm around my waist. "Yes, but to them, your pieces are more than that. They see a beautiful woman going through a difficult time, and it'll speak to them in a way only they can understand."

Madeline strolled up, a bright smile on her face. "You, my dear, have a decision to make," she said. "*Fleeting Bliss* is the subject of a bidding war."

My stomach fell to my toes at the news. *Fleeting Bliss* was the portrait of my mom laughing, surrounded by me and my friends on my seventh birthday. It was the only painting of her smiling. The only one portraying the time before my world flipped upside down.

"I don't understand," I stammered, my voice trembling with disbelief and apprehension. "Can I meet them?"

Madeline shook her head. "You can meet one of them. The other is on the phone. They were unavoidably detained but didn't want to miss out on the painting."

I bit my lip, trying to make sense of the situation. "How do they know they want it if they aren't here?" I asked.

"They've been on video call," Madeline explained, gesturing to a young woman standing in front of the painting.

I frowned, trying to wrap my head around the idea of someone wanting my work so badly that they had a friend call them on video chat. "Are they still on the phone?" I asked.

Madeline shook her head. "They were called into a meeting."

I didn't need to meet the other bidder to decide. My gut told me what to do. "Sell it to the person on the phone," I said firmly.

"You haven't heard their bids," she said with raised eyebrows.

"I know."

Her eyes twinkled as her lips pulled into a wide grin. "Very good."

As I watched Madeline inform the young woman of my decision a sense of sorrow washed over me. As much as it hurt to part with *Fleeting Bliss*, I knew it was time to let go and move on. The past was behind me, and it was time to look to the future.

My stomach clenched at the irony of my situation. Despite my insistence on leaving the past in the past, I still found myself unable to get over what Killian had done all those years ago. No matter how hard I tried to move on, the memories of that time lingered, keeping me anchored to the past.

"What made you chose the person on the phone?" Layla asked.

I shrugged, pursing my lips while trying to find a way to explain it. "I guess because they wanted to be here so badly they sent a friend to video chat with them. Something in my gut told me they will cherish the painting."

Madeline handed me another glass of champagne at the end of the evening, and we toasted to a successful night. During the event, I sold four paintings and received offers from people about commissioning me to design and paint artwork for several hotels and one private residence.

"You were magnificent," Madeline said. "Do you

think you'll accept the offers you received?"

"Oh, I don't know. With my yoga studio, I'm not sure I'd have time to do them all."

"You know I'll cover for you when you need it," Layla offered.

I smiled at her, thinking about what it would mean to paint full time, even temporarily. "Okay. I'll think about it. Thanks, Lay."

Wes, Layla, and I said goodbye to Madeline and headed to an all-night diner. Madeline had declined our offer to join us, explaining that it was time for her beauty sleep. We settled into our booth, ordered way too much food, and talked about the art show.

I left the diner that night with my stomach full of pancakes and my mind buzzing with thoughts about the offers I'd received.

Each time I entered my renovated apartment, the feeling of awe washed over me once again, just like it did on the very first day. Even though it had only suffered minor damage from the fire, the renovation team had gone above and beyond to make it feel like a brand-new space.

The loft had kept its open layout, but now felt even more spacious thanks to the addition of floor-to-ceiling windows. Which were tinted, offering me a view of the city outside while ensuring my privacy within. The exposed brick walls, once hidden under layers of paint, now gave off a cozy, rustic vibe.

My bedroom area, once fully exposed to the rest of the loft, was now sectioned off by a partial wall and a large barn door that provided an option for privacy. They had given the bathroom a luxurious upgrade, featuring a brand-new soaking tub and a refreshing rainfall shower. The walk-in closet, which still served as my art studio, had been revamped with a window and improved lighting.

To save space, they'd replaced my dress rack with a hanging bar and built-in shelves on the walls for storing my folded clothing, shoes, and beloved books. The flooring throughout the loft was the same beautiful walnut as in my studio, but I had added a large area rug for both warmth and style.

There was no doubt in my mind that Killian had something to do with the extra effort the renovation team had put into my apartment.

A pang of remorse hit me at the thought of him. I hadn't heard from him since that day in his room at the bed-and-breakfast. My fickle heart ached at the possibility that he might have forgotten about me, or worse, moved on.

Claudia Lobos' words echoed through my mind: *He always comes back to me.*

The thought of Killian being with anyone else made me want to explode, even though I was the one who had sent him away. I'd told him we couldn't be together, and I had no right to be upset about him dating other women. It didn't matter that I wasn't seeing anyone else; I'd made my choice, and I had to live with it... right?

Every day, it became harder for me to resist the urge to call him. Every day, I picked up my phone to stare at his contact name, which I'd kept labeled as 'Stalker.' I wouldn't change it because he had put it in there, and it would always stay that way.

Feeling tired but restless, I went into my little studio. On the back wall, on either side of the window, hung two paintings: the one of Killian and the one of my studio on fire. They were the only pieces I hadn't included in the recent show. There was no way I could ever part with them, no matter how much they hurt to look at.

When I got back from Vermont, my work had branched out. Instead of my mom, I found myself painting Killian more often, with his dark and intense eyes staring back at me or with his features relaxed as he slept. My favorite piece depicted him gazing at me with a sleepy half-smile on his lips.

I had also worked on other pieces, capturing the essence of people I saw on the streets or in the park. I had even created a few paintings of the city skyline. All of them would be displayed at my upcoming show in three months... except the ones of Killian.

My eyes drifted around the small space, taking in each painting as I pondered the offers I'd received at the recent show. When I first started painting, it was a personal outlet for my negative thoughts. It was never something I imagined would become a source of income. Since that opportunity had presented itself, I needed to decide if pursuing it was truly what I wanted.

MY RINGING PHONE WOKE ME up the next morning, and I answered it with a groan.

"Why are you calling me so early?" I mumbled into the phone.

"Get up and get your ass to the train," she said, excitement clear in her voice. Then she rattled off an address too fast for me to remember. "I'll text it to you, just get here. You're going to want to see this."

I showered and dressed in record time and was on the train within half an hour. I couldn't even begin to guess what she could possibly want to show me. Knowing Layla, it was a new night club or bar... though it was only eight thirty in the morning.

As I approached the address she had texted me, I saw Layla bouncing up and down on the corner. When she spotted me, she began waving her arms wildly.

"Would you relax? You might burst with all this excitement," I said, though a laugh escaped me.

Layla pointed across the street. "Look, do you see that?"

I turned in the direction she was pointing to see a tall apartment building, and my face scrunched up in confusion. "Blue Sky House?" I asked, reading the sign.

"It's a free rehab for addicts," Layla exclaimed, her voice rising in excitement. "They stay there, get counseling, meals, and job training. When they're ready to leave, there's a service that will help them find a job and a place to live, if needed."

I nodded, impressed. "That's so awesome," I said. "Why are you showing me this?"

Layla grabbed my arm, turning me to face her. "Just six months ago, this building was vacant, rundown, and in need of a lot of work. Do you know who had it renovated and dreamed up this amazing place?"

I shook my head, feeling a wave of dizziness wash over me. "No... you can't be serious."

Layla's grin was so big it looked almost painful. "Killian. He did it all for you."

My pulse raced. "Why?"

"Because you got through to him, and he loves you, dummy," she said, still beaming. "There's more." She dragged me two blocks down the road to another building, which had a sign reading Blue Sky Sanctuary. "This is a safe place for women or men to escape abusive relationships. It sets them up with attorneys and around-the-clock protection, should they need it, and if they have nowhere else to go, they can have a room until they find a place... which someone here will help them with."

I stared at the building in awe, feeling my eyes well up with tears. "He did this too?"

Layla nodded vigorously. "Yup. Killian has been busy."

"And wait, there's more," she continued, sounding like a game-show host. "A few blocks from here is another smaller building being renovated. It's going to be an employment center."

I gaped at her. "This was also Killian's doing?"

"Yup. It's going to be called Blue Sky Employment Center."

My head swirled with a flurry of emotions and questions. "How do you know all this? Have you been stalking my former stalker?"

"Don't hate me," Layla replied, and a knot formed in my gut at her somber tone. "I've kept in touch with him."

I gaped at her. "You what?"

"We ran into each other at Whiskey Creek Tavern in Vermont. He looked so lost and defeated, I couldn't just walk away. I've been checking on him ever since."

"I'm not sure how I feel about this," I admitted, trying to process what Layla had just told me. "I know I can't control who you talk to, but it still feels weird. Why didn't you tell me?"

"I'm sorry," Layla replied, her voice solemn. "I should have told you I was talking with him. You and Killian are meant to be together. I guess it was my way of keeping him close for when you're ready to forgive him."

I grunted and placed a hand on my stomach, feeling uneasy. "This is... a lot."

"He's trying to prove to you he can change, that he can make things right. He can't fix the past, Skye, but he can make the future better. You always say to leave the past behind us and focus on the present and future, don't you?"

I muttered a response, my gaze fixed on the sign across the street. "Blue Sky..." I whispered.

The hotel, rehab center, safe house, and employment center were all called Blue Sky.

"He named everything after you," Layla interjected. "Blue for your eyes and sky for your name. Obviously."

I shook my head as if trying to wake up from a bizarre dream. "He told you all this? He barely speaks, yet he confided in you?"

Layla scrunched her nose. "Well, I mostly text with Amelia, which he's aware of. I also check in with him at least once a week to make sure he's okay. I figured if he ever needed anything, I could let you know."

Despite my mixed feelings, I appreciated Layla's concern for Killian. The tornado of emotions continued to swirl within me. For the first time, there was a glimmer of hope somewhere in there that meant maybe, just maybe, I could forgive him and we could start over.

"Sooo... Are you going to call him?" Layla crooned.

"I haven't decided," I replied.

"What about the offers you got last night? Are you going to take the commissions?"

"I haven't decided," I repeated, shoving my hands in my hair to cradle my head. It felt like it was spinning and might pop off at any moment.

"Let's get some coffee and food, and we can talk."

"Yeah, okay." Coffee sounded like a great idea. Caffeine always helped me think more clearly.

Chapter Thirty

Killian

I'd built more in six months than I had in my entire career. Normally, I tore things down and sold off the pieces, but after losing Skye I knew I had to make some changes. To prove I could be the man she wanted, I'd started three new charities. More locations for each one were in the works throughout the city.

My plan was to invite her and Layla to the grand opening of all three so she could see them. Since Skye had made it clear that she didn't want to hear from me, I had to go through Layla to get her to come. No matter what it took, Skye would be mine again.

Amelia knocked on my door and peeked her head in, pulling me out of my thoughts. "You have a call on line one," she said with a pointed look. "It's Chad Walsh's uncle."

"Fuck," I groaned.

Harland Walsh was more than just Chad Walsh's uncle; he was also one of the men Chad had owed money to. Harland was infamous in the state for his ruthless collection methods, which left even the toughest bookies quivering in fear. He wouldn't care about his nephew's death—he'd be more upset he hadn't gotten to Chad first.

Because he wasn't a stupid man, and he was almost as ruthless as me, Harland would have realized Asher Capital had taken over his brother's company under questionable circumstances. Unlike the public and the press who had been fed a sugar-coated explanation for Sterling Walsh's decision to sell his company to mine.

"Asher here," I said into the phone.

"Where's my nephew?"

"What makes you think I know?"

Harland Walsh might have struck fear in the hearts of New York's underworld, but he didn't intimidate me. Not only did I have enough dirt on him to make him disappear overnight, but I also had people on my payroll that would make his enforcers look like amateurs.

"Don't play dumb, Asher. You got the sniveling little shit to make the board sell to you. I know you had something to do with his disappearance."

"Let me guess, he owes you money?" I asked, knowing damn well that was the only reason he was calling me.

"You know he does, and I want it now," he said in his toughest voice.

"I don't know what to tell you, Harland. He's your nephew, you deal with him and leave me out of it."

Harland was calling me because Sterling Walsh had died three days earlier. Walsh had left everything to Chad and apparently included a clause in his will specifically excluding Harland from receiving any inheritance. With Chad missing, any assets left after my takedown would be held in a trust until Chad showed up, which wouldn't happen. Eventually, the assets would revert to the state, and Harland would never see his money again.

"I know you had something to do with Chad's disappearance, and if I don't get my money, I'll make sure anything you care about disappears," he said, in what I assumed he thought of as his most intimidating voice. "Starting with that perky little blonde in The Verve you seem so fond of."

His words sent chills down my spine, and my blood ran cold. A dark rage overtook me, and my vision turned red with fury. "If anything happens to her, I will skin you alive. I'm not being dramatic, I will literally peel your skin from your body, inch by inch, until you beg me to kill you."

"What the fuck is wrong with you?" he asked, fear clear in his voice.

"That's not important. What matters is that you know I'm serious. If you are responsible for even one hair on her head being out of place, I will torture you for days." My voice was low and deadly, but I knew he could hear me. "You'll beg me to kill you, but I won't. I'll leave you suffering in unimaginable pain until you die from shock."

"You're a sick fuck, Asher," he replied. Despite his words, his voice shook and lacked the sharp edge it had when he'd threatened Skye's life. "All I want is my money."

"That's not my problem," I said, making sure he heard the danger in my tone. "Your family troubles do not concern me. In fact, I'd say you're at fault for letting Chad continue to gamble. You should have put an end to it a long time ago."

"Who the fuck do you think you are?" he blustered, but whatever he said next went unheard as I hung up the phone.

"Amelia," I called as I rose from my chair.

"Yes, Mr. Asher?"

I growled and shook my head. "I'm asking you for the last time, call me Killian," I ground out. "Get Leo in here now."

"On it," she said without hesitation.

Ten minutes later, Leo walked into my office.

"You need to keep an eye on Skye again. I need someone to watch over her twenty-four hours a day. The only time she's out of sight is when she's safely in her apartment. Then someone watches every entry point to that building until she leaves again. Is that understood?"

I didn't believe Harland would risk my wrath by harming Skye, but I needed to ensure her safety at all times. Besides, Harland wasn't the only adversary I had out there. Any of them could use Skye as leverage against me.

It made me wonder if Skye would be better off without me. Despite having enemies, when it came down to it, I knew I was the only one who could keep her safe.

Before Leo left, I sent a text to Layla asking where Skye was. Her reply was almost immediate, and she let me know they were having breakfast. Another text followed, this one telling me Skye knew Layla and I had been in contact with each other.

A spark of hope ignited as I read that message. If Skye was okay with her best friend communicating with me, maybe she'd be open to talking to me herself.

I gave Leo Skye's location and told Layla to keep her there for a while longer. She was a smart girl and knew something was up but didn't press me for details. With Leo on his way to Skye's location, I settled back down to complete the plans on the employment center.

The sooner it was done, the sooner I'd get Skye back.

One Month Later

EVERYTHING WAS READY FOR THE GRAND OPENINGS, even though I didn't think we needed a party. Amelia had insisted on it, claiming that it would send a positive message to the community. I had originally thought that opening three charitable venues would have been enough, but I knew Amelia was usually right about these things. Though, *I* insisted we hold the party at the rehab, knowing that would interest Skye the most.

Skye and Layla walked into the Blue Sky Sanctuary two hours after the party had started. I knew the instant Skye entered the room. There was a buzz in the air that hadn't been there before.

It had been over seven months since we last saw each other, and the sight of her still took my breath away.

Her royal blue wrap dress matched her eyes and clung to her curves. Her hair fell in wild curls around her face, framing it like a halo. She was a vision, and I had to resist the urge to claim her right then and there. Every fiber of my being longed to feel her warmth pressed against me, to taste her lips on mine.

When our eyes locked, the rest of the world faded away. When she smiled, it had a calming effect on me, melting the tension in my shoulders. As she approached me, my heart thumped erratically like a teenager on his first date.

"Hi," Skye said, stopping only inches away from me. Over her friend's shoulder, Layla had a huge smile on her face as she gave me a thumbs-up before wandering away on her own. "This is all so amazing. Thank you for inviting me."

She spoke as if we had just met, as if I hadn't tasted every inch of her body, as if I hadn't made her come countless times.

I pushed the irritation aside and forced my lips into a smile. "You're welcome."

"Sorry we were late, the subway had some kind of mechanical issue and sat for ages. We were stuck with a chatty old lady who whined about everything she could think of. I wanted to text you, but the service was awful. By the time the train got going and service came back, we were almost here, so..." She took her bottom lip between her teeth, and she gave a small shrug.

The gesture was so adorable and sexy at the same

time, it made my chest clench. Her nervous rambling proved I still affected her, which gave me hope.

"No worries, I'm just happy you made it," I said, gesturing to the bar. "Would you like a drink? Amelia found a bartender who makes mocktails. Her specialty is a Mock-cow Mule."

"That sounds great. Thanks," she said with a little too much enthusiasm, further proving she was nervous.

Drinks in hand, we toured the main floor, which held the private offices for guest intakes, the common area with plush couches, televisions, a fully stocked kitchen, and the game room, which was equipped with tables for board games and cards as well as pool and ping-pong tables.

"Would you like to see the rooftop terrace?" I asked after I'd shown her one of the guest rooms on the second floor. The rooms were identical on all the floors to avoid jealousy among the guests.

"Oh, that would be wonderful," she beamed, hooking her arm with mine as she seemed to forget herself.

My body tensed as a sudden spark shot up my arm. I lifted my gaze to meet hers, and she appeared equally taken aback. A rosy blush tinged her cheeks, and her lips parted ever-so-slightly. We were alone in one of the guest rooms, and the bed beckoned me to throw her onto it and fuck her into oblivion.

Then she took a step back, her arm slipping away from mine, and just like that, the moment vanished. My frustration simmered, escalating with each passing second. If the three charities I'd arranged didn't prove how much she meant to me, I didn't know what else to do. The only option left would be to keep her locked away in my penthouse, like a tainted version of Beauty and the Beast.

"Right," I said curtly. "We can return to the party if you'd like."

She didn't reply. She just stood there staring at me.

"Skye, are you okay?" I asked, concerned.

She blinked her eyes and licked her lips. "I'm okay. I was just thinking about... something." She smiled and to my surprise, linked her arm with mine again. "Show me the terrace."

Fuck. She made me nervous in a way no one else had ever done. The way she looked at me with those big blue eyes and plump red lips made me want to dominate her and coddle her at the same time.

During the elevator ride, she kept her arm looped through mine, but when we stepped onto the terrace, she let it slip free as she explored the space.

"Oh! This is beautiful," she said, slowly spinning around to take it all in.

A glass enclosure surrounded the elevator, making it look like a glowing gem when looking back at it from the terrace. Twinkle lights, potted trees, and flower boxes decorated the perimeter of the terrace, creating a sense of calm amidst the urban jungle below.

Ample, comfortable outdoor furniture filled the rest of the space where guests could sit down and relax. The fire pit in the center of it all was a focal point, the flames flickering against the night sky.

Skye leaned her elbows on the brick parapet wall and took in the view. We weren't too high up, but there was still a splendid view of the city.

I moved to stand beside her, leaning back against the wall. A small smile played on her lips, and I took the opportunity to observe her as she lost herself in thought.

When she turned to me, her smile had faded.

"Why did you do all of this? Was it just to make me forgive you?" she asked, her tone tinged with suspicion.

"At first, yes," I admitted. "Then the more I thought about it, the more I realized you were right. I needed to take responsibility for my actions and help those affected by them. I knew I could offer a kind of severance package to the employees swept up in the aftermath, but that would only take them so far. That's why I created the employment center. It's there to help them find new jobs or get training for a new industry if they need it."

"Hmm," she muttered, nodding her head. "You've certainly been busy."

"It was all worth it," I replied, cringing at how cliché it sounded. "By the way, congratulations on your art show at the Hearst Gallery."

She studied me with narrowed eyes. "Madeline said you had nothing to do with it, but I'm skeptical."

I raised my hands to show I was sincere. "It's true. I had nothing to do with the show. I've never even met Madeline Hearst."

"Killian Asher doesn't need to meet someone to get

what he wants," Skye retorted.

A small laugh escaped me. "True, but I assure you I had no involvement in the show or your success during it."

Skye arched an eyebrow. "How do you know I was successful?"

"Layla," I said simply.

"Ah, right. I forgot about that," she said, shaking her head and laughing. "She told me she ran into you at a bar in Vermont and has been texting you ever since."

"I hope you don't mind."

Skye shrugged. "I don't. It surprised me you were okay with it."

"She was the closest thing I had to you." It was another corny statement, but something about Skye brought out the sappy romantic in me I never knew existed. "I've missed you."

She averted her eyes, glancing down at the city below. "I've missed you too."

"Look at me, Skye," I said, in a low but firm voice. She turned to face me, her eyes meeting mine. "Do you really mean that?"

"I do."

"Are you saying you'll come back to me?"

Her bottom lip slid between her teeth as she debated how to respond. Just as she was about to answer, a group of noisy partygoers stepped onto the terrace.

"Can we go somewhere to talk?" she asked, eyeing the jovial crowd.

"We can go wherever you want," I replied, eager to hear her response to my question.

She glanced down at her shoes, then looked at me from under her eyelashes. "Take me to your place, please."

The way she was looking at me and the huskiness in her voice made my cock twitch. "Good choice," I said, holding my arm out to her and feeling a surge of satisfaction when she took it.

When we got to the car, Neil smiled when he saw Skye. In all the years I'd known him, I could count the times I'd seen him smile on one hand. Skye had that effect on people. She had a way of making people feel lighter and happier just by walking into a room.

Despite being consumed by darkness myself, it was that light that made her irresistible to me.

Chapter Thirty-One

Skye

K illian and I stood on his balcony, admiring the breathtaking view. From our vantage point, the twinkling lights of the city at night looked like a sea of stars. The view had always been my favorite part of the apartment, other than the man who owned it.

A gentle breeze carried his sandalwood fragrance toward me, and I couldn't help but take a deep breath. After too many months without it, his scent enveloped me, and it felt like coming home.

"Have you decided about the offers you received at the show?" he asked, pulling my attention to him.

"Is there anything Layla hasn't told you?"

"I wouldn't know. I guess we'll have to find out."

"Okay... I accepted the offers for the hotels, but I declined the one for the private residence. Turned out to be an older wealthy man who just wanted to get me alone in his home."

"What's his name?" he asked, his voice taking on a

dangerous tone.

I chuckled. "Easy there, Killer," I said, giving him a playful wink. "I'm not telling you who he is, and don't even think about trying to find out. It's taken care of, and he won't be bothering me again."

His jaw twitched, but he didn't argue. "If he contacts you again, you'll tell me his name."

I nodded because I knew he would find out who it was and monitor the man whether I told him or not. "So, I saw something interesting on social media."

He lifted an eyebrow. "What was it you saw?"

"Claudia Lobos was out with a very handsome man and a reporter asked about you."

"That's interesting to you?"

I shook my head a little. "No, her response was." I pulled the post up on my phone so I didn't misquote it. "She said that you're a horrible brute and no woman should be with you." I glanced up at him with a slight smirk. "I mean, you *are* a horrible brute."

His lips twitched upward ever-so-slightly. "I suppose I am. Though, I still see nothing interesting about it."

"It was interesting to me because it made me wonder what you said to her that night at Harvest & Hearth."

He stepped closer, running his index finger along my chin and leaning in. "I told her if she ever fucked with you again, I'd ruin her career. I'd make it so no one would want her, professionally or personally."

"Oh," I breathed. "That can be taken a couple of different ways."

I knew he had contacts in every industry, so potentially he could block anyone from hiring her. That would take care of her professionally, but it was the latter part of his statement that made me wonder. To ruin her personal life, he could theoretically have nasty things reported about her or... he could have something done to her that would make her unappealing to everyone else.

"Exactly," he said, his lips so close to mine I could almost taste them. "I wouldn't ever actually harm her, but if she believes I might, she'll leave you alone."

"So, you'd ruin her professional life for talking shit to me in a bathroom, but you're okay with her saying nasty things about you to reporters?"

"Yes. I don't care what she says or tries to do to me, but if she so much as looks at you the wrong way, her career is over." He leaned in even closer, his lips grazing my ear. "That's enough gossip. Now tell me, Sunshine, are you ready to come back to me?"

When I hesitated, he curled his hand around my throat. "Keep in mind, I haven't ruled out tying you to my bed and keeping you here against your will."

"Now, *that* sounds interesting," I said, my voice already breathy. "You won't need to do that though."

A primal growl came from his chest as he crushed his lips to mine. His hand on my throat tightened, pulling a moan from me.

"Fuck, I missed you," he groaned before deepening the kiss. His tongue wrestled mine into submission as his free hand unfastened his pants. "You have no idea how much."

"Show me," I said, panting as his hand lowered from my neck to my breast. "Show me how much you missed me."

He picked me up and placed me on the armchair in the corner of the balcony, then fell to his knees in front of me. He slowly trailed his fingers over my ankles to my calves then up to my thighs. His eyes were on mine when he reached the apex of my legs and let out a hum of approval.

"You're not wearing panties," he said, his voice deep and husky. "You planned this."

"Mmm, I did," I breathed. He watched as I lowered my hand to untie my dress, spreading it open to reveal my naked body. "I've thought about this every day and wanted it to be as easy as possible."

I wasn't exaggerating, I had thought about being with him *every* day since we'd broken up. I thought about his warmth, his kisses, his touch. I'd tried to figure out why I was so angry with him, why I couldn't move on from what he had done. When I thought about life without him, I decided I didn't want that. I wanted to be with him.

He pushed my legs apart as far as they'd go, his dark, hungry eyes taking me in. A gasp slipped through my lips when he slid two fingers inside me, his thumb pressing against my aching clit.

"Mmm, you're already fucking soaked for me," he whispered, his eyes fixed between my legs. "So warm and tight."

His fingers moved in and out of me at a slow, methodical pace, as if he was savoring the moment after not being able to for so long. A shudder of anticipation ran over me when his tongue slipped out to wet his lips. He stared at my bare pussy like a starving man, hunger and desire lighting up his gaze as if I were the only thing that could satisfy his appetite.

I held my breath when his head dipped between my legs and let out a deep moan when he circled his tongue around my clit. He pulled his hand away, replacing his fingers with his tongue, and I let myself get lost in the sensation.

He tongue fucked me until I screamed out his name when my climax hit. Hearing his deep groans as he lapped up every drop of my arousal had me squirming with need. I'd just come so hard I saw stars, yet I wanted more of him. I wanted *all* of him.

"Killian, please," I said while trying to catch my breath.

He looked up at me, licking my juices from his lips and I mirrored the action. "Please, what?" The words slipped from his lips like a primal growl, and his gaze burned with a glint that sent a shiver of desire down my spine. It had been too long since I'd seen that gleam in his eyes.

A low hum came from his throat as he slid his fingers through my slick folds. "Do you want me to fuck this pretty cunt of yours?" I pressed my hips against his hand when his thumb moved over my swollen bundle of nerves. "Do you want me to make you come again with my cock filling you?"

"Yes! Oh God, *yes*. Please fuck me."

With a growl, he moved his hands to my waist,

lifting me as he rose to his feet, my legs instinctively wrapping around him. He spun us until my back hit the window, then he slammed into me so hard and fast, I cried out into the night.

He held himself inside me, and I watched his eyes flutter closed. "Fuck, you take me so well, Sunshine. We fit perfectly."

"Made for each other," I said, my voice trembling.

As he buried his face in my neck and inhaled deeply, everything else faded away. There was only us, and nothing else seemed to matter. All that mattered was the touch of his hands and lips on my skin, our bodies pressed tightly together, and the sensation of his cock moving inside me, hard and fast.

What I felt for him was all-consuming. In that moment, he was everything I needed and wanted in my life.

"Killian..." I arched into him, trying to bring him even deeper inside me.

His teeth sank into the crook of my neck, making me hiss in pleasured pain. "I love the sound of my name coming from your lips." He trailed a hand from my hip up to my breast, cupping it softly. "I love the little noises you make when I'm fucking you." He licked a path from my neck to my ear. "I love the way your pussy ripples around my cock when I make you come."

I cried out, the orgasm hitting me like a tidal wave. The pleasure was so intense, it felt as though my bones had melted. If he hadn't been holding on to me, I'd have fallen to the ground.

His lips met mine for a kiss so tender it brought tears to my eyes. "I fucking love *you*," he whispered against my lips.

"I love you too," I said, tears trailing down my cheeks.

We held each other for a long time, caressing and kissing until I felt his arousal pressing against me. This time he carried me to his room where he laid me on the bed before slipping inside me again.

His hands slid under my thighs, lifting my legs as he moved his hips in slow, languorous waves. For the first time, it felt like we were making love.

Later that night, as we lay in bed with our limbs entwined around each other, I regretted ever leaving him. I'd missed out on countless kisses, whispered conversations, and so much more I'd never get back. I reminded myself that the past was in the past, and I still had the rest of my life with him.

The soft glow of the city lights and the moon filtered through the windows, casting shadows across the room as we lay together. It was just enough light for me to see his perfect features as I ran my fingers over his chin and along the line of his jaw, feeling the roughness of his beard against my skin before slipping my fingers into his hair.

He looked at me, his eyes intense in the dim light. "What made you come back?" he asked.

"Layla pointed out that the city would have condemned the building even if you hadn't been involved. My mom probably would've ended up taking the same path, just at a later time."

I leaned in and gave him a soft kiss. "Her addiction was not your fault. When I really let myself think back before she lost the business, I realized she'd already had a problem. She'd been fighting depression for years after my dad died, I was just too young to understand. She had tried to hold it together for me, but in the end she couldn't. Memories of empty bottles of wine and bottles of pills throughout the house surfaced when I finally stopped denying them."

I lowered my hand to smooth it down his muscular arm. "After the studio closed, she had options. She could have found another location for her art studio or moved to Vermont to be near Wes." I paused, taking a deep breath. "Most of all, I came back, because even after all that time apart, living without you was still painful."

"I want to show you something," he said, kissing me and slipping out of the bed.

He led me down the hallway to the room I'd used as my art studio. When he opened the door and flicked on the light, my heart skipped a beat from what I saw.

"How?" I spun around to face him, tears already blurring my vision. "It was you. You were the buyer on the phone."

I turned back to the painting of my mom laughing with me and my friends trying to paint on her. Hot tears streamed down my face as the memory of that day flooded back to me. It was my seventh birthday party, with my neighborhood friends and my mom in all her glory. It had been one of the best days of my life. It was only five years later when all that light turned into darkness.

"How did... I mean, why..." I was so shocked that I couldn't even get the words out.

He stepped up behind me, slipping his arms around my waist and resting his chin on my shoulder. "I know how important it is to you, and I knew you'd always wonder where it ended up, and that not knowing would upset you. Now, it's here whenever you want to see it. We can move it somewhere else, or you can take it down and never look at it again, but you'll always know where it is."

"Killian..." My voice was barely a whisper as I turned to face him, his arms still wrapped around my waist. "This is the most thoughtful thing anyone has ever done for me." Standing on my tiptoes, I pressed my lips to his, pouring all my appreciation and love into the kiss.

He was right. If someone else had bought the painting, wondering where it was and how the new owner was treating it, would have killed me. I knew that because it was exactly what I had been doing until I saw it hanging on his wall.

I nipped at his bottom lip. "Now take me back to bed so I can show you how much I appreciate you."

"As you wish," he said, his voice growing husky.

A laugh escaped me when he tossed me over his shoulder to carry me back to his room. In that moment, I knew I'd made the right choice.

Chapter Thirty-Two

Killian/Skye

Killian

I woke up the next morning to the feeling of Skye's hand stroking my cock and her lips on mine. I fisted my hand in her hair, tilting her head to deepen the kiss while my other hand smoothed down her body to squeeze her ass, then back up to her breast.

"Good morning," she murmured, moving her lips to my neck.

When her teeth sunk into my shoulder, I rolled her over, covering her with my body. The smile she aimed at me made it clear I'd done exactly what she wanted.

She moved her hands over my chest, caressing gently as she grinned up at me. "Yesterday, you mentioned something about tying me to the bed. Why don't you show me what you were thinking?"

"*Fuck.* You'll be the death of me," I said, my voice rough and deep.

Her grin morphed into the sexiest little smirk I'd ever seen. "Well, you're not dead yet, so get to it."

She was a thing of fantasy. It was as though she'd walked out of my dreams and into my life. Sweet, kind, and caring, but also fiery and passionate. A primal groan rumbled from deep in my chest as I got out of bed to grab four neckties.

When I returned to the room, she was already in position. "You're unbelievably gorgeous like this. Spread wide for me like a wanton slut," I said, tying her feet to the footboard. "Is that what you want? Hmm?" I finished tying her hands to the headboard and climbed onto the bed to position myself between her legs. Leaning down until my lips touched her ear I whispered, "Do you want to be my little slut?"

"Yes." She was already breathless.

I drew her earlobe into my mouth, my teeth sinking into it with just enough force to pull a sharp gasp from her. When she squealed in pleasure mixed with pain, I soothed the sting with the tip of my tongue, savoring the taste of her skin.

I crushed my lips to hers in a bruising and heated kiss. It amazed me that my hunger for her could continue to grow, seemingly without an endpoint. I'd never get enough of her, never tire of her scent, her taste, her touch. She was my goddess, and I'd gladly worship her until the end of time.

My lips trailed down her neck to her breasts as my hand slid down her belly. I sucked one nipple then the other, lightly tugging them with my teeth while sliding two fingers inside her. She struggled against her restraints, moaning and whimpering as I worked her toward the edge with my fingers.

"Killian, please," she panted. "Oh God, I need you, please."

I looked up at her with a wicked grin. "A goddess doesn't need a god, Sunshine. So tell me, what is it you *do* need?"

"*Oh!* I need you. I need your mouth on me or your cock inside me."

Her body quivered as I continued moving my fingers inside her, curling them until they hit that sweet spot I knew made her toes curl. "Patience," I whispered, licking and kissing my way down her stomach.

I removed my fingers, and her frustrated groan became a sharp cry of surprise when my teeth glided over her clit. She strained to free herself from the ties when I licked and sucked her sensitive flesh.

"I changed my mind," she cried. "I want you inside me. Please untie me."

I grinned at her. "Hmm, I don't know. I kind of like you like this, spread wide, always ready for me to do with as I please."

"Killian," she whined, wiggling her ass in frustration. "I want to touch you. Now."

"So demanding," I teased, pinching her clit and pulling a pleasure-filled scream from her.

As soon as she was free, I buried my cock inside her, moving in and out of her in powerful thrusts. She was so tight, warm, and wet, and being inside her was pure ecstasy. Her nails bit into my shoulders as her orgasm ripped through her with mine following closely behind.

As I rested my forehead against hers, I struggled to catch my breath. The agony of being without her had been unbearable, leaving me feeling as though my chest was being squeezed in a vise, depriving me of air. Everything had seemed dimmer, less bright.

With her back in my life, back in my arms, and back in my bed, everything felt right again. She'd brought that ray of sunshine back to my dark world.

When my phone rang, ruining the peaceful moment, I reluctantly rose to answer it. As I listened to Amelia tell me about a hiccup in one of the deals, I stared at Skye, still flushed with arousal, and made a decision that would change both our lives.

AFTER NON-STOP INTERRUPTIONS, I wanted Skye all to myself for more than just a few hours a day. So I took her on another trip to my private bungalow, where we'd be in the middle of the ocean, far from civilization where no one could bother us.

We had two weeks in paradise with all the privacy we wanted. The staff made sure we had everything we could ever need, then I sent them home with orders not to return unless we asked them to.

We spent our days lounging by the pool, swimming in the clear turquoise water, and fucking each other on any surface that would hold our weight. At night, we explored and devoured each other's bodies in the open air of our bungalow with the sound of waves lulling us to sleep afterward.

On our last day there, I took Skye to a nearby island known for its luxurious shops and tranquil spas. While she indulged in a day of pampering, I tended to some errands. Later, we dined at a two-time Michelin-starred restaurant, savoring every bite of our exquisite meal before returning to our secluded bungalow.

"Oh!" she gasped when she saw the living area. "What's happening?"

I had asked the staff to decorate the area while we were gone. As we entered the room, the sweet scent of lavender and rose petals welcomed us. The flickering light of countless candles cast a soft glow, creating an enchanting atmosphere.

"What's happening?" she repeated, a sob escaping her when I lowered myself onto one knee. "Oh God..."

"Sunshine, from the moment I first laid eyes on you, I knew you were mine. You bring beauty and light wherever you go. You are the most incredible woman I have ever known, and I'm lucky to have found you." A small sound came from her as she continued to cry silently.

I smiled up at her as I pulled a small black box from my pocket. "Before you, I was consumed by darkness, haunted by the demons of my past and fueled by greed and vengeance. You brought a light into my life I never knew I needed or deserved. You taught me that love is not a weakness, but an act of bravery, that it takes strength to give your heart to someone and trust them not to crush it."

As I lifted the ring from its box, a strange sensation

filled my chest. I'd never felt it before and could only describe it as a mix of joy and anticipation. "With you by my side, nothing else matters. You are my salvation, the light to my darkness, and I will worship you with every fiber of my being, for as long as I live."

As I took her left hand in mine, tears flowed freely down her cheeks. "Skye Larsen, will you marry me?"

Skye

SKYE LARSEN, WILL YOU MARRY ME?

My body shook lightly as I wept, but I managed to nod my head and finally find my voice. "Yes. Yes, Killian Asher, I will marry you."

When he slid the ring onto my finger, my heart pounded so hard I didn't even look at it. I didn't need to see it, all I needed in that moment was him, and I sank to my knees and captured his lips in a searing kiss.

We tore the clothing off each other and when our bodies pressed together, I let our passion sweep me away. The soft glow of the candles and the sound of the ocean floating through the room made everything feel deeper, more meaningful, and more sensual than ever before.

As we made love, it felt like we were the only two people in the world, lost to each other for eternity. Every touch and every caress only deepened our connection until our need for each other completely consumed us. I never wanted it to end and knew I'd remember that moment for the rest of my life.

After, we stayed in each other's embrace, and I finally

glanced down at the ring on my finger, admiring the large cushion-cut blue stone with tiny black diamonds dotted along the twisted platinum band.

"Killian, it's breathtaking," I murmured, tracing my finger along the band.

He propped himself up on his elbow and gazed at the ring with me. "The blue diamond represents you—your eyes, your radiance, and your inner light," he said. "The twisted vine of the band and the black diamonds symbolize our tainted pasts, which, in a way, brought us together."

"My, my Mr. Asher, I do believe you're becoming a romantic," I said, tears blurring my vision.

He let out a low growl. "I'm not a romantic. I'm a realist."

A chuckle escaped me at his solemn expression, and I ran my finger over his frowning bottom lip. "Oh, okay. Well, in that case your description of the ring was very practical," I said with a stiff, serious nod.

My laugh echoed through the room as he tickled me. "You're asking for it, Skye," he said, his voice raspy with his renewed desire.

"If you mean your cock, then yes, I am. I always am." My laughter faded into a moan when his fingers found me still wet and ready for him.

"As I've said, I'll give you whatever you want," he said, positioning the tip of his erection at my opening and slowly sliding inside me. "For eternity."

Epilogue

Skye/Killian

Skye

The second we stepped into Killian's apartment, the peace of our time away morphed into phone calls and text messages. We sat side by side on the sofa in the living room, engrossed in our separate conversations.

Killian's phone buzzed incessantly with urgent work-related messages from Amelia and Lucian, while mine was lit up with excited questions and requests for pictures of the ring from Chelsea and Layla. Wes, on the other hand, had responded with a simple thumbs-up emoji to the news of my engagement.

Chelsea had wasted no time planning a celebration at Harvest & Hearth, which would be that evening. I knew Wes would attend and was probably headed our way already. Because he knew if he didn't show up, I'd never speak to him again. He was my big brother, and I wanted him there to share in my happiness. He may not trust Killian yet, but I did, and that's what mattered.

Layla was already planning the bachelorette party. The group text for the three of us had devolved into mostly just the two of them, as they excitedly worked out the details of both parties. I finally had to intervene, telling them to text each other and leave me out of it. After all, as the bride-to-be, I shouldn't know all the details anyway.

"Maybe we should just move to that island of yours," I said, when another text came through from Chelsea asking me about my color scheme preferences.

"Ours," he replied without looking up from his phone.

"Ours?" I repeated, puzzled.

He finally turned to face me. "The island. It's ours. Or it will be once we're married."

My mouth opened and closed a few times before I could find my voice. "You mean you don't want a prenup?" I asked.

In a flash, his phone was on the table and his hand was curled around my throat, squeezing just enough to let me know he was serious. "Why would I need one? I will never leave you, and I am certainly never letting you leave me again."

His lips claimed mine in a searing kiss before his phone interrupted us. "Fuck," he growled, looking at the message. "I have to go in. I'll be back before you leave for the party."

After Killian left, I retreated to my cozy little art room to get some work done. In keeping with his promise to be open and honest with me, Killian revealed he was not just the owner of his penthouse, but of the entire building. He had even set up an apartment on the floor below for me to use as an art studio, providing me with more space and privacy to work.

Since we'd gotten back together, things had been a whirlwind, and I hadn't had the time to move all my art supplies to the new space yet. Until I did, I was still working in the empty spare room for the time being.

My apartment above the yoga studio was being converted into a larger workspace, while the small one off the entrance was being turned into an extra storage area. As for the extra space, I still hadn't decided what to do with it. I had been trying to convince Layla to become my partner and turn the space into a Barre studio, but she seemed hesitant and indecisive about it. She was not the biggest fan of commitment, but I knew I'd wear her down eventually.

As usual when painting, I'd lost track of time and hours flew by without me noticing, and it was time to get ready. After a quick shower, I did my hair and makeup, and I was just slipping into my dress when Killian stepped into the room.

He took a deep breath and let out a little groan. "I love it when every inch of this place smells like you," he murmured. Sitting on the edge of the bed, he watched me with hungry eyes as I slid the silky material over the lacy lingerie I had chosen to wear underneath.

"I love watching you get ready," he admitted. "It's just a shame I missed your shower."

"I love it when you watch me do anything," I replied, grinning as I sat on his lap. His hands slid around my waist, sending shivers down my spine, while I draped my arms over his shoulders. "Don't worry though, we have a lifetime left for you to stalk me," I added, teasingly.

I looked forward to the years ahead, to his eyes on me, watching me, wanting me, and loving me.

As I looked into those eyes of his, I felt a sense of security and love wash over me. Everything I'd been looking for since I was twelve years old, I'd found in him.

Killian Asher was my stalker, my protector, my entire world. And I'd never let anything come between us again. Never. We were in this together, for eternity.

Killian

THE PARTY AT HARVEST & HEARTH seemed to go on forever. Chelsea had somehow managed to close down the entire restaurant early by promising to make it up to all the canceled reservations with an exclusive tasting menu on a future night. It was a bold move, but it showed how much Skye meant to her.

The constant questions, hugs, and slaps on the back were grating on my nerves, but as Skye mingled with the guests, her eyes sparkling with happiness, I knew I had to tough it out.

When she headed to the bar alone, I sent her a text

telling her to take her panties off before we left for the evening. She turned to look at me over her shoulder, sending me a sexy grin before disappearing into the bathroom.

If I had to suffer through a night of chitchat, at least I had something to look forward to.

As the night wore on, I watched Skye laughing and dancing with her friends, feeling content knowing that she was surrounded by people who loved her.

Wes arrived not long after the party began, hugging his sister and cooing over her ring. However, he made a point to ignore me. He'd been avoiding me the entire evening until I met him in the hallway to the bathroom.

"Wes," I said, blocking his path. "We need to talk."

"I'm not sure we do," he replied, trying to move past me.

I stood my ground. "If it were up to me, I'd never see you again. However, we need to work this out for Skye's sake."

Wes narrowed his eyes, studying me for a few beats before grunting. "Fine. Answer one question for me, and we can call a truce."

I shrugged, curious. "Shoot."

"Where's Paul? My investigator says he dropped off the face of the earth."

A sinister grin pulled at my lips as I looked at him. "Let's just say that I have done, and will continue to do, whatever it takes to keep Skye safe and make her happy."

At first, Wes seemed taken aback by my response. A smile spread across his face as he processed what I'd said. He held out his hand to me. "I wish I could have been there."

I chuckled softly as I shook his hand. "You Larsens are full of surprises."

"The world is better off without people like Paul," Wes said firmly. "All I need to know is that Skye is safe and happy, and since you've sworn to make sure that happens, I'm good." He tugged on our joined hands, and I let him pull me forward. "Hurt her again though, and you'll find out what I'm capable of."

I nodded, keeping my retort to myself. If he thought he could take me out if need be, I'd let him believe it, if only to keep Skye happy knowing her brother and I were in good standings.

Skye's smile when she saw us walking back to the party together was worth the sacrifice of letting Wes think he had even a little influence over me.

After the party was over, Skye and I got into the back of the limo. She leaned against me, tired and a little drunk, and I wrapped my arm around her. As we pulled away from the restaurant, she took my other hand and slid it under her dress.

I hissed in a breath when I felt her bare pussy already drenched for me. "Fuck," I groaned, sliding my fingers inside her. "Ah, you were a good girl and took them off like I told you to. Where are they?" She bit her lower lip as she pulled her panties from her cleavage. "There's no one else like you, Skye Larsen."

"Asher," she moaned as I continued my ministrations. "I'm going to be Skye Asher soon, and then I'll be yours. Completely."

"Mmm, that's right," I said, and a surge of possessiveness burst through me as I covered her with my body, pressing her into the seat beneath us. I'd spent my entire life thinking money and power were all that mattered, until the day I saw her, then everything changed.

Skye was my sunshine, my heart, my *everything*. And I'd never let her leave me again. Never.

Thank you so much for reading **TAINTED DREAMS**! Continue the TAINTED series with **TAINTED HEART** Available on Amazon/KindleUnlimited!

I hope you enjoyed **TAINTED DREAMS**! Please take a moment to leave a quick rating/review on Amazon, Goodreads, and/or BookBub. Thank you so much!

Books by Kimberly Quay

TAINTED SERIES
Contemporary Romance

TAINTED DREAMS ~ a Dark Billionaire Romance

SEASON SHIFTERS SERIES
Paranormal Wolf Shifter Romance

SUMMER CURSED, Book 1

AUTUMN KISSED, Book 2

WINTER UNLEASHED, Book 3

SPRING AWAKENED, Book 4

Fire Banshee Trilogy
Urban Fantasy

BECOMING BANSHEE, Book 1

BANSHEE BEWITCHED, Book 2

BANSHEE BLOOD, Book 3

Follow Along

BookBub, Instagram, Facebook, Goodreads, TikTok, & YouTube as **@AuthorKimberlyQuay**

Sign up for Kimberly's newsletter to receive exclusive giveaways, freebies, and more!

www.KimberlyQuay.com

Acknowledgments

A *huge* "Thank You" to:

Rachel Stanley and Jessica Cantwell for being the best beta readers and friends a girl could have! Your support means *everything*!

Kylie (@buriedwithinpages) for being the best alpha reader, cheerleader, and overall amazing person! Your encouragement and feedback means the world to me!

My husband for always supporting, encouraging, nudging, and inspiring me! Without you, none of this would have happened.

My family, who support me even though I refuse to let them read my spicy books!

Coffee and chocolate for always being there to get me through the rough patches.

And last but *certainly* not least, to everyone who has read my books! Thank you from the bottom of my heart! Without you, I wouldn't have a reason to do what I love.

Printed in Great Britain
by Amazon

22848674R00223